NEUTRINO WARNING

Books by Lesley L. Smith

Temporal Dreams
Neutrino Warning
Kat Cubed
Reality Alternatives
Conservation of Luck

The Quantum Cop Series:
Book 1: *The Quantum Cop*
Book 2: *Quantum Murder*
Book 3: *Quantum Mayhem*

The Space Operetta Series
Book 1: *A Jack By Any Oher Name*
Book 2*: A Jack in the Dark*
Book 3: *A Jack for All Seasons*

Neutrino Warning

By Lesley L. Smith

Quarky Media
Boulder Colorado

Neutrino Warning
Published by Quarky Media, PO Box 3332, Boulder, CO
80307
www.quarkymedia.com

Copyright © 2021 Lesley L. Smith
ISBN: 978-1-950198-34-4 (ebook)

ISBN: 978-1-950198-35-1 (print)

NEUTRINO WARNING

Chapter One

Sometimes, it seemed like Mother Nature, Gaia, was out to get us…

"Snow!" I stopped dead in my tracks inside the physics building's glass front doors, astonished to see a blanket of white outside. Colorado's Front Range rarely got snow anymore. And we never got snow on the Gulf Coast of Missouri, where I grew up.

"Whoa, Kathy. Lookout. Sorry." Jake Moretti, a new physics grad student, almost ran into me. We awkwardly stepped away from one another. My initial impression was that he was adorable with his swimmer's physique and his earnestness. "Yeah, it was a huge blizzard!" He chuckled, looking out the glass doors. "It's cool. Ha ha. Pun intended." He pushed his wire-rimmed glasses up the bridge of his nose. "Why didn't you notice it when you came into work?"

I'd wondered why everyone was suddenly wearing jackets. I'd hardly seen any coats this past winter, so I didn't expect to see any now that March was here. "I didn't come into work this morning." I couldn't even remember the last time I'd left the physics building--but I was not a workaholic. Definitely not. It was just that graduate students had a lot to do.

Jake stopped chuckling. "It was all over the news, too."

"Ellen, what's in the news?" Ellen was the digital personal assistant app on my fon, currently in my pocket. I'd had her since I was a girl. I'd named her after the awesome astronaut Ellen Ochoa from way back in the 1990s.

"March 4, 2098: Blizzard Blankets Colorado," she said.

I interrupted her. "New directive: Give me a news report every morning." I reached for the front doors as if under a spell.

Snow! I needed to frolic outside immediately.

Gopal Khan, my Ph.D. advisor, jostled me as he sped past us on the ground floor landing. "Kathy, what are you doing? The physics department meeting is about to start." He checked his worn watch and glared. "It's mandatory. You too, Jake."

When Gopal got cross with me, which was often for some reason, he reminded me of a bear with his bulky physique and shaggy brown beard and hair. Of course, I'd never actually seen a bear, so I could have been way off.

"But, look." I pointed out the doors. "It snowed."

"I know." He gazed outside for a moment, rubbing his beard. "It's remarkable and pretty. But we still have to go to the meeting."

Ellen said, "The physics department meeting starts in ten seconds."

Gopal flinched. "Now, we're going to be late." He shot me a dark look. "Tell me Lars is already in the meeting room."

I shrugged. "I can tell you that, but I'm pretty sure he went out for a toke, so it would be a lie." I pointed out the door. Lars Karlsson, Gopal's purported second-in-command in the neutrino physics group, had a problem with authority. And marijuana. It had to be because of his overbearing physicist father, Hans. If Hans had been my father, I'd have problems, too.

"Kathy, go outside and see if you can find Lars," Gopal said. "It makes me look bad as the group leader when he doesn't show up for meetings."

I rubbed my hands together. Snow, here I come! "Gosh, Gopal, if you really want me to, I will."

"Hurry up," he said.

I threw open the doors, stepped outside, and squinted. The sunlight reflecting off the snow was blinding; it was like being caught inside a very sparkly diamond. My eyes started watering profusely. A cold diamond; it was definitely cold out here. I shivered. I leaned down, grabbed a handful of (cold!) snow, and made a snowball. I threw it at a red sandstone boulder peeking through the sea of white, and it splattered into a million pieces. It smelled cold and clean out here. Everything seemed fresh and new. I took a deep breath.

"Gopal says, 'Hurry up,'" Ellen interrupted my adventure.

NEUTRINO WARNING

I sighed but started down the path through the snow away from the building: stomp, squish, stomp, squish. I couldn't help grinning; this was fun.

I heard a distant crack of thunder and looked away from my snowy path. I didn't see any clouds. Huh. The snow-covered foothills less than a half kilometer west looked beautiful as they rose majestically into the blue sky.

Focus, Kath! Now, where had Lars gone?

Following footsteps in the snow and the sweet tang of pot smoke, I found Lars behind a big red boulder. "You know smoking will kill you," I said as I approached.

He held the joint carefully with his thumb and forefinger. "I should live so long." He inhaled and held in the smoke.

"C'mon," I said. "Gopal sent me out here to get you. The department meeting isn't optional."

Lars brushed his shoulder-length blond hair out of his green eyes and let out his breath. "Tell Gopal I'll be there in a couple of minutes. This Colorado Gold I got at the farmers' market is excellent. Do you want some?"

"No, I don't want some. And tell Gopal yourself. I'm a physicist, not your errand girl." I stomped my boots in the snow as my feet started to chill.

"Kathy, you haven't finished your dissertation, so you're not a physicist yet." He flashed his perfect white teeth at me. "But you could be my errand girl if you played your cards right."

I snorted. "In your dreams, Lars." I had mixed feelings about Lars. Based on a disastrous relationship in my past, I'd vowed never again to date a fellow physicist. But Lars was unusually good-looking for a scientist. Unfortunately, that also meant his ego was unusually large.

I heard snow squishing under another pair of shoes as Jake appeared around the boulder. When he saw us, he smiled.

Caught in Jake's smile, I got a sense of the sweet gangly teenager he used to be.

"What are you guys doing?" Jake said. "Gopal sent me out to get you."

In the bright sunlight, Jake's intense blue eyes were the color of a pristine alpine lake.

Uh oh. Focus, Kath! "Uh, nothing. We're not doing anything.

We're on our way back to the meeting." I waved my hand around. "Jake, this is Lars; Lars, this is Jake. He's thinking of joining our group." I shivered. My lumpy brown handmade sweater wasn't doing its job, but then how often did it drop below 45 degrees these days?

Jake noticed. "It's chilly out here. Do you want to borrow my coat, Kathy?" He slipped it off and put it around my shoulders. It was cavernous on my tiny frame.

Lars smirked and took another toke.

"Thanks, Jake." I snuggled into it. It smelled faintly of sweat and some kind of cologne. I took a deep breath. "What a gentleman." I shot a glare at Lars, but he didn't notice.

"I don't understand how the blizzard of the last few days could have been because of global warming." Jake pushed a lock of brown wavy hair away from his eyes.

"Easy." I felt a smile take over my face. I loved talking science. "Global warming means there's more moisture in the atmosphere and more energy available for weather systems, so storms have increased precipitation, which can be snow." My nose started to run. I resisted the urge to wipe it on the sleeve of Jake's coat.

Lars stubbed out his now-tiny joint.

Another loud crack of thunder made us look up.

"That's weird." Jake searched the sky. "There aren't any clouds. How can there be thunder?"

The thunder continued to rumble.

Lars stood up and looked to the west, over the boulder. "I think it's from over there."

The rumbling got louder. "What's that?" I pointed west. A massive cloud of white moved down the mountain slope toward us. It was huge, awe-inspiring. Terrifying. "Look!"

"Huh." Lars giggled. "Pretty."

"What?" Jake asked. "Where?"

"There!" I said. "There! West! I'm telling you, there's a huge white mass of something headed right for us!" My extended finger trembled.

"Is it possible?" Jake asked. "Gaia! I've never seen a what-do-you-call-it, an avalanche, before. Shouldn't we get back to the building?" He turned.

10

NEUTRINO WARNING

An avalanche! It had been snowing for days and days in the mountains to the west of us, and now all that snow was heading our way.

I felt a sudden strong gust of cold air. And it was coming straight for us! "There's no time! Take cover!" I grabbed Jake and Lars and pulled them down behind the boulder just as the first icy tendrils of snow kissed my bare neck.

I scrunched up against the boulder and held Jake's coat above my head as the snow started to cascade over it. I couldn't catch a breath and felt as if I was suffocating. The snow fell in bigger and bigger chunks, and the patter of snow landing on the jacket turned into pounding. I tried to angle my impromptu tent so the snow would slide off me and away from the others. Wispy streams of snowflakes drifted down in the slight gap between the jacket and the rock. My ankles and shins were freezing. My legs were already half-buried. I stamped my feet and tried to get on top of the snow.

After what seemed like an eternity, the pounding changed back to pattering. I opened my eyes and peeked out from under the jacket. We lucked out. "I think it's over." Jake and Lars crouched next to me in only a meter of new snow.

They blinked and brushed snow off themselves.

"Cool." Lars stood up.

"We're okay! I can't believe it." Jake wiped snow off his clothes.

"Those rock formations above us must have diverted most of it away from us." I brushed snow off Jake's coat and handed it back to him. "Thanks a lot, Jake."

"So, where'd the snow go?" Jake glanced around.

Lars pointed back toward the physics building. "Look."

Our gaze followed his finger. Snow buried one side of the physics building up to the second-floor windows, and it looked like some of them were broken. That couldn't be good.

"Oh no!" The meeting was on the first floor there. I fumbled for my fon. "Ellen, call emergency services. There's been an accident, an avalanche, on campus at the physics building."

"Message acknowledged," Ellen said. "Calling emergency crews now."

"C'mon, you guys, we have to go help!" I said.

I tried to run to the physics building, but it seemed to take forever as my feet sunk into the snow. It was like some horrible dream where I could only move in slow motion.

After about a million years, Jake and I got to the front door and had to kick the snow away from it to get it to open. Lars was lagging far behind.

Jake and I ran towards the conference room, past broken windows and through snow drifts in the hall.

Inside the conference room, the snow had crashed through all the windows. People were already digging frantically.

Lily, the physics department's administrative assistant, saw us come into the room. She usually seemed like someone's granny with her quick smile, short gray hair, and conservative clothes, but today she barked orders like a drill sergeant. "You guys, come here, dig next to me. A bunch of people were sitting right here."

I went to where she indicated. I dogpaddled through the snow, shoving it behind me. My fingers felt so cold they burned, but soon they went numb.

Soon, some wiggling fingers appeared right in front of me.

I uncovered the rest of the hand and the arm, followed it to the torso, and exposed the face. I recognized Marcello, my old officemate. His thinning dark hair was plastered to his head, and his skin was red and blotchy. He gasped and opened his eyes. I unearthed more of him and found he still sat in a chair. "Hold on, Marcello! I'll get you out." I moved more snow, grabbed a chair arm, and rolled it out.

He gasped and brushed snow off himself. "*Grazie*, Kathy!"

"*Prego*, Marcello," I said.

I saw another chair arm sticking out of the snow. Quickly I turned my attention from Marcello and scooped snow away from where another head might be. Success. It was a woman, Gabrielle, one of the members of the fusion group. I finished exposing her face, but she didn't seem to be breathing.

I yanked the chair out of the drift.

Lily caught my eye. "Is she all right?"

"I'm not sure," I said. "I don't think so."

Lily moved towards us. "Here, let me check for a pulse. I know CPR; I'll take her. Keep digging."

NEUTRINO WARNING

I found another chair arm and tugged on it, but it wouldn't budge. I kept pulling on it. It had to move! I pulled some more. Did it move a little? I was starting to get frantic.

Jake reached over me and started brushing snow away from head level. "Uncover the face first." His voice was high-pitched with stress.

I started brushing snow away from the face area. "Right, I knew that." We uncovered a male head.

I felt his neck for a pulse. Nothing. "I can't find a pulse! He's not breathing!" I was barely breathing myself. I realized we had managed to clear all the way around the conference table. Most of the snow had been spread around the room. We had uncovered everyone. Several people were doing mouth-to-mouth resuscitation or CPR on fallen colleagues.

Gopal stood on the other side of the chair next to me. His neat beard had snow caked on it, and his brown eyes were solemn and unblinking as he examined the man next to me. "Kathy, get out of the way." He lowered the man onto the floor and started mouth-to-mouth resuscitation.

Lily came over. "I'll start CPR."

I scanned the room. "Is everyone accounted for?" There weren't any large piles of snow left. We must have uncovered everyone.

"Lars? Where's Lars?" Gopal asked.

"Still outside," I said. "Or maybe in the hall."

Now that the immediate danger was over, I was panicking. I leaned my head down, resting my numb hands on my knees. Between labored breaths, I said, "Lars is fine."

A piece of window glass fell, shattering on the floor. We all startled at the loud noise.

"Careful, everyone!" I yelled. "Move into the hall if you can."

I took the arm of a very pale Marcello and led him out of the room.

I felt exhausted and couldn't tell if I still had fingers, they were so numb. I put my hands under my armpits to try to thaw them. As I stood in the hall with my shaken colleagues, I heard ambulance sirens approaching.

We trudged down the hall, and someone pulled out a chair for me. "Kathy, sit."

How could I've been so idiotic with that last guy? I knew, I knew, I should have uncovered his face first. Did my mistake kill him? Gaia, I didn't even notice who it was. I leaned forward in the chair as my hands started to burn.

Off in the distance, far away, I heard talking. I rocked back and forth. Who did I kill?

"Miss!" Someone put his hand on my back. "Miss, are you all right? What's your name?"

I gazed at the medic leaning over me. His cheeks were flushed. "Do you know your name? Do you know where you are?"

I nodded. Kathy.

Jake came up. "That's Kathy. I think she called emergency services. She seemed all right a little while ago." He leaned down and peered into my face. "Kathy?"

"Jake. What? What do you want?" I focused on his face.

"Are you all right?" He gazed into my eyes, and his forehead was wrinkled in concern.

I nodded. "I think so. Who didn't I get to in time?"

"You did the best you could," Jake said.

"Who was it?" I asked.

"It was Professor Guy Cassou, one of the French guys in the fusion group. He didn't make it." Jake shook his head.

The medic straightened up. "I doubt you could have done anything more, but if you called emergency services, you saved lives. You're a hero."

"You hear that, Kathy? You're a hero." Jake rubbed my back.

I didn't feel like a hero.

"Anyway, Miss, if you're okay, please move into the other room. We're still assessing the situation." He pointed further down the hall, and we stumbled off in that direction.

Gopal stood in the hallway and checked us off on a list as we went into one of the classrooms. His clothes were soaked. "Thank Gaia, you are all right. Not everyone was so lucky."

I realized I was pretty wet myself. "Who?" My lips trembled so much that it was hard to talk. "Who didn't make it?"

Gopal consulted the list as if such horrible news couldn't be held in the brain. "Uh, let's see, we lost Professor Cassou and his student, Gabrielle." Gopal paused and sniffed, wiping his nose with his palm.

Gaia! That was awful. I nodded, not trusting myself to speak.

Gopal stared stony-eyed at his checklist for a few moments. "It's too horrible to believe …but we lost everyone in the fusion group. They're all gone."

Jake gasped.

"Jean-Phillipe? Everyone?" I asked. Jean-Phillipe was Gabrielle's significant other; they'd come here to Colorado together.

Gopal just nodded.

I collapsed against the doorjamb.

An EMT came up, and Gopal's face turned white as he conferred with him quietly.

Jake and I just looked at each other in disbelief.

I couldn't process this.

The emergency worker shook his head as he walked away.

Gopal's slack face seemed to grow more haggard, and his eyes more haunted as he looked at us. "That was, that was about the department chair, Joe Davidson. He didn't make it either. He had a heart attack."

"No." My eyes finally overflowed. This was just all too much and all wrong. I stumbled to the floor.

"Miss? Miss?" The EMT ran back to me. "Are you…"

Everything went black.

Chapter Two

"Kathy, wake up. You must get out of bed." A perfunctory female voice, Ellen's voice, barged into my dream. Bed was nice; I'd been here for days. I wasn't sick, and I'd recovered physically from the avalanche, but emotionally was another matter. When I was in bed, I didn't have to think or to remember…

I cracked my eyelids and saw sunlight shining on my bright orange-, red-, pink- and yellow-flowered patchwork quilt. Its bright colors conflicted with my dark mood. "Ellen, shut up!"

"I am sorry, Kathy, but that would contradict your earlier instructions. Get up." Ellen's voice got louder.

A thumping noise came from the north wall of my bedroom. My roommate Megan MacDonald yelled, "Shut off your app!" Megan was a computer genius and also a computer science grad student at the university.

Okay, okay. I sat up and scanned the room, looking for my fon. I saw my old wooden desk covered with piles of papers and books. Some of the papers overflowed onto the floor and mixed with piles of laundry, throw pillows, and other flotsam and jetsam of life.

Megan shoved open my bedroom door, banging it against the wall. Her short, curly, brown, and purple hair stuck out every which way. "Shut off your flooding wake-up call, or I'll shut it off for you. Permanently." Her violet eyes flashed in tempo with a throbbing vein on her forehead. Yikes.

"Be my guest." I waved my hand around the room. "I don't know where it is."

"Just order your app to stop--she's your flooding app, after all." Megan glared at me. "She has to do what you say, doesn't she?"

"Stopping before Kathy gets out of bed would contradict previous instructions. Get up!" Ellen said blaringly.

"Ellen, why do you have such strict instructions today?" Megan asked.

"Kathy told me she must get up in time to go to the memorial service for the fusion energy group this morning. Get up, Kathy!"

I shivered and burrowed back under the covers. I couldn't seem to get warm since the avalanche.

"Oh." Megan leaned against the wall and ran her fingers through her unruly hair. "I can't blame you for wanting to stay under the covers." She straightened. "But you've hardly gotten out of bed for days. Don't you think it's time? You need to get up and get on with your life."

She had a point, but I felt so depressed. People, good people, had died just trying to do their jobs. I shrugged. "Would you come with me to the service? I don't think I can face it alone."

"Get up now, Kathy!" Ellen was deafening.

"Yes, yes," Megan said. "Just turn off that stupid alarm!"

"Ellen, where are you?" I asked.

"I am approximately two meters north of you," she said.

I swung my legs out of bed, lunged across the room, and scooped up a pile that turned out to be a quilt. Sure enough, Ellen hid underneath it. I grabbed her and turned off the alarm. "Satisfied?" I turned to Megan.

Her eyes were wide open, and the corners of her mouth were turned down. "Gaia! You look awful."

From what I could tell, my wrinkled pajamas didn't look that bad. I patted my hair; it did feel a bit askew. I turned and looked in the mirror over my dresser. Yikes! My head looked like a giant bird's nest. "As you said, I've hardly been out of bed lately. Does that mean I get the shower first?"

Megan swallowed. "By all means."

I brought Ellen with me into the bathroom for a news update--after the blizzard debacle, I had vowed to stay better informed.

March 8, 2098: Influenza Vaccine Failure:
Government officials warn that this year's flu vaccine has

become ineffective due to an unanticipated antigenic shift in the influenza A viruses.

In a typical year, with an effective vaccine, 20% of the population gets the flu, thousands are hospitalized from flu complications, and approximately 10% of these die from flu. Influenza infections this year promise to be even more virulent.

In light of the vaccine failure, U.S. Health Officials strongly urge residents to utilize good health habits to avoid contracting the potentially lethal flu, including avoiding close contact, especially with people who have the flu. Also, avoid touching your eyes, nose, or mouth, and wash your hands often.

Despite the hot water sloughing off my back, I shivered again.

After a deliciously long shower, I stood in front of the mirror in my bedroom, debating whether I needed a scarf to spiff up my black suit, when I heard a scream from the bathroom.

Megan appeared in my doorway, wrapped in a towel and dripping wet. "I can't believe you used up all the hot water!" That vein in her forehead throbbed, and she shot me her die-under-painful circumstances glare.

I felt guilty. And a little scared. "Sorry."

Megan interrupted her glare with a sneeze.

I looked at her with concern. "Gaia bless you. You should dry off and get dressed before you catch cold."

She shivered. "Are you almost ready to go then? I'll be ready in a couple of minutes."

"Yeah, I just want to dry my hair." I decided not to ask her advice about the scarf. She seemed kind of snippy this morning.

Megan snorted. "Good luck with that. It's an odd-numbered day of the month. No electricity this morning--or didn't you notice the light wasn't working in the bathroom?"

I lifted my shoulders. "I just thought the bulb burned out."

"Girl, you really are out of it."

Ellen interrupted. "The memorial service begins in twenty-five minutes. If you travel at Kathy's average speed, I estimate you need to depart within five minutes."

Yikes!

Eight minutes later, I followed Megan out the front door with my bike. It was like a swamp outside since all the snow had been

18

melting over the weekend. The temperature had quickly risen back to normal levels.

At least the traffic was light. We only saw a few other bikes and the light rail on the century-old streets as we pedaled next to Bear Creek. As usual, I marveled at how wide the roads were; they'd been built for cars, which had apparently been very wide. I was trying to think about anything and everything except where we were going and why.

As Megan and I rode along, drops of water from the street started hitting my back, jolting my attention back to the matter at hand. The snowmelt had begun to overflow the banks of the creek and run into the street. When we reached the southeast corner of campus, water completely filled the street and flowed over the curb. This was a low spot in town. Our speed decreased as we rode through the rising water. I glanced at Megan as she grimly pedaled on, flinching as water splashed up on her. Suddenly, her bike was horizontal, and she splashed into the now foot-deep water.

"Megan!" I yelled.

"Help," she gurgled. She flailed her arms and tried to get up, but the current made it difficult. She slowly slid away from me down the flooded street.

I threw down my bike and tried to run after her as she was swept down the street. "I'm coming!" The water was almost up to my knees as I reached her.

She clutched desperately at my outstretched hands, and I pulled her upright. "Thanks," she said shakily. "It's not that deep. I don't know what happened."

We stood, catching our breath for a moment as the current swirled around us. This had all the makings of a flash flood.

"C'mon, let's try to get over to the light rail shelter," I said. It was about three meters away in the direction the current wanted to take us. It consisted of three plexiglass walls with a roof on top and benches, and a trash can inside. The water was much shallower there above the curb.

She nodded, looking relieved. "Yeah. This water seems to be rising quickly."

Clutching each other, we trudged through the knee-high water and thankfully stepped up onto the curb.

As we entered the station, an automated message was generated. "Warning, this station is not presently in service. Warning. Environmental hazards detected. Warning."

I shook my head. That was an understatement.

"Do you see our bikes anywhere?" Megan asked.

As it flowed by, the water was making a loud whooshing sound.

From the shelter, we scrutinized the area for our bikes. I pointed at a street light with a lot of turbulent water underneath it. "That might be one. I think I see some handlebars. Yes."

"Good." Megan pointed at another area of muddy, turbulent water. "I think the other one might be over there."

Shivering as we sat down on the benches in the shelter, I said, "You know, this isn't the first time I've been caught in a flash flood. Last summer Gabrielle, Jean-Phillipe, two of the students we lost in the avalanche, and I got caught in a flash flood west of campus." I sighed. Poor Gabrielle and Jean-Phillipe. I couldn't believe they were gone.

"Really?" Megan lifted her feet up out of the water and crossed her legs under her on the bench.

"Yeah. We were hiking on those trails behind the physics building during our lunch hour. We were at the top of a ridge when it suddenly started pouring rain and hail. We ran for a tree when the lightning started. That was our first mistake. We realized it was the wrong place to be in a lightning storm, so we slid down the hill through blinding rain and pea-sized hail to a gully. That was our second mistake." As I spoke, the water covered my feet, and I followed Megan's lead and tucked them up under me on the bench.

"We were trying to catch our breath in this gully when a wall of water slammed into us. Now *that* was scary. This is nothing."

"It does sound scary," Megan said. "What happened next?"

In the shelter, the floodwater was rising quickly. The whoosh was turning into a roar. I almost forgot the thread of my story I was getting so nervous. We'd have to stand up on the benches soon. Maybe we should have tried to make a run for it.

"The initial wave knocked Gabrielle and Jean-Phillipe over into the water, but it knocked me into a tree. I grabbed onto it for dear life. The current swept Jean-Phillipe into me, so I grabbed him. He was able to grab Gabrielle. We all made it over to the edge of the gully, but it was too muddy and slippery to climb back up."

"We climbed up some trees on the edge of the gully. Which isn't a bad idea, come to think of it." I jumped up and stood on the bench.

Megan followed my lead and surveyed our situation. "But everything turned out okay, right? And it was deeper than this, right?"

A good-sized branch floated by in the current. The flood here looked a bit deeper now than last summer, but Megan didn't need to know that. After surviving an avalanche, surely, I wouldn't die in a flash flood, would I? Focus, Kath.

"So, then I asked them how the fusion project was going," I said.

In the shelter, standing on the benches, the water covered our feet. I was beginning to wonder how high it could get.

"And then, at some point, Jean-Phillipe put his arm around Gabrielle, and I realized they were a couple," I said.

Megan giggled nervously. "So, what happened then?"

"They talked about their fusion experiment, telling me they succeeded in creating a very large magnetic field in a very small area."

Now, the floodwater approached our knees. It was frigid. My feet were starting to feel numb.

"And the next thing I knew, the rain stopped, and the flood started going down," I said. The water fell as quickly as it rose, and the three of us were on our way in no time."

"How long did all that take?" Megan asked, watching our floodwater intently. "Is the water going down now? I think it's going down."

I thought it was wishful thinking on Megan's part. My knees were immersed. *Brr.* The water was c-o-l-d. "I don't remember exactly--but less than an hour. Plus, the water was much higher then." I was a big liar. It was lower then. We might not make it out of here now.

I took a deep breath and continued my hopefully uplifting story. "Anyway, at the tea break the next day, the three of us regaled the other physicists with our adventures. Gabrielle even praised me for grabbing them and distracting them with the fusion discussion. I didn't have the heart to tell them I was scared, too. I meant to tell them. Now they'll never know." My eyes started leaking.

Megan politely pretended not to notice. "Does it look like the water's going down?" She leaned over. "Look, I can see your knees again! And mine. I think it's going down!"

She was right; the flood was receding. Thank Gaia. "Do you want to go home?"

She shook her head. "No. The memorial is important. But I'm freezing."

"Thank you." I shrugged out of my jacket. "Here, take my coat. It's mostly dry."

When we finally retrieved our bikes and arrived at the outdoor campus amphitheater, a considerable crowd was already there.

The amphitheater was constructed completely of red sandstone: benches, floor, and stage. In happier times, they hosted the university's famous Shakespeare Festival here.

"I'm cold." Megan crossed her arms in front of her. Considering she was wearing my coat, she had to be at least a little warmer than me.

"Me too. It's no wonder--we got rather wet. Between you and me, I was a little worried there for a minute in the shelter. Thanks for coming with me today. I don't think I could have handled all this alone. You're a good friend." I put my arm around her.

"Yes, I am," she said, nodding. "But, so are you. Thank you for rescuing me. You might have saved my life back there. I owe you one."

I gave her a big hug.

There were a lot of somber-looking people sitting on the sandstone benches, watching the speaker on the stage. There weren't many seats left. Thinking of the vaccine failure, I realized people weren't really avoiding close contact. I guess because we were outside? Presumably, if anyone was sick, he or she would have stayed home.

I rubbed my arms. "I don't know where we're going to sit." As we stood in the entrance surveying the crowd, I saw a black-clad arm waving. I scrutinized the head attached to it and recognized Jake.

He motioned us toward him.

"Look, it's Jake. He's waving us over," I said.

Megan wrinkled her brow. "Who?"

"Jake. He's a new grad student in my group. I'll introduce you."

Megan and I snuck through the crowd to him.

When we got there, he pointed at the bench. "Hey, Kathy. I saved you a seat," he whispered. "Why are you so wet?"

"We got caught in a little flash flood," I said quietly.

He widened his eyes. "Are you all right?"

I nodded. "Yeah, thanks for asking. Megan, this is Jake, the new guy in the neutrino group." I waved my hands back and forth. "Jake, this is Megan, my roommate."

"Nice to meet you." Megan scanned Jake, then turned and gave me the raised-eyebrow approval.

Jake finally noticed Megan. "Uh, hi. I didn't see you there. Nice to meet you too. Purple hair!" He smiled so easily, and naturally, we were infected with smiles of our own despite the somber occasion.

"Thanks. Is there room for us both?" Megan whispered.

"Sure, sure, plenty of room," I said. Megan and I squeezed in.

Jake turned to me. "Just to let you know, Kathy, I haven't decided about the neutrino group yet."

I grunted. "Okay." How could he resist such a fascinating project with such fascinating people? But I guessed now wasn't the time to try and convince him.

I turned my attention to the service. On stage, Gopal was speaking in front of a row of pictures on easels. The fusion group members. My breath caught in my throat. All gone, far too soon. My eyes felt hot.

Gopal looked uncomfortable in his black suit, tugging the jacket down. I'd never seen him in a suit before.

"So, in conclusion," he said, "these past few days have been somber for the university and the world scientific community. We will dearly miss these special people, and our hearts go out to their families."

23

LESLEY L. SMITH

"Tomorrow at three o'clock is the funeral for Professor Davidson at the university chapel. Dr. Davidson mentored me when I first arrived here at the university many years ago. His passing is difficult for me, as I'm sure it is for many of you." He wiped the corner of his eye. "I hope to see you tomorrow at the service."

I recalled the first time I'd gone to Professor Davidson's office hours, very nervous after he'd berated our graduate analytical mechanics class for our ignorance. To my amazement, he was a total sweetheart, helping me picture the physical setups of the various ladders, pulleys, pendulums, and the like. It was the beginning of an unlikely friendship--a friendship that was gone now. I had to wipe the corner of my eye.

Gopal cleared his throat. "We may never get over this tragedy, but starting today, the university will have several counselors available for those who need them." He put his finger under his shirt collar and tugged it away from his neck. "After today's service and after tomorrow's service, we will have receptions at the physics department. You are all invited." He sighed and wiped his forehead. "Our next speaker today is Dr. Karlsson. Hans?"

Hans Karlsson glided up to the podium. Unlike Gopal, he looked like he had been born in his black pinstripe suit.

I looked around for Lars, Hans' son, but there was no sign of him.

Hans rubbed his hands together. "The scientists of the fusion energy group will be missed. Their demise was a severe setback to the project. This disaster will put us behind schedule, but I will make every effort to ensure the project stays on track." Gee, he was all heart.

"Is he in the fusion group?" Megan asked quietly.

I shook my head.

"It sounds like he's campaigning for something," Jake whispered.

Hans didn't seem sad at all. He reminded me of a politician trying to convince us to elect him to something.

I tuned him out and thought about the people we were there to remember. In contrast to Hans, Gabrielle and Jean-Phillipe were charming. They loved France and always had an amusing anecdote ready about their homeland despite their emigrating. They spoke French whenever possible; I often heard their cheerful *Bonjour*s in the halls.

It was the ultimate cruel irony that these people had died in an avalanche. They'd moved here because southern France, in fact, all of southern Europe, was fast becoming uninhabitable because of the heat. There was no snow there; that was for sure. I wiped the corner of my eye again.

Megan patted my shoulder.

"Allergies," I whispered to her.

Sure." She nodded her head and patted my shoulder again. "I think it's almost over."

"Good." I shifted in my seat, cold, wet, and depressed. My friends didn't deserve to die.

Hans droned on, smiling and smoothing his hair. I tried to ignore him.

The members of the fusion group were heroes. They tried to develop a pollution-free energy source to possibly save the planet from global warming and gave their lives for it. Nuclear fusion was a safe, low-cost energy source. It could eliminate the need for any fossil-fuel-based power plants or vehicles. It could power as many desalination plants as needed--ending any freshwater shortages. It could even power chemical plants that remove carbon dioxide from the air.

I sighed, hoping that someday I could make that kind of positive difference in the world.

Megan poked me. "It's over." People were starting to get up. "I guess we missed most of it."

"Well." Jake shook his head. "That was really something."

Megan grunted. "That Hans is a real piece of work."

"Let's go." I turned to the aisle. "Maybe we can get a hot drink at the reception."

We didn't move fast enough and got caught in the crowd. I felt like a cow being funneled into the slaughterhouse in one of those old western movies. Moo. It made me wonder what cow tasted like. Since they were endangered now and kept only in zoos and special preserves, I'd never know.

As we slowly approached the physics building, I was surprised to see they'd already replaced most of the broken windows. Since most of the snow had melted, you could hardly tell there'd been an avalanche. Somehow, that didn't seem right.

Eventually, we made it into the building. Usually, I loved the physics building; it was one of the only places I knew of that had electricity all the time. It filled me with a sense of purpose and possibilities.

Today, black outfits and blacker expressions overflowed the lobby in a sea of sorrow, and the muted conversation ebbed and flowed like the tide going in and out.

Jake spoke up. "Can I get you something to drink, Kathy? You too, Megan?"

"Yeah." I grunted. "Something hot if they have it. Thanks."

"Sure. That would be nice, Jake," Megan said. As Jake elbowed his way through the crowd, Megan said, "Did you say he's new? He seems to be your age."

"I think he took some time off school before college," I said.

"He's sweet," she said. "I think he likes you."

Megan knew I didn't like talking about this stuff because I was so inept at it. All my previous relationships had ended poorly. Why had she brought it up? "I wonder what kind of drinks he'll bring back?"

Megan sneezed. "I may leave when Jake comes back. I'm not feeling so well, I think it's a cold, and I have to go to work at three o'clock. We're still trying to repair the network problems that the avalanche caused."

"I understand if you think you have to go." I gave her my most pathetic expression, the one with sad eyes and a delicate frown.

"Aw." Megan chuckled and hugged me. "I've seen that face before. I think you'll be all right."

A few minutes later, Jake showed up, juggling three glasses of red liquid. "Sorry, it took so long."

Megan took a glass. "No problem. It was kind of you to go. Thanks." She elbowed me.

"Yeah. Thanks." I took a glass. "What is this?"

"It's supposed to be fruit punch," he said.

I sipped the sweet, but not fruity, concoction. "What kind of fruit?"

Megan smiled. "Red." She gulped her punch and had a

26

bright red mustache when she lowered her glass.

"Jake, did you get any napkins?" I asked, pointing at Megan's face.

He pulled out a stack of wrinkled navy-blue napkins from the pocket of his black sports coat.

Megan wiped most of her new mustache off.

"And that's not all." He fished around again. "I got sandwiches too." He held one out with a big dent in it. "They're only a little smushed."

Megan smiled. "As tempting as that is, I need to go. Nice meeting you, Jake. See you at home, Kathy." She made a quick getaway.

I took a dented sandwich from Jake. "More for us." One hand held my cup and the other a sandwich wrapped in wax paper. I held it up to my face, attempting to nudge open the paper with my nose. I needed another hand. "Let's go to my office."

Later, after we had trekked up to the deserted sixth floor and finished the cheeze and veggie sandwiches, Jake leaned back in a wooden chair, "What were they like, the French guys? I didn't know them."

"They were all really nice and good scientists too. In fact, Jean-Phillipe and Gabrielle and I were caught in a flash flood together last summer." I told him the story.

Jake appeared suitably impressed. "Wow. Weren't you scared?"

"Nope. I knew we'd be okay." I paused. "No. Actually, that's a lie. I was scared. We helped each other through it."

Jake nodded. "Cool."

"They told me at the tea break last week…." I trailed off. They wouldn't be coming to any more tea breaks, excited about some new milestone they'd reached. I wiped my eyes with my crumpled napkin.

Jake pushed his glasses up. "They told you what?"

"They said they've been making good progress."

"Cool." We were silent for a few minutes. "It's neat how they said, '*Bonjour*,'" Jake said.

I nodded as I checked the time. "It's time for our group meeting. Do you want to come? If so, we better get down to the lab."

As we walked into the neutrino lab, Jake and I spontaneously said *'Bonjour'* to Gopal.

Gopal smiled in spite of himself. *"Bonjour."* He'd already lost his jacket and tie and unbuttoned the collar of his formal white shirt. He sat on a lab stool surrounded by banks of computers and other electrical equipment. We sat down on lab stools too.

"Jake, does the fact that you're here mean you want to join the neutrino group?" Gopal asked.

Jake glanced at me and grinned. "I'm leaning that way."

Of course. We were an excellent group. I flashed him a 100-Watt smile.

"You may want to hold off on that decision," Gopal said.

Why would he say a thing like that?

After a couple of minutes of waiting for Lars, Gopal shrugged. "This is stupid. This week's tough enough without waiting around for a *prima donna*." He shot another glance at the door. "Anyway, the physics Faculty Forum met yesterday afternoon and discussed what to do about the fusion energy program. It's one of the most important research programs at the university. Some good news: we're going to try to get some new fusion physicists here as soon as possible. The Chinese and the Europeans both said they would try to send some scientists since it's an emergency." He stopped to take a breath. "With the avalanche damage, we'll need some so-called new computers, so the faculty gave us the go-ahead to order some. It's too bad supercomputer research, and development stopped in the mid-twenty-first century because of all the natural disasters.

"Yeah." I nodded. "But the faculty actually agreed on something?" I asked, glancing up. The Faculty Forum I had attended had been surprisingly vociferous. Gopal usually seemed so grumpy at them that I made a point of avoiding him afterward.

Gopal grimaced. "On the fusion project stuff, yes, we agreed. You don't want to know about the 'discussion' about a new department chair."

I nodded. That sounded more like it.

He paused and drew his eyebrows together. "We also decided to shift some people to the fusion group immediately to try to assess the situation and get the equipment back in shape. In terms of apparatus, our group has some stuff that is similar. So..."

I was starting to get a bad feeling about this. "Yes?"

"So, we're it. The neutrino group is suspended, at least for the time being."

Of course, I wanted to help the fusion group, but my group was suspended? My degree was suspended?

He turned to Jake. "Jake? I hope we can count on your help with the fusion project."

Jake nodded.

"Gaia." I could see four years of my life circling the drain. "Can't I work on fusion after I finish my dissertation? Or part-time? You know I've spent years on my neutrino dissertation, and I'm almost done. I only need a little more data. Is this decision final?"

I waited, heart thumping, for his response.

Gopal locked eyes with me. "Yes. It's final."

Chapter Three

Monday morning, since I was running late, I got the news update from Ellen as I rode my bike to work. It had been about a week since Gopal gave me the bad news. He claimed it was only a temporary setback and that I could return to my research as soon as the replacement fusion scientists arrived. I hoped he was right

March 15, 2098: Class One SARS Outbreak: The Beijing Morning ePost says the infectious disease early warning system in China's capital has announced another Class One outbreak of the deadly Severe Acute Respiratory Syndrome, known as SARS. Class One is the most severe type of outbreak and is only invoked when more than 100 people are infected by a disease that expands by more than 20 percent in two months.

Three public hospitals, including Ditan Hospital, which handled many of Beijing's SARS cases in last year's outbreak, and one military hospital have been designated as treatment centers for the current SARS outbreak.

China has issued emergency instructions to hospitals nationwide to isolate patients suffering from SARS and again banned the cooking and selling of the civet cat, the animal considered the primary human source of SARS. "Any person found possessing one or more civet cats, alive or dead, will be dealt with most severely," a government official said.

SARS is a viral respiratory illness caused by a coronavirus and was first reported in Asia near the turn of the 21st century. In general, SARS symptoms begin with a high fever, and other symptoms include headaches and body aches. Some people also have respiratory symptoms, diarrhea, and/or a dry cough. Most patients develop pneumonia. SARS spreads through close

NEUTRINO WARNING

person-to-person contact via respiratory droplets.

Severe Acute Respiratory Syndrome has emerged many times in China's southern provinces and typically soon spreads by travelers worldwide. The disease has killed thousands of people worldwide and infected tens of thousands more.

In related news, U.S. public health authorities say that all airline flights from China are prohibited from landing on U.S. soil for the foreseeable future. If safety concerns force such flights to land, passengers and airline personnel will not be released from quarantine unless and until they can be certified SARS-free. Relations between the U.S. and China are becoming more and more strained.

Before I knew it, I'd made it up to my sixth-floor office in the physics building.

I stopped outside the men's room and took a sip of tea from my travel mug. I glared at the battered wooden door with its prominent 'MEN' sign. The closest ladies' room sat five floors below me. One of these days, I would commandeer this bathroom and put a big 'WOMEN' sign up. None of the professors who had offices on this floor ever came up here anyway.

I shifted my too-full backpack and made it the rest of the way down the hall to my office. Luckily the door stood open, so I didn't have to fish out my keys. I shared my office with the rest of the neutrino group students; I guessed that was the former neutrino group now. The neutrino lab was all the way down in the basement.

New-guy Jake sat inside the office. Apparently, he was an early bird.

There were four once-stately but worn wooden desks placed on three walls of the room. An avalanche of papers buried my desk; the other desks were clear. My desk had an ancient scrawl-covered chalkboard above it, and the other walls had a variety of posters advertising the scientific meetings of yesteryear. A huge window with a ratty orange plaid couch underneath it stretched along the fourth wall. Outside the window, there was a fire escape. Occasionally, I crawled out on said fire escape to get some air and take a little break.

"*Bonjour.* Morning, Kathy." Jake gave me a big twinkly-eyed smile.

I set my load down atop the pile already balanced precipitously on my desk. It wobbled but held. I sank down in my old office surplus metal chair, which also wobbled but held. I smelled chalk and too many musty papers.

"*Bonjour.*" I missed Gabrielle and the others we'd lost. Contemplating him, I took another sip of tea. Something about him seemed different today--maybe it was just that we weren't at a funeral. I went to five funerals last week besides the big memorial service at the campus amphitheater. "You seem more cheerful today." Maybe that blue shirt brought out the color of his eyes? Or, again, maybe it was the lack of a funeral.

His head wiggled up and down like one of those old-fashioned bobblehead dolls. "I'm looking forward to getting to some physics." Of course, as the new guy, Jake hadn't known the people that died.

I nodded. "I hear that." I took another sip.

"So, I haven't talked to you since Professor Davidson's funeral last week." He brushed a wavy lock of hair back from his face.

Now it was my turn to be the bobblehead doll. "Yep."

"That was sad when Gopal lost it and blubbered like that," Jake said. "I felt bad for him."

"I agree. Me too." But it did take the attention off some other people who might have been on the verge of blubbering, like me, for instance.

"Did you hear that big argument at the reception afterward?" he asked.

I shook my head. "Argument?"

"Dr. Karlsson and some other bigwigs were yelling at each other. Gopal screamed it 'wasn't appropriate' and stormed off."

I leaned back in my chair. "No. I must have left before then. Do you know what it was about?"

Jake pulled his chair over to mine, sat, and leaned toward me. "I think they argued about who's going to be the new physics department chair," he said softly.

I leaned toward him. "Interesting." I gazed into his eyes. He looked really cute up close.

Lars appeared in the doorway. "Good. Hey, Kath." He

stopped short in the doorway. "Oh, hey, Jake." He paused. "I'm not interrupting something, am I?" He smirked and brushed his hand through his blond hair.

I jumped up. "What?" I scrunched up my face. Just what was he implying? "No. What are you talking about? We were talking about physics. Right, Jake?"

Jake backed away a little. "Uh, yeah, right."

Lars leaned against the doorjamb, scowling. "By all means, continue. I know how you love to talk about physics, Kathy."

I took another sip of tea and cleared my throat. "So, as I was saying, the main piece of fusion equipment is a Tokamak, in which plasma is heated and confined by magnetic fields." Yes, I had been cramming fusion physics.

"What's the plasma again?" Jake asked, playing along.

"High-energy positively-charged heavy hydrogen ions and negatively-charged electrons make up the plasma. Pay attention," I said and then glanced at Lars, who'd crossed his arms.

Lars gave me an amused look, the corners of his mouth tugging upward.

I continued in lecture mode. "When these heavy hydrogen ions fuse together to form alpha-particles, they release energy. The goal is to reach ignition when the power from these alpha-particles gets high enough to maintain the plasma temperature, and the reaction becomes self-heating." I glanced at Lars again. "Alpha particles are...." I grabbed some chalk and started drawing some alpha particles on the chalkboard.

Jake scowled at me and interrupted. "I know what an alpha particle is: a helium nucleus, two protons, and two neutrons. I do have a bachelor's degree in physics, you know."

Lars came in and sat on his pristine desk. "What are you guys talking about this crap for? How come you're not down in the neutrino lab? I just tried to get in, and my key didn't work."

I noticed his left eye twitched. Uh, oh. That usually meant he'd had a run-in with his father. "The neutrino lab?" I asked in what I hoped was an innocent tone. Lars had a rude awakening coming; namely, the neutrino group was defunct, but I didn't want to be the one to tell him. Since he was almost ready to defend his neutrino dissertation, I had a feeling he would take the end of the neutrino project worse than I had--if that was even possible.

"Well, duh." Lars frowned.

"Lars, I hate to tell you, but--" Jake said.

I interrupted. "You should go down and talk to Gopal. He's been trying to get a hold of you."

"Tell me what?" Lars scrutinized Jake. He sidled over next to him and gave him his best smile. "C'mon, buddy, what's up?"

Jake looked at me, shrugged, and looked back at Lars. "Yeah, you should talk to Gopal."

"As your boss, I could order you two to tell me," Lars said.

I snorted. "The only thing you're the boss of is your so-called harem, and even that's iffy." Damn. Why had I brought that up?

At the mention of a harem, Jake perked up. "What's this about a harem? That sounds interesting."

Lars folded his arms and grinned. "Ah yes, my 'harem.' I happen to have a couple of openings if you're interested, Kathy...."

He did seem to have a lot of dates, but his harem was basically a figment of his imagination. "Dream on, Lars." I forced myself to smile. He used his charm as a weapon. I wasn't going to let him get to me. I knew better.

Lars turned to Jake, "Jake? I'm an equal opportunity employer." He flashed him a wickedly bawdy grin.

Jake turned beet red from the edge of his collar to the roots of his hair.

How cute. I couldn't help relishing Jake's discomfort a bit.

"What? Er, no, I don't think that would be appropriate." Jake shook his head a little.

Lars laughed and lightly punched Jake on the shoulder. "Chill, kid, I was joking."

Jake leaned back in his chair and relaxed a bit. "Oh." He smiled tentatively.

"Mostly." Lars grew back that wicked grin.

I felt relieved Lars' evil powers of persuasion weren't focused on me. Truth be told, I wasn't sure I was totally immune to them. Few people were. "So, anyway, go. Go see Gopal; he's waiting to see you."

Lars chuckled. "All right. I'll go ask him about this little mystery if it's too much for you two." He sauntered out of the room.

Jake let out a sigh of relief. "What was that? Was he flirting with me? I think that was inappropriate; he's my boss!"

"Not really your boss. Gopal's your boss." Hmm. Since I had a few years of seniority over Jake in grad school, at least, did that make me his boss, too? Did that mean he and I couldn't get together? Did I want to get together? I shook my head. Get a grip, Kath! "Don't worry about it, Jake. Lars flirts with everyone. It's a power play for him. He just tried to get you off balance." And it totally worked!

Jake leaned back in his chair. "Well, sure, I didn't think he was flirting. I mean--"

The fon on my desk rang. I answered it.

"Bad news, Kathy," Gopal said on the fon. "Because of the SARS outbreak and the fatalities from the last one, the government won't let anyone from Asia into the country."

I groaned. "So, the Chinese fusion experts that were supposed to come to help us...?"

"We're out of luck." Gopal sighed loudly. "Can you and Jake go down to the fusion energy lab and check it out? The university's Safety Committee signed off on it, but they don't have your expertise. Just a sec. Hi Lars. I've got to go, Kathy. Lars finally deigned to show up."

"Jake, it looks like it's back to the desalination plant for us," I said, hanging up.

He pushed up his glasses. "Huh?"

Yes, possibly, I was the geekiest person in the room. "Salt mines." I forced a grin. "We have to get back to work." For a few moments, I sat there trying to psyche myself up for entering the lab of my dead friends.

We eventually made our way down to the fusion energy lab in the northwest corner of the basement.

I braced myself and opened the unlocked door. Breathe, Kathy, breathe. I had to do this; Gabrielle and the others would want me to do this. I took one cautious step inside, examining the dim lab. The large, high-ceilinged room seemed very moist and chaotic, with a lot of equipment against the east wall. "I don't like the looks of this." I sidestepped a puddle. The garden-level windows had been repaired where the snow had crashed through, but I could definitely feel a lot of humidity in there. Frankly, I was surprised the Safety Committee had deemed it safe.

"I don't think we should go in," I said. I wasn't procrastinating. "I'm going to go to the circuit box under the stairs and make sure the power is off to the room." Water and electricity don't mix. "Jake, can you stay here and make sure nobody goes in?"

He nodded. "Yeah."

A little while later, I returned, my electrical mission completed, and we ventured inside. Water pooled on the floor. Except for the big metal cylinder bolted in the middle of the room, most of the equipment had been pushed against the east wall by the avalanche. The snow must have crashed through the windows. If I recalled correctly, from what Gabrielle had said, most of the equipment was sensitive, so this wasn't a good thing.

"Let's unplug everything so I can restore the power," I said, "and we can turn on the lights to see what we've got here." We made quick work of it, and soon I returned from another successful mission to the circuit boxes.

With the lights on, the situation looked dismal. The room was flooded, with a thin layer of water and broken glass all over the floor. The expensive cutting-edge apparatus was now an expensive, jumbled, possibly broken puzzle.

"Well, crap monkey!" Jake scowled.

An involuntary laugh escaped from me. "What? What the heck is a crap monkey?"

He faced me. "Oh, you know, it's a bad situation, a crap monkey."

Again, I couldn't help laughing. "No, I can't say as I do know."

He smiled back at me. "Yeah, okay, I just made it up. This looks bad, though."

A voice in the doorway echoed his thoughts. "It sure does." Gopal's face resembled a Red Giant star. "What's going on here?"

I pointed at the disarrayed equipment. "It looks like the avalanche did quite a bit of damage," I said. "We turned off the electricity to the room."

Jake nodded. "We should be safe. We were just getting ready to inspect everything."

"Yeah," I said. "What happened with Lars?"

Gopal rubbed his beard ruefully. "I told Lars about the neutrino project being canceled for the time being. He didn't take it well."

I felt relieved that Gopal had borne Lars' wrath instead of me, but I quickly pushed those thoughts out of my head.

"Hans was up to his old tricks yelling at Lars again this morning," Gopal said. "I could hear him from my office all the way down the hall. I feel sorry for Lars. But I had to tell him I couldn't avoid putting him on probation since he's been MIA for over a week. He didn't take that well either."

Poor Gopal and poor Lars. Sometimes it seemed Lars was caught between a rock and a harder rock, what with his ambition and his dad's.

Gopal continued, "So anyway, the reason I came down is I've made a decision about the group. I decided to make Kathy the de-facto group leader." He smiled at me.

I must have heard him wrong. "What? Me? I can't be the group leader." I don't want the responsibility! "What about Lars? What about you? What about the Europeans who are coming?"

"Lars is unstable. He's proven that he can't be trusted. When the Europeans get here, we'll revisit the situation."

Gopal gingerly rubbed his beard. "The faculty noticed your quick thinking during the avalanche. We need someone who can think on his, er, her, feet for this important project and get it going again. It's a high-profile project. It has the potential to really help the human race."

I wasn't sure I was ready to be in charge of something so important. "But what about you?"

"I will be the official head, but it looks like I'll be stuck doing a lot of bureaucratic nonsense until we get this department head issue resolved." His gaze unfocused, and his attention went somewhere else.

"But if Kathy is my boss, then we can't… I can't ask her…." Jake trailed off.

"Can't ask her what?" Gopal contemplated him.

I stared at the two of them. Good question. Can't ask me what?

Jake hung his head. "Nothing. Never mind."

I couldn't be in charge; I'd never been in charge of anything. "But I don't have the experience."

Gopal frowned. "Kathy, you've been saying you're ready for more responsibility for quite a while now."

I'd meant it when I'd said it, but now faced with the possibility, it seemed intimidating. Woman up, Kath! I swallowed. "I appreciate it. But…"

Gopal's face was turning red again. "What's the problem? I shouldn't have to tell you how important the fusion project is."

"I know it's important." That was the problem. "Are you sure?"

"You're all we've got. You have to step up." He held his hand up. "You're in charge. That's final. Congratulations. Just don't disappoint me."

"Uh, thank you." I gulped. "You won't be disappointed." I hoped.

Chapter Four

On my way to work Tuesday morning, Ellen gave me a news report.

March 16, 2098: Flooding along the Mississippi River continues: The Mississippi River and its tributaries are above flood stage in Wisconsin, Minnesota, and Iowa. Waters are expected to continue rising in the coming days. Government officials in these areas have declared states of emergency, and many residents have been piling sandbags to try to protect homes and businesses. This year, the region has received higher-than-average precipitation, with some areas receiving more than double their typical amounts. Individual storms have often dumped volumes of rainfall that completely overwhelmed local streams. The Mississippi is closed to all traffic from Minneapolis, Minnesota, to Muscatine, Iowa.

"Rising waters are hazardous," said a director of the central office of the National Weather Service. "Do not under any circumstances drive or walk into moving floodwater."

Several people are reported missing and feared dead.

I felt a lot of trepidation when I unlocked the door to the fusion energy lab. I still missed my friends from the group and still couldn't believe they were gone.

The awful news about the Mississippi flooding put my nervousness about the new job into perspective, but I still couldn't believe I was in charge of the group. I knew in my gut Lars would not be happy about our reversed roles, but I hoped he wouldn't be too nasty.

When I'd told Megan about my new job, she'd laughed uproariously until I convinced her I wasn't joking. Then she'd gotten very quiet and said, 'Well, good luck with that.' That about summed it up--I needed lots of luck. I wanted to have a positive impact on this project; it was important.

Since we're almost out of fossil fuels and they're so bad for global warming, their use is highly restricted. We desperately needed more alternative energy sources. Nuclear fusion was ideal because it made pollution-free energy out of water. If we could develop cheap fusion energy, we might be able to stop global warming from getting worse. Or, who knows, maybe we could even reverse it. Optimism segued to nausea when I thought about the huge responsibility.

Yesterday after Gopal's announcements Jake and I had mopped the floor, swept up the glass, and generally picked up. Facilities Operations had finished the repairs, which apparently didn't involve cleaning up. Jake had worked hard but hadn't said much. Frankly, he'd seemed kind of mopey. Men, can't live with 'em, can't boss them around without them getting grumpy. At least after our work yesterday, it didn't look like a disaster area in here anymore.

I set my rucksack on what I'd claimed as my new desk and sat down on my new cushy chair. The equipment here was much more shiny and new than in the neutrino lab down the hall-- avalanche notwithstanding.

Yesterday, I'd also discovered a power kill switch in the fusion lab for emergencies, so my rigmarole with the circuit breakers had been for naught. Live and learn. Yep. I had a new motto. I would--

Jake came into the lab. "*Bonjour.*"

...lick this whole fusion manager thing. "*Bonjour.*" Mmm. He looked yummy. Egad! That wasn't managerial. Or maybe it was? No. I was just hungry for breakfast; that was it. "Morning, Jake. Good job yesterday." I smiled managerially.

"Thanks. Are you all right?" He peered into my face. "You look a bit odd."

Okay, maybe I should nix the managerial smile. "Sure, thanks for asking. And you, how are you?"

"Fine." He sat down at a desk and leaned back in his chair, balancing on the two back legs. "So? Any sign of Lars? Are we going to do some physics today? What's on the agenda?"

What's on the agenda? Did I even have an agenda? Action

item one: get an agenda. I said the first thing that popped into my mind. "How about breakfast?" I wasn't avoiding a confrontation with Lars.

"Fine with me." Jake smiled. "I can always eat."

We decamped to the student union cafeteria. As usual, teenagers and twentysomethings with technicolor hair filled it to overflowing, with a few grown-ups and little kids in animal costumes thrown in for good measure. The costumes must be for Earth Day at the end of the week. Maybe the kids were here to practice the Parade of Species?

As we walked in, Jake waved his hand toward the grill areas. "Carnivores or herbivores?" he asked.

The carnivores line had a giant picture of a Tyrannosaurus Rex, and the herbivores line had a picture of a Brachiosaurus-- both painted in tones of cerulean and shocking pink.

"What do I look like? A thousandaire?" I darted around him into the herbivores' line. "Herbivores, of course."

He followed me into the line.

We stood there for a few minutes, as the line didn't go anywhere. It felt awkward. "So...," I said.

"So...," Jake said at the same time.

We laughed uneasily. Why did I feel so nervous?

"You go ahead." Jake waved his hand toward me.

"What are you going to do this weekend for Earth Day?" I asked.

Jake shrugged. "Not much. I don't have any family."

"Bummer." I frowned. Not see your family on Earth Day? Not have any family? That seemed incomprehensible. And depressing.

"My roommate and I will probably just have dinner, maybe invite some friends over," he said. "How about you?"

"Luckily, my folks are coming from Missouri to visit; I haven't seen them in ages." I made a split-second decision. "But you and your roommate must come over to my place. I insist. You can even invite some friends if you like."

Jake shot me a grin as the line inched forward. "Thanks. That sounds nice. I'll have to check with Dave, though."

At that, our conversation reached another standstill, not unlike the food line.

"Do you really think dinosaurs were blue and pink?" I asked.

Jake glanced up at the herbivore sign and chuckled. "Oh, yeah. These signs are pretty garish."

I liked the way his eyes twinkled when he was amused, and that smile of his was hard to resist.

He pointed over my shoulder. "But look, there's a green dinosaur."

I turned around to see the child in front of us in a miscellaneous dinosaur costume. "Well, yeah, it's green, and I guess it's a dinosaur, but I couldn't tell you what kind; maybe gimme-breakfast-asaurus."

Jake laughed, and his eyes twinkled again.

I wasn't staring at him.

"Yeah, or I'm-hungry-asaurus," he said.

I roared with laughter. People turned around and looked at me to see what the commotion was. I wasn't overreacting; Jake was funny.

My emotions were all over the place lately. Take it down a notch, Kathy!

"Lily, the physics administrative assistant, is a wizard at making costumes," I said. "You should see some of the ones she's making now. She makes them for her daughter, her daughter's friends, and even some adults."

"Next!" someone in front of me yelled.

I turned around to face the front of the line.

"Yes, you missy. What do you want?" A very large fellow in a greasy formerly-white apron pointed his spatula at me.

I guessed it was my turn to order. I hadn't even thought about what I wanted yet. "I guess I'll just have a cheeze and bakon omelet and some potatoes with cheeze and onions and toast on the side. And some fruit." Breakfast is my favorite meal.

"Is that all?" Jake muttered. He ordered two eggs and some toast. "So, have you ever had real meat from an animal?" he asked as we stood there waiting for our orders.

"Sure, all the time." I waved my hand.

He frowned and pushed up his glasses. "Really?"

"Okay, I exaggerated. When I was little, we had chicken at home on winter and summer solstices, Earth Day, and the fall equinox. But I haven't had it much since I left home and went away to school--unlike these undergrads--they're probably rich." I waved my hands at the folks in the carnivores' line.

"Yeah, same here."

"My parents might get some for this weekend. In fact, I bet they will." What a yummy thought.

"Order up! Hey, missy!" the employee said. "Your food is ready."

Wow, that seemed quick. I guess it wasn't as crowded here as it appeared. We got our food, paid with our university cards, and went to the seating area. Feeling famished, I dug right in.

Jake leaned back in his chair and snickered. "You're something, Kathy. You're the real thing; you're not fake. I like you."

That seemed kind of out of the blue. "Okay? Thanks?" I may have had a goofy grin. He liked me.

All too soon, we were done eating, and it was time to go back to work.

By the time we got back to the physics building, I had an agenda for the day: we needed to assess the equipment's status and see if we could find the physical lab notebooks and fons and access the fusion group's computer files. Basically, we needed to figure out what stage they were in with the research.

Back in the basement, we heard yelling in the fusion lab. I stopped in the hall. I didn't want to get into the middle of anything.

Jake took a few more steps before glancing back at me and halting. He raised his eyebrows.

I raised mine back at him and shrugged.

We both shook our heads. It had to be Lars and Hans going at it in the lab.

"I forbade you to go into physics, but you did it anyway!" one man yelled. "You're such a flooding screw-up." That must be Hans.

"How can you say that?" another man yelled. I was betting that it was Lars.

"We were too easy on you," Hans said. "You should have seen my dad with me. He was strict. Your mother coddled you; I never should have let her have a say in raising you."

"Don't you dare say anything bad about my mother!" Lars

said.

"Did you ever stop and consider how it makes me look when you can't seem to accomplish anything?" Hans said. "You've been in grad school for years. How long is it going to take you?"

"It's not my fault there was an avalanche!" Lars said.

"If you're going to work on the fusion project, I need results!" Then, an older blond man stormed out of the lab, barreling past us, red-faced, with his lips pressed into a microscopic line. Yep, it was Hans Karlsson. I don't think he even saw us. Thank Gaia, my folks were nothing like Hans.

After Hans started up the stairs, Jake faced me. "Was that Lars' dad?" he said under his breath.

"I'm afraid so." We walked the rest of the way to the lab very slowly.

When we entered the lab, a red-faced Lars was leaning over some equipment. He straightened and tapped his watch. "Tick, tock, boss. I wondered when you'd show up." His voice was fake-cheerful, and his smile looked more like a grimace.

So much for making a good impression on my first day as The Boss. I wanted to see if his left eye twitched, but I felt a bit afraid to get closer. "Uh, nice to see you, Lars. We were here... working...earlier. See, our stuff is here." I pointed at my bag. "We just took a little break to get some food." Why am I justifying my behavior to him? I'm The Boss. My brain knew he was upset about his dad yelling at him, but the rest of me was very nervous about dealing with him.

"Went out for breakfast, huh? Poor kids." He smiled genuinely this time. "I had breakfast in bed--served by the beautiful Brittani and the scrumptious Stephani."

Ugh. More information than I wanted. But better them than me.

Jake chuckled. "Cool." He stepped closer. "So, you, ah, like women then?" He peered into Lars' face.

Lars smiled in my general direction.

Uh oh. He wasn't going to try to flirt with me, was he? My flirting muscles were way out of practice. I decided to change the subject. "Lars, how are you doing with the new ...situation? As far as I'm concerned, we're all a team. Everyone is valuable." I stepped away from him and put a table between us.

"How do you think I'm doing?" His eyes flashed. "I'm on flooding probation--I might lose my job. My dissertation is in a shambles. And my dad--don't get me started on my dad. He flipped out when he heard. And I have a new boss--no offense, Kathy." He crossed his arms.

I crossed my arms, too. "None taken," I said through a fake smile. At least not an infinite amount of offense taken. He was just upset about his dad, right?

"While you were gone, Gopal stopped by and said the computer place in Iowa was flooded, and we can't get any 'new' computers," Lars added.

"Oh no!" That was bad news. I sank onto a lab stool. With the global economy essentially dead, refurbished electronics were the best we could get. And now we couldn't even get those.

Lars continued. "I was just hooking stuff up to see if it still works, Boss." His eyes narrowed when he emphasized 'boss.'

I held up my hands. "Whoa. I would rather you didn't just hook stuff up. We need to be careful here. Are you even familiar with this equipment?"

"Yes." Lars fluffed his shoulder-length hair. "But, of course, some of us have personal lives, so we may not know every little detail."

I scowled. "Yeah, well, how about you keep your personal life personal. We don't need to hear any more about Brittani and Stephani or their ilk."

"Jealous, huh?" he said.

Jake piped up, "I wouldn't mind hearing...." but trailed off when I shot him my die-in-a-horrific-shark-attack glare.

I needed to calm down. I carefully considered the situation. "If you guys don't know anything about the fusion equipment, start with the computers. Maybe we can get them to work. Try to get them up and connected to the network. I'll look for the lab notebooks and fons--even though we might not be able to access the fons."

Lars glared at me for a couple of seconds, but I guess he was too worn out from fighting with his dad or breakfast in bed to kick up a fuss. He shrugged.

Jake and Lars got to work connecting computer components.

I scoured the large, rectangular room looking for notebooks and fons. I looked around the giant cylinder in the middle of the room, in the piles of books, papers, and miscellaneous electrical equipment piled against the east wall and on the book-filled shelves that were still standing.

Nothing. I stood in the room with my hands on my hips, elbows out. We were drowned if we couldn't find the lab records. I would be a big fat failure at this project and disappoint everyone.

Jake came over. "No luck, huh?" He shoved his hands into his pockets.

I sighed and shook my head. "Nope." The fusion lab records had to be here somewhere. We had to find them. As far as I knew, the fusion grad students didn't have a separate office in the building.

"Well, I've got some more bad news: as we suspected, the computers don't seem to work," Jake said. "I guess they got wet. I hope they backed up all their data on the Mass Storage System." He frowned.

I knew it had been a long shot, but I felt my stomach drop like precipitation from a cumulonimbus cloud. Computers were a necessity for our fusion mission.

Glancing around, my eye grazed the row of desks. Did I check them? Of course, I did. I think I did. Didn't I? I rushed over to my new desk and flung open the drawers. It contained Gabrielle's stuff. There was a framed picture of her with some people I didn't recognize; they all had their arms around each other and looked so happy. My breath got trapped in my throat. Those people would never be happy together again.

My stomach fell into my shoes as I was reminded of the tragedy yet again. I guess there was no helping it; we were going to have to go through their things. "Jake, please go see if Lily has some shipping boxes. Somebody should have returned these personal effects to their families. Ask her if she can come down and help us."

"Okay." Jake nodded and bounded out the door.

"What should we do about the computer situation?" Lars asked.

It did seem to be a conundrum. "If we submit a work request

46

to the computer group, it could take a long time. Maybe Gopal could tell them the project was a high priority?" I sat down and drummed my fingertips on the desk, thinking furiously. "Megan might be able to pull some strings for us."

"Megan? How's old purple hair doing? Is she still into girls?" Lars asked, smirking as he sat down and swung his feet onto a desk.

"You're just upset that she didn't go for you when you flashed her your pearly whites," I said.

Lars flashed his pearly whites at me. I ignored him as I patted down my pockets, looking for Ellen. I couldn't find her. "Ellen, where are you?"

"I am in a dark place with some books and papers." Her voice sounded muffled and coming from the top of my new desk.

I found her in my backpack. "Ellen: dial Megan."

Soon, I heard Megan's voice and saw a blob of purple in the tiny screen. "Hi, Kathy. How's the first day as boss going? You're not still nervous, are you?"

I glanced at Lars. "Nervous? Whatever gave you a crazy idea like that?" I rushed on. "I'm here with the new fusion group, and we are having computer problems."

"Okay," she said. "What's up? Maybe I can help?"

"They don't work." I exhaled.

She laughed. "That is a problem. Yes, I think I can help. For you, I can expedite an emergency work request--that ought to get someone there this week."

"Nothing sooner? Like today?"

She guffawed. "I can't perform miracles."

"Okay," I said. "Thanks for your help. Please input the request."

"You owe me," she said. "I think I foresee you doing a lot of dishes in the near future."

"I didn't know I'd called a psychic line--but okay." I sighed.

"Anything else?" Megan asked.

"Uh." My mind went blank. Too much pressure! "I guess not. Thanks a lot, Megan." We signed off. One disaster was averted, but we still needed the fusion lab notebooks and fons.

"I guess I'll be going then." Lars sat up. "We can't work without computers."

I had a brainstorm. "Wait, I know! Let's get the computers from the neutrino lab."

Lars didn't immediately jump up and follow my instructions for some reason. He scowled. "What makes you think our computers will be in any better shape than these?"

"Geography. That side of the building didn't get hit by the avalanche."

Lars tensed as if to get up but then relaxed. "We can't get into the neutrino lab, remember?"

Jake came back with Lily and some boxes. Lily was a vision in gray: gray hair, gray eyes, a gray silk blouse, charcoal gray slacks, and silver jewelry.

Jake was a vision in cute. Focus, Kath! I approached them.

"Oh, dear." Lily put her hand in front of her mouth. "I can't believe we didn't get this stuff taken care of for the fusion group. University protocol says the department chair should take care of it, but obviously, since he's gone too… And we don't have a replacement yet. It must have fallen through the cracks. And what about their houses? Oh, dear."

Jake gave her a gentle smile. "It's not your fault, Lily. A lot has been going on lately. Can you handle this, or will it be too difficult? Of course, we'll help if you want."

She lowered her hand and squinted her eyes in stubborn resolve. "No. I can handle it. They deserve to have someone looking out for them--even now."

I nodded and rubbed her arm. "No one could do a better job of it than you. While you're at it, could you please look for their lab notebooks and fons? We need them to continue the experiment.

Brainstorm! "Say, Lily, can I borrow your keys? We need to get some equipment out of the neutrino lab."

"I guess that would be all right." She lifted the chain around her neck over her head. "It's for the fusion experiment, right?"

"Absolutely," I said.

Lars, Jake, and I succeeded in stealing, er, borrowing, the computer equipment from the neutrino lab, complete with all the associated bric-a-brac.

In the meantime, Lily had been busy sorting and packing. She approached me with a beaming smile on her face and a box of stuff. "I think I may have found something."

I glanced into the box to see it had some fons and notebooks underneath them. Hurray! We were saved! "You fly, Lily! Look, you guys, Lily found them!"

Jake and Lars rushed over to us.

"Dry!" Jake exclaimed.

"These fons are kind of a long shot, but they would be the most helpful." I took one of the proffered tiny black fons from Lily. "Since they're voice-activated, most fons only work for the owner." I tried punching some buttons and saying "Activate." and "Emergency override." Nothing happened.

Jake peered at the fons. "Some people do password protection for their fons in case something happens to them--so other people can access their data. Maybe Gabrielle and Jean-Phillipe did that?"

"If they did, we're still out of luck because we don't know their passwords." I paused. "That's a good idea, though; we should do that with our fons."

Lars shot me a cryptic look.

I sighed, disappointed. We had to access the fusion data. "Jake, please check the rest of these fons to make sure we can't access them."

"Sure thing." He scooped them up.

Lily gestured toward the notebooks at the bottom of the box. "Here, I have a good feeling about these notebooks."

I gingerly took one of the (dry!) notebooks and opened it slowly, as if the fate of the planet depended on it. Because it might.

Chapter Five

Hurray, the notebook wasn't too soggy. I found a beautiful, glorious schematic diagram of the Tokamak apparatus inside it. "Thank Gaia!" We were saved! Maybe we could come up with a new energy source for our dying planet after all. And it might not matter if we couldn't find the fon passwords.

Lars opened another notebook. "Here's the overall laboratory set up with the Tokamak surrounded by instruments!" He almost jumped with excitement. Thank Gaia, the fusion team kept old-fashioned paper records like we were supposed to. These days, you never knew when the computers might go down.

The rest of us eagerly looked at the indicated diagrams. In them, various equipment, including two kinds of spectrometers, some bolometers, photodetectors, computers, and a laser interferometer, surrounded the Tokamak.

Lily backed away, patting her gray hair. For some reason, she didn't seem as enthralled about the diagram as the rest of us. "So, I should get back to work. I don't understand all this stuff."

I took in her uneasy expression. "You know what the big apparatus in the center is, right?"

"Uh, sure. It's the Toka-thingy." She pulled an errant lock of hair back behind her ear.

Lars laughed.

I shot him a dirty look. "Exactly. We put the plasma in there and try to ignite it."

"It sounds dangerous." She crinkled her forehead.

"It is a little bit dangerous, but it's worth it." I grinned.

"What's that other stuff in the diagram?" She pointed at one of the pictures.

I was all for everybody knowing more about science. "The spectrometers are machines we use to measure, well, to measure spectra."

Lily turned down her mouth and wrinkled her brow.

"By spectra, I mean electromagnetic waves, including visible light--which you know about, and also less-energetic stuff like infrared light and radio waves and more-energetic stuff like ultraviolet light, x-rays, and gamma rays."

"You don't say." Lily started shuffling towards the door. "Well, this has been interesting, but I better get back to the office--who knows what's going on up there without me."

Jake reached for a couple of boxes. He was sweet. "Let me help you with those." Jake and Lily exited, arms full of boxes, on their way up to the physics department office.

"Lars, can you get started with the cables and detectors around the Tokamak using the diagrams we found?" I asked. "I'll get the computers from the neutrino lab hooked up."

Lars saluted me. "Sir, yes, sir!" He was annoying, but I'll take sarcastic obedience over slacker disobedience any day.

We got to work. I tried to connect the various computer parts to each other and the network. It was slow going--I guess I should have paid better attention when we took them apart.

Jake returned to the lab at an inopportune time; I stood in front of the computer pieces throwing them dagger looks.

"Kathy, do you need some help there?" he asked.

"Yes," I said. "Please. Help me hook up this stuff."

"Lucky for you, I'm a whiz at machinery," Jake said.

Together, we got the small computer network assembled.

Periodically, I'd hear a grunt or two coming from Lars, but it seemed like he was making progress, so I decided not to poke the beast.

I logged onto a computer and accessed the physics network, but then I was stumped. I couldn't access any of the fusion group's files. Ugh! I shot some more dagger looks at the system, but it didn't seem to care. If we couldn't access their data files, we were drowned. I scooted my chair back from the computer.

Lars swore softly while standing in front of one of the

interferometer stations.

I went over to him but stayed a safe distance away. "What's up?"

"This piece of crap doesn't seem to work," Lars said. "I'm not sure why." When it worked, the interferometer combined two beams of energy to create an interference pattern that enabled us to measure the tokamak's effectiveness.

I raised my hands in the air. "Well, don't look at me. I'm not going to troubleshoot an interferometer. I could barely get the computers going."

Jake gave me a raised-eyebrow look from across the room.

I ignored it. "And I can't access any of the fusion group files."

"I hate to say it," Lars sat on the edge of a desk, "but I think we need more help." He looked down at the floor, shaking his head.

Jake joined us. "I agree. Don't you guys know anybody that could help out?"

"As a matter of fact...." Lars shook his forefinger. "Brittani is a great lab tech. She's an electrical engineering major. I bet I could convince her to help us somehow." He flashed us his lewd and lascivious grin, and I cringed a little.

"I bet Megan would help us with the computer troubles." Jake pushed his glasses up his nose. "She seems nice."

Jake was right, but I wasn't thrilled about getting stuck with more household chores. But I guessed it couldn't be helped. "Ellen: Call Megan."

Megan answered. "Hi, Kathy. What's up?"

"I," I glanced at Jake, "er, we cannot access any of the fusion group's files on the physics network or the Mass Storage System. Is there any chance you guys could reassign ownership to me and reset the passwords?" My voice did not get all whiney at the end there like I was begging. Please, please. We needed this.

Phew. The loss of my friends hit me suddenly again. So unfair. My eyes started filling with tears. I blinked rapidly.

"We've never had a situation like this before, where all the people involved...." She quickly changed tacks. "I should be able to do that."

I cleared my throat. "It's sort of an emergency," I said. "We need it as soon as possible."

"I'll see what I can do," she said. "But considering all the other favors I've been doing for you lately, I foresee you cleaning the bathroom in the near future--and being second in line for the shower for the rest of the month."

I sighed. "Thanks."

Once I'd gotten that settled, Lars jumped up abruptly. "I'm leaving. It's almost past lunchtime, and I'm starving." He raced out the door like some Nordic Olympian.

"Sure, let's break for lunch," I yelled after him. "Go ahead."

I looked at Jake. "I usually go to the lunchroom here in the physics building for lunch. Do you want to join me?"

Jake shrugged. "Sounds good."

A little while later, Jake and I entered the lunchroom. It was a plain twenty-foot by twenty-foot room with mismatched tables and chairs, a beat-up refrigerator, several vending machines, and a long counter with a microwave and coffee machine. A few other physicists were in there eating.

After I got a sandwich, I said, "There's Marcello."

He had his head bent over his plate, and the top of his balding head reflected light.

Eyes full again, I said, "*Bonjour.*" My emotions were all over the place these days.

"*Bonjour.*" He gave us his big crooked-teeth smile.

"Jake, do you remember Marcello?" I said. "I think I introduced you. Marcello and I shared an office when we first started grad school years ago. Can we join you?" Marcello and I were at similar stages in our careers.

"*Si.*" Marcello waved his hand at the empty seats. He and Jake greeted each other.

"So, how are you guys holding up?" Marcello asked. "Have you recovered from all the...ah...events?" He picked up his fork.

I nodded as I unwrapped my favorite sandwich, cheeze salad, and took a big bite.

"So, Kathy, I guess congratulations are in order. You are now the group leader, *si*?" Marcello waved his fork around.

"Yes. Thanks," I said with my mouth full.

Jake examined Marcello's plate. "Say, what do you have

there? That looks good. Is it some type of pasta? Where did you get that?"

Marcello gave us a big smile. "*Sì*. It is delicious. My beautiful wife, Allessandra, cooked it for me. So, alas, you cannot get any around here."

Jake put down his sandwich untouched. "Can I have a bite?"

Marcello patted his stomach and laughed. "*Sì*, Alessandra does tend to pack a lot. You can have the rest if you like."

"I like," Jake said, grinning and grabbing.

"I guess I will be going," Marcello said. "It was nice to see you again, Kathy, Jake." He stood up.

"Wait, Marcello, I want to ask you something." I grabbed his arm.

He sat back down. "*Sì*? What is it?"

I chewed and swallowed, throwing a look at Jake. "The fusion energy lab isn't in very good shape. Since you're such a physics genius, I wondered if you could help us." My dad always said a little flattery could go a long way.

Marcello rubbed his lower lip with his fingers. "*Sì*, it is, of course, an essential project. It was kind of your group to step in and fill the void."

I didn't need to tell him we weren't given a choice, right?

"Still, I have a lot of my own work to do," Marcello said. "What is in it for me?"

"Since you like home cooking, I could cook--" I said.

Marcello raised his hands. "Santa Maria, no. Please do not try that again--at least not on my account. Those carrot, ah, … cookies of yours were very interesting."

I paused and considered my options. Marcello was a physics genius; if he joined our team, we'd have a much better chance at success. "Please consider helping us achieve nuclear fusion; it could save the planet." Come to think of it, I was surprised he hadn't already been asked to help.

"It is a crucial experiment, and you did save my life in the avalanche." He sighed. "I guess I owe you. *Sì*. I will help."

"*Grazie*!" I stuck my hand out. "It's a deal." We shook on it. I felt relieved. The fusion project needed all the help it could get.

Look at me, recruiting help even during lunch. Maybe I

could handle being The Boss.

After lunch, when we got back to the lab, Ellen told me I had a message from Megan. "Mission accomplished, Kath! I got the files and passwords assigned to you. I'm a hacking goddess! You're welcome."

Megan flies!

Ellen gave me a news update on my way to work the next day.

March 17, 2098: Severe flooding in Europe:

Thousands of Europeans braced for yet another wave of flooding as drenching rain continues to fuel the worst natural disaster to hit central Europe in years. Floodwaters have killed dozens of people, and thousands have been evacuated from their homes. Church bells and fire sirens were sounded to warn residents. Thousands of Germans along the raging Oder River were ordered to evacuate yesterday after another earthen dike burst in the Oderbruch plain, a low-lying area sixty kilometers north of Frankfurt an der Oder.

The flooding is growing particularly critical in Ratzdorf at the confluence of the Oder and Neisse rivers, which form part of the border with Poland.

Due to excessive rains in the last few days, virtually all central European towns have been crippled by power outages, overflowing sewers, and severe damage to roads, railway lines, and bridges. With hundreds of thousands of acres underwater or projected to be underwater soon, officials fear diseases such as dysentery and typhoid will spread because of sanitary drinking water shortages.

In related news, German scientists have compiled an over 1000-year historical record that suggests recent devastating floods that left central European cities from Dresden to Prague buried in water are part of an upward trend caused by global warming. The University of Leipzig study focused on the Oder and Elbe rivers. Together these two rivers drain rainfall from over 150,000 square kilometers of Central Europe. The Leipzig study spokesperson said, "We found evidence for over 350 major floods on the Oder, with the earliest in 1269, and over 500 major floods on the Elbe, with the earliest in 1021. We applied statistical tests to this data and discovered positive trends: the frequency of major river floods in these areas is increasing."

I shuddered. How horrible! And right before Earth Day, too, the biggest holiday of the year. At this rate, there won't be anyone left in Europe.

Jake, Lars, and I finished putting together the equipment. We connected the bolometer array to the Tokamak on the side opposite the lab windows, with two spectrometers on the opposite side of the Tokamak. We put the carbon dioxide Interferometer next to the bolometers. Next to that, we put the visible light spectrometer, and of course, we hooked everything up to the now accessible computers.

I didn't take any, or at least not much, pleasure whatsoever in bossing the two of them around.

Unfortunately, when we tried firing up the equipment, none of it worked.

Jake plopped down on a lab stool. "So, we're zero for," he scanned the lab, "everything."

Lars sat on a desk with his arms crossed. "I told you none of this junk would work."

I rubbed my forehead. I hated it when Lars was right. Of course, he really hated it when I was right, so it all evened out. "Fine. Call your friend, Brittani."

Lars saluted me sarcastically. "Sir, yes, sir. I'll go get her."

"No. Please just call her." I sighed. "We need to keep working."

Lars walked to the door. "She might need some …
convincing." He grinned wolfishly and left before I could stop him.

"Okay," I called after him. "Go get her."

Jake stood up. "I'm pretty good with machines. I could open some of them up and try to fix them. What do you think?"

It was music to my ears. "By all means. Go to it."

Marcello appeared, smiling and showing off his chin dimple. "*Buongiorno*, Jake, Kathy. How's it going so far?"

Jake stood. "*Buongiorno*, Marcello." He gestured around the room. "We've made some progress, but we're waiting for a lab tech right now."

Marcello nodded. "*Sì*, it was to be expected the delicate electronic equipment would not appreciate being flung about the room. Congratulations on the progress you have made so far."

He was being overly nice. "Is something up, Marcello?" I took a step toward him.

"Bah." He shook his head. "I am the bearer of bad news. The European scientists you were expecting...."

I immediately thought of the morning news. "Gaia!" I said. "They're not dead, are they?"

Jake gasped.

Marcello pursed his lips in surprise. "No, Kathy, why would you say such a thing?"

"I heard on the news there's more European flooding," I said. "The way things have been going... They're okay?"

"*Sì*, they are okay, but they are stranded in Germany and will be unable to join us for the foreseeable future."

That was a blow. I sank on a nearby lab stool. "The most important thing is that they stay safe and help their countrymen stay safe." It almost seemed as if Gaia herself was working against us. But I wasn't going to cry; I was The Boss, and bosses don't cry.

"I guess the project is up to us now," Marcello said.

I nodded.

Jake looked at me with trusting eyes. "So, what's next?"

I couldn't let him down, so I pulled myself together and stood up. "Marcello, can you help us out this afternoon?"

"*Sì*. I believe so. What did you have in mind?"

"We could review the computer files and see how far the fusion group got with simulations and data and such," I said. "Jake, please look at the equipment as you suggested."

Later in the afternoon, as Marcello, Jake, and I worked, Lars returned with a statuesque blonde woman in tow. Marcello and Jake turned, and their jaws fell open for a moment when they spied her, and then they rushed over to her.

"Santa Maria." Marcello reached her first. "*Buona giornata*, lovely lady, my name is Marcello." He held out his hand. When she held out hers in response, he grabbed it and raised it to his lips. "It is a great pleasure to meet you."

"Thanks," she said. "I'm Brittani. It's nice to meet you, too."

Jake wasted no time in introducing himself either. "I'm Jake. It's nice to meet you." As he shook hands with her, he seemed mesmerized.

This bothered me more than it should have. Who knew guys liked lab technicians? What did they see in her? Maybe it was that long blonde hair, or those big breasts, or those long legs.

Lars chuckled. "Down, boys. She's all mine."

Brittani put her hand in front of her mouth and giggled.

I walked over to her. "Hi, Brittani. I'm Kathy. Nice to meet you. Thanks for helping us out." I smiled. "We appreciate it." I waved my hand around the lab. "As you can see, we have a lot of electronics that need repair. Anything you could do would be most appreciated."

She flashed her perfect teeth at us. "Nice to meet all of you, too." She turned to Lars. "You weren't kidding when you said there was a lot of equipment here." She held up what I thought was her purse.

"Luckily, I brought my equipment." She glanced around the room. "Where can I set up?" No, not a purse, a toolbox.

I waved toward a lab table. "Over there is good."

As she walked over to it, the guys' eyes followed her.

I walked back over to my desk and accidentally knocked over my teacup. A miniature brown lake pooled on the desktop. Men, you can't live with them, can't work with them without getting totally aggravated. As I stared at the spill on my desk, I started to get a very intriguing idea about the experiment...

I vaguely remembered something about liquid that Gabrielle had mentioned. I picked up Ellen. "Ellen, please do a literature search on Tokamak and liquid."

"Message acknowledged." She paused. "Search complete. There are several relevant articles. The most promising seems to be 'Liquid Lithium Increases Efficiency in Tokamak'."

"Good. Show me that one." As I read, I got more and more excited. This idea might be just what we needed to make fusion energy viable. If we had a clean energy source, we could rid ourselves of global-warming-inducing fossil fuels once and for all. I could imagine the headlines: 'Human Race Saved!'

Chapter Six

I was in the fusion lab two days later, engrossed in designing Tokamak improvements, when Ellen interrupted.

"Incoming call from Maria Garcia, your mother. Do you accept?"

I looked up from the computer simulation Ellen and I were working on and realized it was later than I thought. "Sure. Hi, Mom."

"Hi, Kathy."

In the background, I heard an energetic "Hi, Kathy-bird!" from my dad.

"Hi, Dad!" I couldn't help smiling.

"Honey, we're waiting for you at the train station. You didn't forget about us, did you?"

Crap! I flushed. "Of course not, Mom. I'm just running a little late. Happy Earth Day!"

"Happy Earth Day." Mom sighed. "Shall we go ahead and take the light rail over to your house?"

"Uh, good idea. That might be easiest. See you soon." My parents were here. Earth Day flies!

I intercepted them at the light rail stop closest to my house. From a distance, I recognized their small statures. I could also tell they had a surprising amount of luggage for a short visit.

Dad dropped his bags and grinned as soon as he saw me. Then, he took large, loping strides until I was enveloped in his arms. "Kathy! *Hola, mija!* It's so good to see you!" he said into my hair. "It's been too long!" All my great-grandparents had immigrated to the U.S. from Mexico, and my parents occasionally whipped out their Spanish. Usually, when we were greeting or leaving one another.

I grinned as I breathed in his unique scent, a mysterious mix of soap and sulfur. I looked into his face, noting the fine laugh lines at the outside corners of his blue eyes. "*Hola*, Dad. It's good to see you too."

He held me at arm's length so he could see my face. "Happy Earth Day!"

"Happy Earth Day!" I smiled, taking in his usual wild brown hair and rumpled outfit. His shirt collar stuck up on one side, and part of his shirt was tucked in, and part wasn't. He seemed to have some kind of brown stain on the front of his jacket.

"How are those students treating you this semester?" I asked. "Have they blown anything up?"

He chuckled. "Not yet this semester--unless you count the time when some troublemakers combined sodium carbonate and diluted sulfuric acid."

"It didn't really explode, did it?" I asked, concerned.

"No flames, but they made a *huge* mess." Dad chuckled again.

Mom set her luggage down carefully, stood in place, and held out her arms. Her appearance was impeccable, from her smooth dark-brown hair and tan skin to her beautiful marbled-brown dress and matching shoes. In some ways, Mom and Dad were opposites. "*Hola*. Don't keep me waiting!" she said.

I hopped over and hugged her. "Sorry, Mom. Happy Earth Day!"

"Thanks. And to you." She looked me over. "You need a haircut, dear. And what are you wearing?" She shook her head. "Oh, well, you're your father's daughter."

"I'll take that as a compliment," I said. "How are your students this semester?"

"You know my college kids are a lot easier to deal with than Chris' high school kids." She smiled. "I can't complain. How's work going with you? How do you like the fusion project? Anything new?"

"Yes. Wait until you hear my latest idea. I'm going to try to use a liquid wall in the Tokamak."

"You don't say?" Mom's brown eyes sparkled. "Now, that sounds interesting. Tell me all about it." Mom and I linked arms and started walking toward home.

"Don't mind me," Dad said. "I'll get the luggage, this massive amount of luggage. No worries."

"Thanks, Pop," I said.

"Yes, thank you, dear," Mom said over her shoulder.

In no time, we were at my house. As we went inside, Mom said, "So did Megan get off okay? She went to visit her folks?"

"Yes," I said. "I'll tell her you asked about her."

"We're sorry to miss her," Mom said. "She's such a nice girl."

Dad huffed and puffed as he brought in the bags. "Megan's colorful!" He chuckled at his own dad joke. No one else did.

Mom glanced at her watch. "We need to put away this food as quickly as possible so we can make it to the Moonlight Mourning event."

"Food?" That sounded good. My stomach growled. When was the last time I had eaten?

"Of course, we brought food," Mom said. "It's Earth Day, isn't it? Did you shop?"

"I meant to…." I stammered. "I still can, later."

"No need. I took care of it." Mom started opening the bags. "Kathy, dear, where do you want this stuff?"

"Kitchen," I said.

"C'mon, Chris," she said. "Help us carry this stuff into the kitchen."

Leave it to Mom, she unpacked a feast worthy of a king: two chickens, sausages, several loaves of special holiday bread, wheels of cheeze, cookies, and two Earth Day cakes. Now, all the luggage made sense.

Mom brushed her hands together. "So, that's done. I assume you've got some fresh veggies in your cold frames?"

I nodded. "I should have some greens and carrots in the backyard. And I still have potatoes and dried beans left from last season. But how many people are you expecting for dinner tomorrow?"

"Surely, you invited several friends?" Mom said. "It's not a proper Earth Day feast unless there are lots of folks celebrating together."

Who did I invite? Oh, yeah, Jake and his roommate. I smiled. "So far, I have only invited a couple of friends."

Mom smoothed her dress. "I'm sure we'll find some people at the festivities to invite." She glanced at her watch. "Don't we need to get going for Moonlight Mourning? Are you riding this year?"

I deflated a little. I hadn't thought about Moonlight Mourning today. I did need to ride; it was a good remembrance of the people we'd lost.

Mom and Dad glanced at each other, and someone came to a wordless understanding. Would I ever have what they had?

"It's important to start Earth Day by remembering all the friends and relatives we've lost," Mom said.

"C'mon, Kathy-bird," Dad said. "It might not be the most fun thing to do, but you know it's the right thing."

"If we don't celebrate and remember people we've lost, how can we truly celebrate Earth Day and look to the future?" Mom asked. "Besides, you lost several friends recently, didn't you? You have to ride. Get your bike. We'll be fine. We can watch the procession from your front yard."

"I know you're right," I finally said.

The sun had just set when I reached City Hall, and stars were beginning to appear in the eastern sky. Town Square was jammed with black-clad bike riders. I looked down at my jeans and t-shirt; I should have changed.

"Welcome!" the mayor, a middle-aged gray-haired woman, yelled out. "Happy Earth Day!"

"Happy Earth Day!" the crowd boomed back to her.

"Do we have any new riders this year?" she asked.

A smattering of hands went up in the large crowd--mostly junior-high or younger kids.

"Good." She cleared her throat. "As you all know, tomorrow is our Vernal Equinox, also known as International Earth Day. It is the first day of spring, a day of hope and renewal. We will make Earth healthy and happy again someday if we all work together."

The crowd cheered.

"But tonight, on Earth Day Eve, if you will, all of Earth's citizens look back on the mistakes humans have made so we do not repeat them. We will stop global warming, not ignore it."

"We will stop global warming," the crowd chanted.

"'Why moonlight?' some of you youngsters may ask," she said.

"Why moonlight?" a couple of people in the crowd yelled, and the rest of us alternately groaned or chuckled.

"I'm glad you asked." The mayor shot us a smile. "Many places are simply too warm for their citizens to carry out the procession during the day. We ride at night so all our brothers and sisters around the world can ride with us as the same moonlight guides us all. Every person on Earth is united on Earth Day Eve."

"Every person on Earth is united tonight," the crowd chanted, and I joined in as I wiped a tear out of the corner of my eye. Ugh. So many tears lately.

"Why bicycles?" someone in the crowd yelled.

The mayor nodded. "'Why bicycles?' you may ask. Seventy-five years ago, the visionary Jacob Moretti rode his bicycle around the world to publicize the perils of global warming. Sadly, people didn't pay enough attention to him back then, but we do now. We follow his lead and resolve to get around under our own power."

I repositioned my bike against my legs.

"Now, I will read the Mourning Statement. Afterward, we'll have the moment of silence and commence the traditional silent bike ride around town." She cleared her throat again. "We gather tonight to mourn and remember the extinct plant and animal species and the millions of people lost in the last century through direct and indirect effects of global warming."

"We mourn and remember," the crowd chanted. I looked around a little. In many ways, it was a diverse bunch of all ages and races. However, the group was homogeneous in its fervent hope that planet Earth could be healed before it was too late. I nodded.

"We mourn and remember the peoples and cultural treasures of coastal Europe, Africa, and Asia," the mayor said. "We mourn and remember those lost from river flooding, mudslides, tidal waves, and disease."

"We mourn and remember."

"We mourn and remember Alaska, Texas, Louisiana,

Arkansas, Mississippi, Tennessee, Kentucky, Indiana, Illinois, Alabama, Florida, Georgia, South Carolina, North Carolina, Virginia, Maryland, Delaware, New Jersey, New York, Connecticut, Rhode Island, Massachusetts, New Hampshire, Maine, and Hawaii and regret that they were devastated by the advancing oceans."

"We mourn and remember."

"And finally, we mourn the wonderful family members, friends, and neighbors we lost here this year to disease and avalanche. They will never be forgotten."

It hit me harder than I expected. "We mourn and remember." My eyes filled with tears as memories of Gabrielle, Jean-Phillipe, and Guy, buried in lethal whiteness, came tumbling back. "They will never be forgotten," I whispered, glad I came.

The mayor's statement was met with respectful silence. A warm Chinook wind ruffled my hair. After a minute, the mayor picked up her bike by the podium and started riding out of Town Square. The folks closest to her got on their bikes and followed her out. Bike by bike, we followed them, an eerie silent river of people winding through town. The full moon lit our way, the only sound the thudding of wheels on pavement.

We passed groups of people standing on the edge of the road, mostly little kids and the elderly, who couldn't ride themselves. They saluted us as we rode by. Some of the children seemed confused, but the old folks stood stoically at attention. Most of them, even the older men, had tears streaming down their cheeks. I looked away and tried to focus on pedaling. Poor Gabrielle, Jean-Phillipe, Guy Cassou, Professor Davidson, and the others the town lost in the avalanche. Their passing was so sad and unfair. I would miss them.

I could barely see where I was going, what with the tears pooling in my eyes. Last year I swore I wouldn't do this again; it was too upsetting. We needed to put all this in the past and look to the future. But how do we move forward when so many people have been left behind?

After our first lap around town, I left the diminishing procession when it passed my house. My folks stood outside, waiting for me. They each gave me a hug when I disembarked from my bike.

NEUTRINO WARNING

"We're proud of you, Kath," Mom said.

"Yes. We know that wasn't easy for you," Dad said.

I was drained. "I don't think I'm up for the Sunrise Service in the morning. Can I meet you guys at the Pancake Breakfast?"

Dad rubbed my back. "Yes. Don't worry about it, honey. We can manage it on our own. We've been to Sunrise Service here before."

Mom pursed her lips. "I guess we can meet you at the Pancake Breakfast. But no later, okay? The Parade of Species is just the antidote you need after tonight." In the parade, kids dressed up as animals that weren't extinct.

I sighed. "Fine. So, can I get you anything? Are you all settled into Megan's room?"

"Yes, dear," Mom said. "We've stayed here before."

"I'm wiped out," I said. "I'm going to bed then. Goodnight."

Mom held out her arms.

I gave her a quick hug and a peck on the cheek. "'Night, Mom." I turned to Dad. "'Night, Dad."

Dad gave me a gentle smile. "Goodnight, Kathy-bird. Sleep tight."

It was tough, but I managed to drag myself over to the Pancake Breakfast at the campus amphitheater before it ended. I felt like I had a mourning hangover.

I had just snagged a big stack when I felt a tap on my shoulder.

"I might have known I'd find you here by the food," Jake said with a twinkle in his eyes.

I didn't have the energy to protest, so I just grinned and finished chewing the food in my mouth. "You caught me. I thought you'd be my mom when I felt the tap."

Jake raised his eyebrows. "Do I look like a woman to you?"

Someone cleared his throat. It was Dad. He and Mom stood behind Jake.

"'Morning. Glad you made it, Dear," Mom said.

I sighed. "It's eight o'clock, Mom. On a Saturday."

Jake piped up. "Yeah, that's a miracle for her."

"And how would you know that, young man?" Mom asked with mock consternation.

Dad elbowed me and whispered, "Nice going, Kath."

I blushed.

Jake blushed. "No, no. It's nothing like that."

"Nothing like what?" Mom asked.

"Give him a break, Mom." I pointed at Jake. "This is Jake Moretti, a new grad student in the fusion group." I pointed at my folks. "Jake, this is my mom, Dr. Maria Garcia, and my dad, Chris Garcia. They're both scientists and teachers."

"Nice to meet you," Jake said.

Mom brightened. "You're a physicist! Nice to meet you, Jake. Please call me Maria."

Dad shook Jake's hand. "Please call me Chris. Very nice to meet you, indeed, Jake. I'm glad to see Kathy's making some new friends. I hope you're prying her out of the lab sometimes?"

Jake chuckled. "That's not so easy."

"Moretti?" Mom said. "You're not related to Jacob Moretti, are you?" He was the famous climate activist from years ago.

He nodded. "Yeah. He was my great-grandpa."

Wow. I didn't know that.

Mom and Dad nodded. "Neat," Dad said.

"So, Jake, tell me what research you're working on," she said.

Dad smiled. "Like mother, like daughter."

I didn't know what he was talking about--I was nothing like my mother.

"Thanks for asking, Maria, but I'm just starting," Jake said. "We should have plenty of time to talk later, though. Kathy invited me and my roommate, Dave, over for dinner."

Mom nodded. "Excellent. Then, maybe we should adjourn over to the parade route on central campus so we don't miss any of the parades."

When we arrived at the wide-open, grassy central quad, a booming 'Buongiorno' and a crooked smile greeted us. I introduced Marcello to my folks, and he introduced us to his wife, Allessandra. She looked like an Italian supermodel: thin, with long glossy brunette hair and big brown eyes.

"So." Mom rubbed her hands together. "What are you two doing later? Can we entice you to come over and share in our

Earth Day celebration?"

Marcello pursed his lips for a second. "Kathy is not cooking, is she?" I wasn't sure I liked where this was going.

Mom shook her head and laughed. "I will be cooking."

"It is very kind of you to invite us," Marcello said, "we would like to come, but we have invited a guest, Gopal Khan, one of the physics faculty, to our celebration."

"*Sì*, the poor fellow is on his own," Allessandra said. "No family."

"We must invite him as well. You must all come over," Mom said. "I insist."

Dad and I exchanged raised eyebrows. "Sure," I said. "Sounds good."

Jake grinned. "You *are* just like your folks," he whispered to me. What did that mean?

"*Grazie*, Maria, we would be happy to accept," Marcello said.

Allessandra squealed in delight. "Look, the parade has started." She pointed at the squiggly line of kids dressed in animal costumes marching down the sidewalk. "They are so cute! Look at that little red bird in front."

We quickly stepped over to the sidewalk. I loved the Parades of Species. When I was a kid, it was my favorite event. I'd felt so important representing the animals and marching in front of my parents and neighbors. It should put me in a better mood.

As the first kid passed us, the crowd of spectators broke into a raucous cheer.

Mom said, "Is that red bird in front a Cardinal?"

I studied the bright red suit with the triangular crest. "Yes, I think so."

Dad smiled. "I agree. *Cardinalis cardinalis* is one of my favorite birds." Every bird was one of Dad's favorites.

I should focus on how much fun these kids were having.

The creature passing us now had a dark gray-brown furry body, a white rump patch, a small black-tipped tail, and big ears. It must have been a mule deer. The little face peeking out of the costume had a radiant smile. The boy's smile was missing his two front teeth. He had freckles. He held hands with a smaller creature next to him. The two of them together were adorable.

The smaller boy flashed us a beaming smile but passed out of sight before I deciphered what kind of animal he was.

All the kids seemed to be having the time of their lives.

Jake poked me gently. "Hey, look, there's gimme-breakfast-asaurus," he said with a smile.

I forced the corners of my mouth up in an attempt to return his smile.

"And look, there's I'm-hungry-asaurus!" he said.

His smile was charming. I smiled back at him.

Dad grinned at us. "Hey, you guys better pay attention. With kids involved, you never know how long these parades will last. They can fall apart pretty quickly."

We clapped and cheered for the next group of kids.

Then the procession started to go the slightest bit awry.

"Uh, oh," Mom pronounced. "This does not bode well."

We continued clapping and cheering, but the marchers' lines became clumps of marchers and then just a jumble. The kids stopped to talk to one another, wandered off to talk to their parents, sat down, and/or generally indulged in all manner of other kid-favored activities.

I giggled. I couldn't help it; they were adorable.

A couple of harried teachers tried to round them up. "This is not how we practiced it. We are supposed to march in a line. It is essential. Children! Pay attention!"

They were having none of it.

Parents gave up and sought out their offspring.

"I guess that's about it. A short one this year." Mom turned to Marcello, Allessandra, and Jake. "You all are welcome to come over any time. We shall plan on dinner at five o'clock. Allessandra, may I talk with you for a moment?" They stepped aside to discuss the feast, presumably.

"That might be the shortest parade yet," Marcello said.

Dad grinned. "Nope. One year when Kath was little, back in St. Louis, the kids didn't even start marching because some contagious crying jag erupted. It was chaos."

"Kathy and chaos?" Jake said. "That's hard to picture."

"Kathy didn't act up," Dad said. "She stood in the middle of the parade route, stamping her feet, and wouldn't budge.

She said she was there to march, and she was going to march, drown it! We couldn't get her out of there. Finally, we had to let her march around by herself. She looked adorable in her little penguin costume."

Dad, Jake, and Marcello laughed, and after a moment, I joined in. "The parade is important; it's an antidote to Moonlight Mourning." Actually, I felt a lot cheerier now.

"I would have enjoyed seeing that," Marcello said.

"Me too," Jake said.

"We might have some old footage around," Dad said.

"All right," I said. "That's enough of that. Nix the embarrassing stories, Pop."

"Are you sure it is okay that Allessandra, Gopal, and I come over?" Marcello asked. "I realize you might not want to hang out with your boss in your free time."

"It's fine," I said. "I like Gopal. Besides, Mom is a force of nature. Once she makes up her mind about something--watch out."

Dad nodded.

I just hoped the day wouldn't entail any more surprises.

Chapter Seven

Therefore, on Earth Day, Dad and I spent the afternoon following orders: setting up the table and chairs, shopping for beverages and ice, picking veggies, washing, chopping, stirring, you name it. I tried to sneak off to the lab a couple of times, but Mom kept an eagle eye on me. The house filled with the smell of cooking chicken, onion, and spices--the scents of home.

When Marcello, Allessandra, and Gopal arrived, Mom was thrilled and put them all to work in the kitchen. Since the reinforcements had arrived, Mom ordered me to set the table and 'make it pretty.'

Closer to dinnertime, someone knocked on the front door. I opened it and saw Jake and a guy I didn't know. "Happy Earth Day!" I said. "Hi, Jake. Glad you could make it." I turned to face the stranger. He was tall and chubby with curly blond hair and strangely long sideburns, which I'd seen somewhere before. "Hi, you must be Jake's roommate. I'm Kathy. Welcome. Come in, you guys."

He grinned. "I'm Dave. Thanks for inviting us." They stepped inside.

Before I could close the door, Lars poked his head in the door and flashed his perfect smile at me. "So, Jake, is it okay?"

Ack! I felt the corners of my mouth turn down. "Lars! This is a surprise." Who invited him? I glared at Jake.

Jake swallowed. "We ran into Lars on the way over. He got into a big fight with his dad and didn't have anywhere to go for dinner. I told him he could join us --if it's all right with you, of course." He smiled while wrinkling up his forehead.

Way to put me on the spot! "Of course, everyone is welcome," I said. "It's Earth Day, after all."

NEUTRINO WARNING

Lars stepped through the doorway. "Thank you for inviting me, Kathy. I'd hate to be on my own tonight."

Was this Lars look-a-like being nice?

He walked past me in the direction of the kitchen. "I'm hungry."

Jake followed him. "I'm going to say hi to Allessandra."

Dave said, "I think I figured out where I know you from. You came with Megan a few times to see my band, right?"

Ah ha. That's where I'd seen those sideburns: on stage. I pointed at him. "You're in that 'Statue' band that Megan likes!"

"Right." He tilted his head, staring into my face. "If memory serves, you're the girl Jake took a shine to last semester."

"I don't think that's right," I said. "Jake and I just met this month on the day of the avalanche."

He shook his head. "No. I'm pretty sure Jake noticed you several months ago when you were hanging out with Megan."

I thought I would've remembered meeting Jake. Dave must have started partying early.

From the kitchen, Dad leaned into the family room. "Ah, the rest of the partiers." His smile lit up his eyes and his laugh lines. "Well, come on and meet everyone." He waved us toward the kitchen.

I peeked into the kitchen while Dave and Dad introduced themselves.

Mom, Allessandra, and Marcello congregated around the stove, faces flushed, eyes sparkling, laughing about something. A meter away, Jake seemed captivated by the tableau. Lars looked bored.

Gopal leaned against a cabinet, his smile pasted on. He caught my eye, and I motioned him to join me in the living room. We went and sat on the couch. "Thanks," he said. "I was kind of out of my element."

I smiled. "I always think of cooking as a chemistry experiment: combine chemicals in exact proportions, mix, and heat."

"You're right. Cooking is like chemistry. I never thought of it like that before." The corners of Gopal's lips rose. "And, as I recall, I was pretty good at chemistry."

That about exhausted our small-talk abilities.

71

"Are you going to help us in the lab with the fusion project?" I asked.

"I'm trying," he said. "Right now, I'm bogged down in other stuff. I've been meeting with university officials to get us more resources. I'm trying to meet with national officials but haven't managed it yet. Bureaucracy is a pain."

I nodded. We grinned at each other awkwardly.

"So, Gopal, I've been thinking about an improvement for the Tokamak," I said. "Gabrielle told me they were considering a liquid wall. I examined the published papers and her notes, and Ellen and I even did some preliminary simulations. It looks really promising."

Gopal leaned back on the couch. "I think I've heard something about that. Did you replace one or more solid surfaces inside the Tokamak with liquid lithium?"

I nodded. "Yes. The fusion energy experiment is crucial, and this improvement would make it more likely to succeed."

Gopal sighed. "Kathy, we can't get caught up in some complicated new thing. We need to focus on getting the existing apparatus up and running."

"We should ensure the experiment has every possible opportunity for success," I said. Yes, I was feeling pressure to succeed.

"Well, I disagree, and I'm your supervisor." Gopal's eyes flashed.

I was ready to launch into a follow-up attack when Dad, Jake, and Dave joined us in the family room.

Dad seemed to sense some tension as he observed the two of us. "So, what's going on out here?"

Gopal rubbed his beard and relaxed back on the couch. "Uh, Kathy was giving me cooking tips."

"Kathy? Cooking tips?" Dad's eyebrows ascended.

"Don't look so shocked, Dad," I said. "It was just my 'cooking as chemistry' idea."

Jake snickered and pushed his glasses up the bridge of his nose.

Dad looked us over. "It seems to me that we have a quorum of partiers. What do you say we break out the refreshments? Would you guys like something to drink?"

There was general assent, and beer was the beverage of choice in the living room.

"Stay put, Dad. I'll go get it," I said. "I am supposed to be the hostess, after all."

No one argued with me--unfortunately.

They sat on the sofa as I ventured into the cooking arena. "Is anyone in here ready for something to drink? Wine, perhaps?"

"Yes, dear," Mom said.

"*Sì.*" Marcello seemed to be scowling at Lars.

Lars, who now stood very near Allessandra, said, "Wine for me, please."

Allessandra giggled. "*Sì. Grazie.*"

"Wait. Don't move," I said. "I'll get it." Why was it cooks always preferred wine and non-cooks always preferred beer?

I served everyone their drinks and joined the non-cooking beer drinkers in the family room. I wanted a chance to convince Gopal to implement my Tokamak idea but deduced it might be more polite not to interrupt the current conversation.

I thought they were talking about music. However, when I sat down, the conversation stopped abruptly. "Was it something I said?"

"Uh, no." Dave flushed.

"Dave was just regaling us with stories of band groupies." Dad grinned. "Maybe not the best topic for mixed company."

Jake shook his head. "I need to join a band. I had no idea."

"Yeah, I think Jake is lonely." Dave poked Jake with his elbow. "So, uh, I'm working on a new song. It's about a woman who acts the opposite of a groupie. I chase after her, and she doesn't react at all."

"That sounds right up Kathy's alley. Maybe she can help you," Jake said.

What was that remark about? I shot Jake a puzzled look. "Sorry, I'm not a musician, Dave."

"I have the tune," Dave said. "I'm just working on the lyrics."

"Hmm," I said. "Not reacting… That reminds me of a physics thing."

Jake grinned.

"Neutrinos!" Gopal exclaimed and smiled.

73

I nodded. "Exactly. Tiny neutral particles that barely react at all."

Dave leaned toward me. "That sounds promising. What about 'Neutrino Woman'?"

"Sounds good to me," I said.

There was a moment of uncomfortable silence as we groped for a new topic of conversation.

Dad said, "So Jake, what's your family doing tonight? They couldn't come to visit?"

Dave shook his head and made a chopping motion across his neck with his hand.

Jake cleared his throat. "Chris, I don't have any family. My parents passed several years ago, and I never had any siblings."

How sad! I put my hand on Jake's arm.

"Jake's great-grandfather is famous, though," Dave said. "Jacob Moretti rode his bike around the world to raise awareness about global warming."

Jake nodded. "Yep. So, my parents told me anyway."

"No wonder you were anxious to help us with the fusion energy project," Gopal said. "You were following a family tradition to try to solve global warming."

Mom cleared her throat behind us. "We are ready to eat."

As we got up, I asked, "Is there anything else I should know about you, Jake?"

He just grinned and wiggled his eyebrows up and down.

We all helped carry the platters of food from the kitchen to the dining table. The large worn wooden table had been covered with a nice brown tablecloth (hand-me-down from Mom), mismatched plates, napkins, silverware, a bunch of colorful fall leaves I'd gotten outside, and some candles in the middle. I thought it looked nice if I did say so myself.

Once we sat down, Mom pushed out her chair and stood up. She raised her wine glass. "We thank Gaia and her bounty for this glorious feast."

The rest of us raised our glasses, cheering, and all took a sip.

Mom remained standing, holding up her glass. "On a personal note, I'd like to raise a glass to our firstborn, Emma, who we lost twenty-five years ago to illness. Emma, we're thinking of you."

We raised our glasses. "Emma." I never knew her. She died when I was a baby. I always thought it'd be fun to have a sister, though.

"And finally," she said, "I would like to say that I am very thankful to have this opportunity to break bread with my beloved husband, Chris, our daughter Kathy, and all you wonderful friends."

That one got a big cheer.

I stood. "Thank you, everyone, for coming, especially Mom and Allessandra, for doing the cooking--so I didn't have to do it," I said, laughing a little. "And now, since I am the official hostess, I say we dig into the food before it gets cold and resume the toasting later." I sat down.

Snickering, people started passing food around. Dinner was perfect, as expected, with Mom in charge. There was roast chicken, herby Earth Day bread, oven-fried crispy potatoes, red curry lentils with sweet potatoes, steamed mixed vegetables, and more.

After eating, we finished making all the usual Earth Day toasts, giving thanks, and making resolutions. I promised the group to do an excellent job with the fusion energy project, and in my heart, I resolved to succeed and help save planet Earth, no matter what.

After the resolutions, we ate again as per the Earth Day overeating tradition. A good time was had by all.

.

Afterward, when we were all stuffed to bursting, the beer drinkers took on clean-up duty in the kitchen and the wine drinkers relaxed in the family room.

We were about finished cleaning up the kitchen when Mom rushed in. "Oh, dear, we forgot to put out the food for the birds and squirrels and such. Kathy, could you put it out?" She rustled around in some bags on the counter.

This would be a perfect chance for me to bend Gopal's ear again about the Tokamak improvements. "Yeah, okay," I said. "Gopal, can you help?"

"I'd be happy to help," Gopal said.

Mom shoved a massive bag of dried corn, berries, and

seeds on me.

I folded over the top of the large bag she gave me. "C'mon, Gopal."

When we got out the front door, Gopal sat down on the walkway.

I started filling the feeder closest to the house.

"So, out with it," he said. "Give it your best shot. I know you just wanted me out here to try to bulldoze me."

I cut my eyes to him. "Bulldoze is a strong word." I filled another feeder. "I merely wanted to suggest that a liquid wall would make an excellent addition to the Tokamak. I would be more than happy to show you the supporting documentation."

He stood up. "I believe you. That's not the issue."

Huzzah! "So, we can do it?"

"No," he said quietly but firmly.

"What?" I said.

"I said 'no,' and you heard me say it. We have to focus on the basics before we go off on some tangent."

"You're being stubborn. You just admitted my idea sounded good. Don't you want the experiment to work? Don't you want to achieve nuclear fusion? This could help the planet a lot. It could save the planet!" I may have raised my voice a tad.

"I hope you know you're the only person I would let address me in such a manner." Gopal rubbed his beard. "I am your supervisor, however, and I don't deserve that. Tone it down, young lady! As the boss, I make the decisions, not you."

"You're right," I said. "I'm sorry. But this is a revolutionary new idea for the Tokamak. Just let me try it. It will work." I felt like this was my big chance to help save the planet.

Someone cleared his throat.

I glanced at the open front door.

Lars stood in the doorway. "Maria said you might have some extra Earth Day wildlife food. I'm about to leave."

I nodded. "Yeah. Let me get you a bag."

"I think I'm going to go also," Gopal said. "Please thank your folks for me. It was a lovely evening--for the most part."

"Couldn't we talk a little more?" I asked.

"It wouldn't do any good. My decision is final." Gopal strolled down our front walk to the street.

NEUTRINO WARNING

As I watched him go, my hopes plummeted like dirty dishwater sucked down the drain.

Chapter Eight

It was difficult, but I resisted the urge to implement my great liquid wall idea. I figured we could always do it later.

I was working late in the lab one night, finalizing the testing procedures, when Lars appeared on the scene. Drown it. I thought I had the lab to myself.

"Hey, there, Lars. What are you doing here tonight?" I attempted a smile. It may have been my imagination, but lately, Lars had been working unusually long hours, often staying after the rest of us had left. And he hadn't blatantly disobeyed me once. It was all very suspicious.

"Oh, I thought Brittani was working tonight." He glanced around the room. "I guess not." He leaned back against a lab table, crossed his arms, and flashed me his brightest smile. "What are you doing here tonight?"

"Oh, you know me," I said. "I work too much."

His smile faltered. "I apologized for that remark more than once." The smile resumed.

"What do you want, Lars?" I asked. "Did you lose your lady of the evening?"

He snorted. "As a matter of fact, I did." Grinning, he added, "How would you like to join me for dinner?"

I felt the corners of my mouth turn down of their own accord. I couldn't figure him out. "To what do I owe this offer?" Was he up to something nefarious? But how could dinner be nefarious?

"Yeah," Jake said from the doorway. Apparently, he'd just gotten here. He was frowning. A lot.

"I still owe you a meal for the excellent Earth Day feast you put on," Lars said.

"Me, too," Jake said, walking into the room.

Huh. That was true. And I had to eat. But I'd much rather go with Jake. I turned to him. "So, you're buying, Jake?"

He stood up straight. "But, of course."

"I guess I do have to eat dinner," I said. "Sorry, Lars. Okay, Jake. Let's go." Dinner was my favorite meal, especially free dinner. I grabbed my bag.

"You guys go ahead," Lars said. "Don't mind me." We weren't.

Jake and I decided to go to the little Italian place across the street from campus, Caffe Lavena, that Marcello recommended.

I was surprised to see the sun still in evidence and birds flitting about as we walked across campus. The evening air was still coolish, even at the beginning of May.

As we entered the restaurant's large glass doors, the smell of garlic and oregano was divine. My eyes adjusted slowly to the dim interior, and I made out a mural near the front door. It included a large stone-paved courtyard with dozens of people sitting in chairs surrounded by fat gray birds and some old-fashioned stone buildings, one of which had a giant clock tower right next to a large body of water. There were some odd flat-bottomed boats, each with a man standing on its back with a pole.

A rotund restaurant employee with a big smile rushed up to us. "*Buona sera*. Two for dinner?" His dark hair was slicked back above his hawk-like nose.

I nodded.

"*Sì*," Jake said.

"*Benvenuto*. Welcome to my place. I'm Gino." He showed us to a table with a flourish and gave us menus once we were seated. "May I recommend the special of the day, *Risi e Patate*?"

I put down the menu, which I couldn't decipher anyway. "Sure. Sounds good to me," I said, grinning.

Jake smiled. "Rice and Potato? *Sì*, that sounds good."

"And some Chianti?" The restaurateur collected our menus.

I shrugged. I wasn't drinking more than a glass because I needed to finish up some stuff in the lab tonight. "I'll take one glass."

Jake looked amused. "*Sì*, some Chianti also."

Gino nodded and took a step away from our table.

"Excuse me. What's that mural in front?" I asked.

"Ah. You do not recognize the famous Piazza San Marco of Venezia?" He looked shocked.

I shook my head. "Uh, is that in Italy somewhere?"

He sighed. "Sadly, Venezia, you may know it as Venice, no longer exists." He looked so upset I was afraid to ask him anything more about it.

"Thanks," I said.

He went to put in our orders.

"I didn't know you knew Italian, Jake," I said.

"Marcello has been kind enough to give me some pointers." He grinned. "But enough of him. Let's focus on our nice dinner." He looked like the cat that had found a whole flock of canaries. I started getting nervous. What exactly did he think was going on here?

The waiter returned with the wine and poured us each a big glass before setting the bottle down.

Jake leaned back in his chair. "It seems like you've been working long hours lately." He smiled. He had a friendly smile; it lit up his whole face. "I'm glad you took the time to relax. I'm looking forward to getting to know you better."

Gaia, this event had all the makings of a date. What had I gotten myself into? I sputtered as a sip of wine went down the wrong way. After I finished coughing, I said, "I haven't been working any longer hours than usual."

"I have some questions." He put his glass down carefully on the tablecloth. "I guess when you were in the neutrino group, you worked long hours too, but something's different now." How would he even know that? "You seem relentless about your work. What's up?"

"The fusion project's important," I said. The fusion project could save the world, so it had to work. But relentless didn't sound good. Was he implying I was a workaholic? Was I a workaholic? I quickly looked at my glass of wine. "But as for relentless, I don't know what you're talking about."

"Then, tonight, when I showed up, you seemed very nervous," he said. "You weren't working. What's going on with you and Lars?"

"I was working. Nothing's going on with Lars. He got there

right before you," I said. "So, how are your classes going? Or your roommate? Or his band? How's his band doing?"

His eyes twinkled. "Nice try, Kathy. I won't be distracted so easily."

Apparently not. Drown it! "I promise I was working," I said. "Lars showed up right before you. I don't know why." I felt heat spread across my face. I didn't know what else to say, so I grabbed my wine and chugged the rest of it. The warmth spread to my stomach.

"Could I have some more, please?" I held up my glass.

Jake poured me another glass of wine.

I drank it. This was going horribly. I'd been banking on a quick, easy dinner, and instead, I was facing the inquisition.

He shook his head a little, finished off his glass, and poured himself another drink. "Now that you have some liquid courage, maybe you're ready to explain to me why we can't date."

"Uh, did I say that?" I considered bolting.

"I want to date you," he said.

"Uh…" I eyed the door.

A waiter appeared, bearing *Rici e Patate*. "Here we go." He placed the plates in front of us. "Enjoy. Can I get you anything else?"

Saved by the plate. I immediately started eating.

"No, thank you," Jake said to the waiter.

The dish was delicious, with lots of Parmesan cheeze, olive oil, fresh tomato, and rosemary. "This flies," I said with my mouth full.

"I'm glad you're enjoying it," he said dryly.

We focused on dinner for several minutes. My reaction to the evening had me very confused. Jake was so nice and so polite; he was a nice guy. What was wrong with me? Why couldn't I just date him? Wasn't this basically a date? Why did I feel panic? What was my problem?

I drank some more wine, which was a mistake. I wasn't used to wine, and apparently, it was more potent than beer. I was definitely starting to feel tipsy.

I stood up. "Excuse me. I'm going to go to the restroom." I wobbled a little as I turned to go.

He stood up. "Are you all right?" He contemplated me.

"Yeah, thanks," I said. Look at me, totally paranoid. Maybe I should give him a break. I got halfway to the restroom when I realized I had forgotten my bag. I went back to get it.

My bag was out on the table, and Jake was rummaging through it.

"Jake!" I said. "What are you doing?"

His eyebrows shot up, and his mouth fell open for a moment. "Kathy! I heard Ellen say you had an incoming call."

Maybe I wasn't crazy. "Give me that." I snatched the bag and stalked away. Once I got to the surprisingly large ladies' lounge, I sat on one of the couches and took my fon out. "Ellen, did I get a call? Did you say anything at the table?"

"Yes," she said. "Gopal called, asking for an update."

Ugh. I needed to calm down. And I should give Jake a break. I splashed some cold water on my face and wiped it off.

Still, he shouldn't have messed with my fon. "Ellen: implement password 'crap monkey.'"

Ellen said, "Acknowledged."

I walked back to the table and sat down, still fuming, and started shoveling in food.

When I glanced at Jake, his fork was frozen in mid-air. "I've never seen anyone eat so quickly."

I pointed my fork at him, and some rice fell on the table. "Going through my bag was not cool. You know that, don't you?"

"Yes." He nodded solemnly. "I'm sorry. You'd just gotten through saying the fusion project is so super important. I was worried it might be something about it."

Well, that did make sense. Calm down, Kath.

"So, what about it?" he asked. "You and me. There's something between us."

I scooted my chair back from the table. "Gee, this has been fun, but I need to get going. I should get back to work."

He looked surprised and hurt. "Going? But we still have some wine left. And what about dessert? I thought we were having an important discussion about our relationship."

My heart started beating in my chest like it was trying to break out of my rib cage; I felt panicky.

But I also felt bad about hurting his feelings. And dessert was tempting.

NEUTRINO WARNING

Maybe he read something in my face because Jake flagged down Gino. "Yes, we'll have a Tiramisu and chocolate cream Cannoli."

Now I couldn't leave. "I do like chocolate," I said.

"I know." He smiled.

I slowly finished my dinner and my water. I did not drink any more wine.

"So, what do you think?" he asked. "About you and me dating?"

"Well," I said slowly, "I haven't told you this, but I had a horrible experience when I was in grad school...."

"A romance with a fellow physics student?" he leaned towards me.

"Yes." I wrinkled up my nose. "We were together for a while...." Ugh. I didn't want to talk about this; it was so embarrassing. It had been my first serious relationship; I was totally, naively in love. I thought we would get married.

I'd helped my ex a lot with school and research. But it turned out he'd only dated me because I was a better physicist than him. He'd built up his reputation using my work. "It didn't work out. It's why I'm so cautious now. Is it okay if we don't talk about it more?"

Jake looked disappointed, but he nodded. "Of course. I would never pressure you." I believed that about him. He wouldn't pressure me.

Our desserts arrived, and we shared both of them. They were delicious. Creamy, crunchy, chocolatey. I resisted the urge to lick the plates clean.

I glanced at Jake across the romantic candle-lit table. If this had been a date, it would have been just about perfect. Except for my emotional baggage.

A little later, outside the restaurant, we paused in the cool night air. The moon was just rising over campus. I smelled something flowery.

He stepped right up next to me. "Thanks for a nice night." He looked down at me.

A sudden fear struck me that he was going to kiss me. And simultaneously, I feared that he wasn't going to kiss me. "Thank you," I whispered.

He leaned in and pressed his lips to mine. Time seemed to stop; we were frozen in a moment of perfection.

He leaned away. "That was also nice."

"Yes," I whispered.

He stared at me, and I could tell he wanted to ask me about us dating again. But he restrained himself.

I felt relieved and ...sad.

Finally, he said. "Can I walk you home?"

"Uh, no," I said. "I think I need to go back to work."

When I returned to the fusion lab, no one else was there. I sat down at my desk. I did have a bad memory for stuff like passwords; I should write it down somewhere while still remembering it. But if I wrote down the password in the fusion lab, Lars or someone else would probably find it, and I didn't want that. I had a brainstorm. I could put it upstairs in our old neutrino office; we never went up there anymore.

I trudged up six flights of stairs only to find that I had no writing implements. There was paper everywhere, overflowing my desk, on the floor, you name it, but no pens or pencils. There was no way I was going to go all the way back down to the basement to get a pen. I checked all the desks.

"Crap monkey!" I said.

Ellen said, "Kathy, you don't need to use the password."

"I know that." My eyes cut to the chalkboard over my desk and slid down to the brightly colored chalk in its little tray. Ah ha. I did have one writing implement. But I should be careful; I would not write the password on the chalkboard. I should write it somewhere less public...

The next night as Lars, Jake, and I finished up some minor tests on the Tokamak, Lars kept looking at his watch. "So, are we ready for a test, finally? I can't hang around here all night. I have a date or two this evening to make up for last night."

Jake looked up with a big grin. "Oh yeah? Two dates tonight? Tell me about it."

Lars flashed his brightest smile. "I would, but you're too young." He glanced at me. "Besides, the Empress of the Lab has forbidden such talk." We'd all been spending all day, every day in here, and I'd finally given him an ultimatum to quit talking about his personal life.

I nodded. "That's right." At least Lars didn't seem to be holding my dinner refusal and quick exit against me. How unlike him.

"Can I flip the switch and finally turn on the Tokamak, your Royal Highness?" Lars smirked.

We had the testing sequences programmed into the computers. We had checked and double-checked all the components and all the connections many times. Recently we successfully injected a bit of magnetized Hydrogen plasma into the sphere.

I thought all the work we'd been doing recently would improve our performance and was anxious to see it--without Gopal around. That way, if there was a small snafu, we could fix it before he heard about it.

There was no way to check the whole thing and see what kind of plasma currents and magnetic fields we could generate without giving it a try. "I guess so. I think it's ship-shape," I said. "We have to get it going sometime."

"All right!" Lars rubbed his hands together and sat down at a control station. "I'll initiate the plasma injection sequence."

"Sounds good." I ran around and checked to see if all the peripheral equipment was powered up and ready.

"Wait," Jake said. "Maybe we should call Marcello and Gopal first? And Brittani? They put in a lot of work and deserve to be here for the first real test." Jake had migrated over to Lars and was scrutinizing the computer screen over his shoulder.

"That's a good point, Jake," I said.

"Jake, give me some space." Lars lifted his hands off the keyboard and turned to me. "Let's do it now. Or are you afraid to test it, Kathy?"

"No, I'm not afraid!" I glared at him.

"This is just a test, right?" Lars said. "We don't need Brittani and the others here."

I agreed; it would be better to do an initial test with fewer witnesses around. Yes, I was a little nervous.

Jake had wrinkled up his forehead and was shaking his head. He took a step toward me. "Kathy, I'm not sure...."

I glanced at him. "Don't worry. We're ready. I was about to initiate a test anyway." That was my story, and I was sticking to it.

"I guess if you're sure," Jake said.

I sat down at another workstation and checked that all the data acquisition software was primed and ready. It seemed to be. "Data acquisition ready."

Lars nodded. "I'm almost ready, too."

"Wait!" I said. "I need to check that the high-speed video camera is ready to record the plasma." This all seemed so exciting! I danced over to the camera we had set up in front of the tiny viewing window. "Looks good." I stepped back. "Fire her up."

Lars said, "Okay, I'm initiating full injection of the magnetized plasma in five, four, three, two, now!"

I ran back to the data workstation. "Data acquisition is ready. Electromagnetic field on." The external electromagnetic field was supposed to keep the plasma in the 'sweet spot' of the Tokamak and initially give the plasma a little push and get it moving, so it created currents of its own. These plasma currents would, in turn, create an electromagnetic field, which would increase the plasma currents. Hopefully, they would increase the electromagnetic field, and so on, until the electromagnetic field became so intense it resulted in nuclear fusion.

"Is it working?" Jake looked over my shoulder.

"It'll take a second to register the plasma current if we're successful," I said. In our initial test, we were just looking for plasma current and maybe a small electromagnetic field. "Give it a chance to get going." I held my breath as I peered intently at the meter readouts on the computer screen. Gradually, an almost imperceptible hum came from the Tokamak, and the instruments started registering values.

"We have plasma current!" I clapped my hands together.

"We do?" Lars' eyes were wide open, and his eyebrows shot up to the middle of his forehead.

"The data is starting to come in, and it looks good," I said. The humming from the Tokamak got louder and louder.

"It is? It does?" Lars' voice was so high it squeaked.

Jake joined me at my computer and pointed at the screen. "Whoa! Look at those huge magnetic field readings! Is that right?"

"No. Something must be miscalibrated." I shook my head. Drown it! Perhaps something was broken from the avalanche?

"What? What are the magnetic fields?" Lars got up from his station and came over to look at the screen. "What the flood?"

Then, I heard an earth-shattering crack, and a giant yellow spark arced from the Tokamak to the ceiling. Another spark followed.

"Shit! Shit!" Jake yelled, pointing at the sparks.

Another huge spark arced out, and we heard a thunderous hissing sound. The Tokamak emitted more loud hissing sparks from the top where it was coupled to the power source. The air took on the pungent smell of ozone.

"Jake!" I said. "Hit the power kill switch!"

He ran over to the wall and punched the big red button. "Got it!"

The room lights went out, but yellow tendrils of electricity continued to arc out of the machine. It looked like an enormous electrical hydra.

"We have to get out of here! C'mon you guys!" I yelled.

Jake took a step toward the door and then hesitated.

"Go, Jake!" I said.

He ran to the doorway. "Are you coming? Hurry up!"

Streams of electricity flowed off the Tokamak, buzzing loudly as they contorted through the lab.

Lars stayed at his station.

"Lars!" If somebody got hurt, I couldn't take it. There'd been too many deaths and injuries around here already. I went over to Lars and grabbed his arm. "Now! Let's go now! It's not worth dying for!"

Lars shrugged me off.

Gaia! "Lars, if you buy it here at your workstation, people might think you made a mistake."

He turned and met my eyes. "Me? You're the so-called boss!"

"You can yell at me in the hall!" I said.

The electric hydra continued its evil hissing dance, waving electrical tentacles around the room.

"I will." Lars' eyelids tightened, and he pressed his lips

LESLEY L. SMITH

together.

I dashed after Lars toward the dim emergency lighting of the hall.

As an electrical tendril approached, all the hairs on my body tried to make a run for it.

Lars turned around to look at the Tokamak, and I got caught in his furious scowl. He snarled and pushed me back into the lab before rushing ahead through the doorway.

"What are you doing?" I stumbled and fell to my knees near the door of the lab.

A yellow snake of electricity flew over my head and slammed into Lars' back. He jerked spastically and crashed to the ground just outside the lab doorway as the hissing noise from the Tokamak stopped.

The abrupt silence was deafening.

"Lars?" I crawled over and felt his neck. He seemed to have a pulse, albeit a weak one.

Jake kneeled next to me. "Is he alive?"

I nodded. "Yes. Barely." I activated Ellen. "We need emergency medical assistance at the fusion lab."

"Acknowledged," she said. "An ambulance is being dispatched. I will direct them to your location."

"Kathy, are *you* all right?" Jake asked.

"Yes," I said. "I think so. How about you?"

Jake pushed his glasses up the bridge of his nose and said, "I'm okay."

"Ellen, I need you to figure out what went wrong with the equipment as soon as possible."

"Acknowledged," she said. "My wireless networking is still operational. I can access the data."

I sank to the floor in the hallway next to Lars. Why did it seem I was constantly calling the EMTs these days?

Jake rubbed my shoulder. "He'll be all right."

I couldn't help it, a few tears escaped. "I hope so," I whispered. He'll be all right. He'll be all right. I repeated it in my head like a mantra.

We stayed there on the floor with Lars until three men in big boots and uniforms clomped down the hall.

The front man yelled, "There are people on the floor up

ahead!"

Jake stood up. "There's only one injury here." He pointed down at Lars.

The EMTs knelt and felt Lars for a pulse.

The fireman reached us and checked out the lab with a giant flashlight. "Looks clear," he said into his radio. "There's evidence of an electrical fire, but it's out now. Let's get some more men in here to make sure, though."

He'll be all right. He'll be all right. He'll be all right.

The next thing I knew, someone helped me to my feet. "Miss? Just come with me."

"Kathy," Jake said. "Her name is Kathy."

"Say, I know you guys, don't I?" a man said. "You were involved with the avalanche a few weeks back, weren't you? Wow, you're having a bad spring."

Somehow, I ended up sitting outside the physics building with a blanket around me. It was dark out, and I mean really dark; all the streetlights on campus were out. The moon was the only source of light.

Someone touched my shoulder, and I jumped. "Hey!"

"Relax, it's just me, Jake," he said. "You must be doing better if you're talking."

"How's Lars?" I asked.

"They took him to the hospital, but the paramedic told me he has a good prognosis."

Thank Gaia. "That's a relief." My hand shook as I rubbed my forehead.

I couldn't make anything out in the gloom. Were there any other people around?

"They also said we were okay. Uh, Kathy, I've got some bad news. I think we managed to take out the power all over campus." Jake adjusted his glasses.

"That is bad." I shook my head.

"Wait, that's not the bad news. The Fire Marshall asked who was in charge, and since you seemed so out of it, I told him to call Gopal. He's on his way here. We're supposed to wait for him."

My failure was complete. Gopal wouldn't forgive me for this. A tear rolled down my cheek. I wiped it with my sleeve.

"Aw. It's not so bad." Jake wrapped his arms around me. It felt warm and safe.

I may have cried into his chest for a few minutes before I managed to get my act together.

Finally, I backed away from him. "I don't know what's wrong with me. I didn't ask you how you were doing after all this. You're all right, aren't you?"

I could just make out his nod in the dim light. "Ship-shape, as my boss would say." He nudged my arm with his shoulder.

"Sorry, I might have gotten your shirt wet," I said.

We sat in companionable silence in the cool night air until Gopal rode up on his bike.

"What the flood?" He wheezed and stopped to take a breath, holding up his forefinger. "What the flood have you been up to?"

"I take full responsibility-" I said.

"What did you do? Do you know the power's out all over town? I got a call from the Fire Marshall! I had to drop everything, call Hans, and rush over." He petered out. "I have to sit down for a minute." He sat next to us, breathing heavily.

I prayed no one else got hurt.

"Dr. Karlsson's coming?" Jake glanced around.

Gopal rubbed his beard. "I hope not. But, knowing him, probably." He turned back to us. "Are you two all right?"

I nodded. "Yes, I think so. Right, Jake?"

Jake agreed. "And Lars is supposed to pull through, too."

"Lars?" Gopal's head spun around. "Where is he?"

"He went to the hospital," I said meekly. "He experienced an electrical trauma. But he's going to be okay, according to the paramedic."

"Electrical trauma! Hospital! You better start at the beginning." Gopal's face got all blotchy.

"We just turned on the Tokamak for a test run," I said. "And we did follow the testing protocol." I didn't meet his eyes.

"And then?" Gopal asked.

"And then nothing," I said. "We just did what we were supposed to do, and all hell broke loose."

Hans rode up on his bike, breathing easily, every hair in place. "What is the meaning of this? What is going on here?"

NEUTRINO WARNING

I stood and held my hands up. "Lars will be okay. They took him to the hospital."

"Lars? What?" He turned to Gopal. "Gopal, I hope there weren't any damages to the fusion lab as a result of this fiasco."

"Has there been equipment damage?" Gopal turned to me and asked.

Definitely! "Dr. Karlsson, don't you want to go to the hospital and see Lars?" I asked.

Hans's face became slack for a moment. "Lars? What does this have to do with him? Never mind." He frowned at me. "Well? Has there been equipment damage? I don't have to remind you this project is important."

So, why did he just remind me, then? I'd had it with him. Didn't he even care that his son was hurt? Cool it, Kath! I took a deep breath and tried to steady my shaking hands. "We will have to assess the situation carefully before we can answer that question. I take full responsibility for this unfortunate incident." I exhaled slowly. "Now, you'll have to excuse us. We're going to check on Lars. C'mon, Jake."

"Call me when you find out something more about Lars," Gopal yelled after us. "And there's a meeting in my office first thing in the morning!"

Jake and I retrieved our bikes. Riding through town with only moonlight to guide our way reminded me of the Moonlight Mourning event; it was sobering.

When we got to the hospital, it was a madhouse, and the emergency generators were on, giving the whole place a sickly greenish-yellow glow. A plethora of nurses rushed back and forth, and patients packed the waiting room. We went up to the admissions desk and asked about Lars.

"And you are?" the large gray-haired woman behind the desk asked. "I can only give out information to relatives."

"I'm his sister, Olga, and this is his brother, Bjorn." I pointed at myself and Jake.

Hhmpf. She sniffed. "You don't look like an Olga and a Bjorn."

Jake grinned at her, turning on the charm. "Please, ma'am."

"Let's just say our grandparents were a diverse lot," I said. "Please, how's Lars?"

The nurse sniffed again, consulting her computer. "Well, you're out of luck, he's not allowed any visitors yet, but it says he's out of the woods. You can see him tomorrow." Her mouth set in a grim line. "Now, move along. There's a line of sick or injured people behind you."

I turned around, and sure enough, a motley assortment of mostly minor injuries had queued up behind us. As I walked away from the counter, every overheard comment was like a stab in the gut.

"And then the power went out, and bam, I rode right into that sign!"

"Oh, man, I hear you. I was chopping up veggies for a late supper, the lights went out, and my daughter screamed, and let's just say this isn't a carrot I have on ice here."

"Gaia, that's harsh."

"U.S. Energies dropped the ball on this one. They swore this kind of stuff had ended."

"Yeah, I wonder what screwed things up this time?"

"Ellen, how's that calculation going?" I asked quietly.

"Still working," she said.

Jake and I quickly slunk out.

Outside, I paused and took a deep breath. After the hospital, the air felt beautifully fresh. Some bugs chirped in the undergrowth.

"I feel bad that all those people might have gotten hurt because of our experiment." Jake pointed his thumb back toward the hospital.

"Me too." He had no idea how horrible I felt. I sighed. I didn't know what else to say; it had been a long night. We stood there a minute.

I examined him in the moonlight. With that wavy brown hair of his and those little wire-rimmed glasses, he looked very cute. I shook my head. Get over it, Kath!

"Can I accompany you home?" He grinned for a second.

That sounded like trouble. That grin was definitely trouble. But I recalled how nice and safe it had felt to have his arms around me a little while ago. "Sure. Let's go." Yes, I was weak.

When we got to my place, Jake jumped off his bike and laid

it on the grass.

"What do you think you're doing?" I narrowed my eyes in suspicion.

"I'm walking you to the door," he said. "I think you were in shock earlier."

I shrugged and pushed my bike up the walkway through the front garden. At the door, I leaned my bike against the ivy-covered wall and fished in my pockets for keys. I checked all my pockets, but there were no keys. "I don't have my keys." Comprehension dawned. "They're back at the lab."

Jake stood very close. He smelled good--like flowers. Or maybe that was the lilac bush we were standing next to.

He leaned in, and we hugged. "It'll be okay, Kathy."

"Thanks, Jake," I said into his shoulder. "I hope so."

He stepped back and grinned. "If you can't get inside, maybe you need to come to stay at my place."

Gradually, my brain took on solid form again. "Uh, no. That's not a good idea."

I recalled that I had a roommate that could let me in. I pounded frantically on the front door. "Megan! Megan, open up! It's me, Kathy."

Jake leaned in again. "Are you sure?"

I intercepted him by putting my hands on his chest. "No, this is a bad, bad idea. We work together. I'm your boss." His chest felt good through his thin shirt, firm and warm.

"We're back to this? You're only my de facto supervisor. Gopal is the official boss." He stepped away, shaking his head a little. "But it's your call."

When Megan opened the door, she did not look happy. Her purple hair was all askew. She squinted at me and yawned. "Kathy? Do you know what time it is? Did you lose your keys again?"

I picked up my bike and pushed past her.

She continued squinting. "Jake? Is that you? What are you two up to?" She turned to me. "Kathy? You said--"

"What did she say? Did she say something about me?" Jake asked eagerly.

"Thanks for taking me home, Jake. I'll see you in the morning," I called over my shoulder.

Megan closed the door and leaned back on it. "What was that about?"

"Nothing. We were just working late. There were some developments at the lab. Jake just offered to take me home since it's so late."

Megan yawned. "I knew I liked that guy." She shambled off to her room. "'Night."

"'Night." I knew I liked him too. Drown it!

Chapter Nine

I was sneaking into the bathroom when a scuffed boot flew across the hall and slammed into my leg.

"Ow! That was uncalled for!" I limped into Megan's room. "What did you do that for?" I asked the big lump under the covers.

The lump spoke. "You were sneaking into the shower after you swore I'd get first dibs on it." A purple head popped out from under the blankets. "And you have to clean the kitchen. You didn't do it yesterday."

I held up my hands. "You're right. Have at it." I pointed toward the bathroom. The lump rustled.

I brought Ellen with me to the kitchen for some company. I set her on the counter and filled the kettle to start making tea. At least the power had been restored sometime while I slept. "Anything new on your analysis, Ellen?"

"Analysis complete, Kathy," she said. "My leading hypothesis for the accident is the Tokamak shifted slightly when the avalanche hit, causing the insulation along the power coupling to crack."

I leaned against the counter. "That sounds like it should have been preventable. But thank goodness, it should be fixable, at least." I took a deep breath. Thank, Gaia. "So, Ellen, what's in the news?"

May 5, 2098: Injuries due to Power Failure:

Work continued through the night to restore power after blackouts hit parts of Colorado. The hardest hit were light rail services throughout the region. Hospitals and airports successfully transitioned to emergency generators, limiting the loss of life. Still, dozens of injuries were reported primarily due to traffic accidents and accidents in private residences and businesses.

I hadn't realized the damage was so extensive. My hands shook as I tried to scoop the tea into my cup.

"We did that, didn't we?" I felt so guilty.

"Yes," she said.

"Is there any other information about the blackout?" I asked.

"No," she said.

"What's the next story?" I asked.

Scientists Confirm Earlier Spring Onset.

"Okay, let's hear that," I said.

Scientists confirm spring has been coming four-tenths of a day per year earlier throughout the last fifty years. They utilized indicators such as earlier bird egg-laying trends, amphibians spawning early, earlier spring river thaws, oak trees leafing out earlier, and cherry trees blossoming earlier.

Part of the day? What the heck did that look like? I turned my attention back to breakfast.

Somehow, I managed to get to Gopal's office on time. He wasn't there yet, but Jake was. I waved hello and sat on one of Gopal's rickety wooden chairs.

"About the other night." Jake pushed up his glasses.

I was starting to get the clue that he did that when he was nervous. "Shh. The less said about the other night, the better," I whispered.

"Oh, right, the accident." Jake cocked his head at an angle and raised his eyebrows. "Did you hear it spread across Colorado, and people got injured?" he whispered back.

"We knew some people in town were injured from our trip to the hospital." I still felt guilty. The whole point of the fusion project was to help people, not hurt them.

Feeling confused, I squinted my eyes. "I thought you were talking about the kiss." I leaned toward him.

"I *was* talking about the kiss." He leaned toward me.

"The kiss was a mistake," I said. "Forget about it."

"Forget the kiss?" His face fell. "But it seemed so unforgettable." His voice trailed off.

"Let's just say it shouldn't have happened," I said. The last time I'd gotten involved with someone like Jake, it had been a disaster. I wasn't going to go through that again. I couldn't.

Jake leaned back in his chair, frowning.

No Siree. Shouldn't have happened. And, no, I wasn't trying to convince myself.

We sat there for what seemed like an eternity, not saying anything else. I stared at the floor. Really, what else was there to say? After a while, I wondered what had happened to Gopal. He was so late, it was getting ridiculous. I peered in Jake's direction.

He leaned further back in his chair and almost fell when his fon alarm went off. He grunted and turned it off. "I have to go to class. Tell Gopal I'm sorry I missed him." He bolted out the door.

Possibly I hadn't handled that as well as I could have. Great. Something else to feel guilty about. I sat there for a couple more minutes trying to calm down and then marched down to the physics department office where Lily was holding down the fort. "Where is everybody?" I asked, glancing around the office.

She was sewing something furry at her desk and turned and gave me a glance. "Hans and Gopal and the other department big-wigs had to go to the university president's office for a teleconference meeting with some even bigger wigs."

I sat down on an empty chair next to her desk. "Oh?" I thought I sounded quite nonchalant. "You don't happen to know why, do you?" Please don't say the power failure.

She put down her sewing and studied me. "Perhaps it was about how you guys may have shut down the power grid last night?"

Ugh. She said, or at least meant the power failure.

She leaned towards me. "I probably shouldn't tell you this, but Gopal and Hans had quite a row this morning in the office. Hans advocated kicking you all out if you were responsible for the blackout."

That would be a nightmare come true. I'd made sacrifices for my career. "Uh, is there any evidence that we were responsible for the blackout?"

Lily pushed a lock of gray hair behind her ear and sighed. "My impression is they are still investigating. Gopal said they should at least find out what happened first, and then probation would be the first step."

"Probation?" I gulped. "What kind of probation?"

She put her hand on my arm. "You'd probably lose your financial support. I'm not sure what they could do academically since you're done with classes. That would be up to your academic advisor, Gopal."

"So, what do you think'll happen?" I asked.

Lily frowned and shook her head. "I know what should happen, but I doubt they'll ask me. They should make Gopal department chair. That Hans is just not right. He doesn't even seem to care that Lars got hurt. I knew Hans was a cold fish, but he values his career more than his son."

Another reason to feel guilty: I hadn't thought about Lars once yet today. "How is Lars?" I asked. "Have you heard anything?"

She dipped her head. "Yes, I called Mrs. Karlsson a little while ago. She was about to leave for the hospital, and she said he was doing better."

"Good. That's a relief." My relief was tempered with guilt. "Maybe I should go down to the fusion lab and see how bad things are."

"It couldn't hurt. Let me know what happens, okay?" She reached for her sewing.

I nodded. "You'll probably know before I do, but sure."

In the basement hallway, everything appeared the same as usual. It didn't look like a man almost died here last night or like we massacred the power grid. That didn't seem right. Shouldn't monumental events leave monumental evidence?

Slowly, I approached the scene of the crime and peeked my head through the doorway. I eyed the power kill switch. We'd killed the power, right? That meant the power should be off. But I could have sworn that currents spewed out of the Tokamak after the power was off.

Weird. I mentally reviewed the events of last night. How could there be currents with no power? And then, when we were all running away, why did Lars shove me backward?

It almost seemed like he was shoving me into danger...

I tramped around the lab, unplugged everything except the

98

computers and hit the power switch. That should turn the power on in the room.

I tried the room lights, and they worked. Huzzah.

I shoved a ladder over near the Tokamak. There was definitely a lot of charred-looking material near the top. If I squinted, I could just make out a tiny crack in the power coupling insulation layer. How had we all missed it before? Maybe the accident last night made it worse?

"Ellen, I think you're right," I said. "I think the avalanche messed up the insulation here."

"You should repair it as soon as possible," she said. "That is a safety hazard."

I paused. Was she being sarcastic? No. Couldn't be. Apps weren't sarcastic, were they? Finally, I said, "I noticed."

After consulting Jake briefly by fon, I found some spare electrical insulation and duct-taped it along the power coupling and the top of the Tokamak. It looked crude, but it should do the job. Maybe. I wouldn't know until it was powered up.

I traipsed over to one of the computer workstations. With bated breath, I turned it on. Nothing happened with said computers. Well, crap monkey.

"Ellen, call Megan," I said.

Soon I heard, "Hi, Kathy. Wait! Let me guess. The power outage screwed up your computers?"

"Uh, yeah," I said. "Did I call the psychic line again?"

She sighed. "No, join the club. Computers are screwed up all over campus. Even our computers at the computer center are screwed up."

"Is there any chance..." I started to say.

She laughed so hard that she started coughing. "Any chance we can fix yours before everyone else's? No." Clearly, the IT department didn't know how vital the fusion project was.

How the flood were we going to figure out what happened without computers?

"So, anything else?" she asked impatiently.

I had a light-bulb-over-the-head moment. "Did you make any progress with those other computers we brought over, the fusion lab computers?"

"Just a sec." I heard talking in the background.

"You are one lucky daughter of Gaia. We finished working on the original fusion lab computers yesterday and packed them up. So, they should be fine."

"Woohoo! That was some rush you put on them." I was impressed.

"Are you being sarcastic? We did rush. We had to order a bunch of parts, rebuild components, and all kinds of stuff. You're not implying that we don't do a good job after I just offered you the only computers that work on campus, are you?"

She sounded snippy. I could imagine her eyes flashing and that vein on her forehead pulsing even though I couldn't see it on the tiny screen. "Certainly not, Computer Goddess. I am yours to command. What do we need to do to possess these computers?"

She said, "Damn straight, I'm a Computer Goddess. Just come pick them up. I can't spare anyone to deliver them."

"Yes," I said. "I hear and obey."

I went back up to the physics department office. Lily and Jake were deep in conversation, with Jake leaning over her desk. What were they talking about? Jake wasn't telling her about the kiss, was he? I didn't want Lily trying to convince me to date Jake, as well. Resisting him was hard enough already. I rushed over to interrupt them. "Hey, what's up?"

They immediately stopped talking.

Jake shrugged.

"Good news," I said. "Megan says the original fusion lab computers are fixed. We lucked out because the ones in the lab don't seem to be working. We have to go over to the computer center, though, and get them. Are you available now, Jake?"

He looked down and shuffled his feet. "Yeah, I guess so."

Lily contemplated the two of us, leaning forward. "Hey. What's going on here? What aren't you telling me?" She pointed from me to Jake and back again.

"There's nothing else to tell about the accident as far as I know," I said, choosing my words carefully. "Right, Jake?"

"Oh no." Lily drew her hand up in front of her mouth. "You're not saying it wasn't an accident, are you?"

I shook my head.

"No," Jake said. "I'm not saying that. Maybe someone made

100

a mistake, is all." He glared at me. "We all make mistakes."

What was that look for? I was getting confused. What mistake? "The *accident* last night seems to be because of the avalanche. Although, we should have noticed the insulation problem earlier." Guilt, guilt, guilt.

"There was an insulation problem?" Lily asked.

Jake nodded.

"Uh, possibly. We're still investigating," I said. "If we fetch the fusion computers, we can check and see if any data made it to the Mass Store."

"Wouldn't any data from the accident have been wiped out in the power failure?" Lily asked.

"Au contraire, madam!" I said. "That is exactly the purpose of the Mass Storage System. Most of the physics experiments generate huge amounts of data, too much data to store locally. We send it offsite to this gargantuan data storage facility which guarantees the data's integrity no matter what happens. They have an uninterruptible power source." I was not pedantic.

"Yeah, no matter if it's an earthquake or flood or avalanche or even a power failure, it should be okay," Jake added.

Lily got up and started walking to the storeroom off the office. "Here. Use these carts and, by all means, quickly get the computers. I want to know what's going on."

She wasn't the only one.

Jake and I pushed the carts across campus to the computer center. He seemed quiet, too quiet.

"The lab accident is a little murky for me," I said. Lars' behavior was especially murky. "What do you remember?"

He just shrugged.

"So, about earlier today, in Gopal's office, I'm sorry. I didn't handle it very well." I focused on the cart.

"Yeah, I'm sorry you didn't handle it very well, too," he said.

That sounded like he was criticizing me, not apologizing. "And?" I asked.

"Is that all you have to say?" he asked.

"Well, yes. I still don't think me and you are a good idea." I petered out.

"Whatever!" He scowled and picked up the pace.

I had a hard time keeping up with him. Jeez, guys were

moody.

When we got to her cubicle, the Computer Goddess definitely seemed out of sorts. Her arms were crossed in front of her, and that forehead vein twitched like a drug addict in withdrawal. "There's a rumor going around that the power failure started in the basement of the physics building, in the fusion lab, to be specific," she said. "Is it true? Did you guys blackout most of the state and cause us days, weeks, maybe even months of extra work!"

"Ah." Jake glanced at me. "Did you hear we could have been killed? Lars was almost killed."

"We aren't sure what happened yet," I said meekly. "We think it was due to the avalanche. If the power outage did start in the fusion lab, will you still give us the computers?"

She uncrossed her arms. "Was Lars really hurt?"

I nodded. "Yes. He's still in the hospital."

"We got checked out by the paramedics, and Kathy went into shock." Jake shifted back and forth from one foot to the other.

"Really?" Megan's vein stopped throbbing so noticeably. "Why didn't you tell me last night? Or this morning?"

"I sort of forgot," I said.

"Forgot!" Vein throbbing resumed. "How do you forget something like that?" she asked.

I blushed but most definitely did not look at Jake. "I guess I had something else on my mind."

"Yeah, and she handled it badly, too," Jake said.

"What? What did she handle badly?" Megan asked.

Jake blushed. We had that in common.

"Clearly, I have no choice but to give you guys your equipment, or I may never get to the bottom of this. You better tell me the whole story later. Come on; your computers are over here." Megan waved to her left.

Jake and I lugged the machines back into the lab. We disconnected the broken neutrino lab computers and connected the repaired fusion lab computers. I discovered it was much easier to connect computers together if you pay attention when you disconnect them. Go figure.

NEUTRINO WARNING

Before long, we sat in front of the new, er, former, fusion lab computer, task completed.

The next few moments could sink or save our careers. We desperately needed some data files to prove we'd done an actual experiment rather than just causing a horrible life-threatening disaster. "Are you ready?" I felt nauseated as I reached for the computer.

Jake seemed too nervous to speak and just nodded.

I turned it on.

Chapter Ten

I hoarded my breath. The computer beeped and chirped. A drop of sweat dribbled down my face, and I wiped it absentmindedly.

After an eternity, the login screen appeared. I quickly typed in my username and password.

"Access Denied."

"Shit!" I pounded the desk with my fists.

"Calm down," Jake said. "Are you sure you didn't type in your username or password wrong? Try again."

This time I typed carefully, pausing after each character. I pressed 'Enter' and felt faint.

The login screen went away, replaced by a workspace. I quit holding my breath and glanced at Jake. "So far, so good."

He crossed his fingers.

I accessed the Mass Storage System and looked for fusion data files with time stamps within the last fourteen hours. "There are at least a couple of dozen files here. Thank Gaia!"

"That's good news," Jake said.

I opened one of the magnetic field data files. The values were huge. Too huge. My finger shook as I pointed at the screen. "Jake, what do you make of these?"

He pushed his glasses up his nose and peered at the numbers. "Wow. Those are gigantic magnetic fields. That can't be right, can it?"

I pursed my lips. "I don't think so. We were expecting much smaller magnetic fields. But let's check the other files and see if they're consistent."

I opened up the digital video file of the interior of the Tokamak. It showed the inside of a silver cylinder. The plasma stream lit up like a river of yellow-white electricity, and plasma current began to flow. Every once in a while, the floor of the Tokamak rippled slightly. "Hurray! We got a plasma current!" That was our first goal on the way to controlled fusion energy. I continued watching, and much to my dismay, suddenly, the plasma current folded back on itself and flowed in the opposite direction.

"That's great that we got a plasma current, but why is it so weird?" Jake jabbed his finger at the screen. "Why is the bottom surface rippling? And why does the plasma current turn around? I thought it was just supposed to flow around in a circle inside the Tokamak."

"The rippling is weird." I stared at the screen. "It looks like liquid lithium. But we don't have that." I didn't add that I'd asked Gopal if I could do it, and he'd said no.

"What? Liquid?" Jake asked. "Does Gopal know about this?"

When I glanced up, Jake was scowling at me. "Uh, yes," I said. "He knows about liquid lithium and its usefulness in a Tokamak."

"You didn't answer the question." Jake frowned.

I ignored that little detail. "I think we need to look inside. Grab the tools."

With Jake's help, we made short work of taking off the exterior access panel. And, sure enough, the bottom of the tank seemed to be made of liquid. "Well, shi-oot," I said. "I didn't know that was there." I turned to Jake. "Did you?"

"It's not supposed to be there, is it?" he asked.

"No," I said. "I don't get it. How did it get there? I didn't put it there. Did you?"

"No," he said, shaking his head. "Lars, Brittani, and Marcello are the only other people working here."

"I don't think Marcello would do it without asking us first," I said slowly.

"Is there a chance Gopal asked someone to install it?" he asked.

Recalling how annoyed he'd been when I suggested it, I seriously doubted it. "I seriously doubt it." The two of us stood there for a few moments. The perpetrator would have to remain a mystery for the moment, although all signs pointed to

Lars. I guessed he'd paid the price if it had been him, though, considering he was in the hospital.

"There's charring at the top," I said. "Do you want to see my repairs?" I pushed the ladder back next to the machine.

"Yeah," he said. "I can check them."

A little later, the two of us were back in front of the computers. "As for the plasma current turning around, it's unexpected," I said. "It might be a mistake--although I don't know what."

"Hey, check the plasma current data file and see what the numbers say." Jake's elbow accidentally poked me.

I became acutely aware of how close to each other we were sitting. I scooted my chair over a bit, away from him, and found and opened the plasma current data file. The first numbers looked reasonable, but the following ones quickly grew much larger than we'd been anticipating. I scrolled down, and the numbers decreased. I scrolled down further, and the plasma current went negative.

"What the heck does a negative plasma current mean?" Jake raised his eyebrows into the middle of his forehead.

I pushed my chair back from the workstation. "I don't know. We weren't expecting a negative plasma current. This data might be all screwed up!" I rubbed my forehead, then reached for the computer keyboard again. I felt a headache coming on. "We'll just have to dig in and figure out what's going on."

Jake's elbow poked me again.

I shot a glance at him. He sat over a foot away. "Did you do that on purpose?"

He blushed and smiled sheepishly. "Do what? I didn't do anything. Not me." He doth protest too much. I felt a grin coming on.

His fon beeped. "Oops. Saved by the beep." He grinned. "Sorry, gotta go to class. Are you going to see Lars at the hospital later? I'm going to stop by there."

I frowned. Stop by the hospital? I did want to make sure Lars was all right. And I wanted to know why he pushed me back into the lab. And I really wanted to know if he installed the liquid lithium. "I guess so, but I thought you were going to help with this analysis?"

"Get Ellen to help you. Let me know what you figure out, though." He gave me a jaunty wave before slipping out the door.

Men, can't live with them, can't get them to do your work. I sighed, got Ellen, and pulled my chair back to the computer, determined to get to the bottom of this mess. I accessed the data, printed out everything that could be printed, and started studying it.

After a while, my stomach rumbled like a strike-slip fault about to blow. I checked the time and realized I'd been so immersed in work that lunchtime had come and gone. That just wouldn't do. Lunch was my favorite meal, after all.

I went up to the snack bar armed with a sheaf of graphs, plots, and some time-stamped video stills thrown in for good measure. I needed to pick someone else's brain; mine was worn out.

I bought a sandwich with assorted accompaniments. Scanning the almost empty room, I spied Marcello at a table in the corner.

He caught my eye but ducked his head down and focused on his plate, pretending he didn't see me.

I marched over to him anyway and dropped assorted foodstuffs and papers onto the table. How dare he pretend not to see me! "*Bonjour*, Marcello."

He raised his head. "*Buona giornata*, Kathy." He peered down and took another bite of pasta.

I plopped down on an adjacent chair. "What's with you?"

He chewed slowly, swallowed, and finally gave me a piercing stare. "I cannot believe you ran the first major test without me. I thought we were a team. Did all my hard work mean nothing to you?"

The blood drained from my head. He was right. How could I do that to him? "Uh." I fiddled with my sandwich, playing for time. "You're right. I'm sorry. We should have waited for you. Lars--"

"Lars. I might have known." He spit a tiny piece of pasta out of his mouth in his excitement. "I can not believe you are under his spell." He grimaced and waved his hands around vigorously.

"I'm not under anybody's spell." My fist hit the table.

Marcello snorted. "Bah. My Allesandra flirted with him! I do not understand why he so enchants women."

"I'm not enchanted." How dare he say such a thing?

"He is a bad man." He shook his head, and his few meager strands of black hair waved back and forth.

I had my own suspicions on that point. Shoving me was the action of a bad man. Had he done other bad things?

"You didn't install liquid lithium inside the tokamak by any chance, did you?" I asked.

"No," he said, eyebrows rising up his substantial forehead. "Did someone do that?"

"It appears so," I said.

"Were they supposed to?" he asked.

"I don't think so." I took a bite of my sandwich.

"Did it cause the accident?"

"I don't know."

He shook his head as if in disgust.

We silently bit, chewed, and swallowed for a few uncomfortable minutes. I focused on the table, glancing up at Marcello once in a while.

Marcello stopped eating and peered over at me. "So, what happened last night? Were you guys the ones who caused the blackout? Did Lars truly get hurt?"

"Yes, Lars got hurt," I said. "Some kind of huge electrical current from the Tokamak knocked him out."

Marcello shook his head in disbelief and pored over his lunch again.

I leaned forward. "And Marcello, I didn't realize it at the time, but there were still currents coming from the Tokamak after the power had gone out in the room."

His head perked up. "After? Are you sure? But that would be incredible. It would mean..."

"That could mean we'd ignited the plasma and started a self-sustaining fusion reaction," I said. "We couldn't get any data after the power cut out, but the data before that seems to indicate plasma ignition was about to happen. Ellen and I did a preliminary analysis." I fanned the papers out on the table.

Marcello examined every plot, every graph, every picture I'd brought. Soon he forgot all about his pasta and his aggravation. "Santa Maria. I cannot believe it. This is fantastic. It all looks great, except for this stuff." He tapped the plasma current data. "And these photos." I had laid the photos of the interior of the Tokamak out in chronological order. "Are you sure these time stamps are correct?"

I pointed at the corner of the photos. "Those are the time stamps right there. The camera puts them on automatically. I wouldn't have the first clue how to change those, even if I wanted to."

He looked me over appraisingly. "I believe you." He smiled wide, showing off his crooked teeth and the big dimple on his chin.

We pondered the pages.

I tapped my forefinger on one of the papers. "This stuff is all consistent with the plasma current changing direction, but nothing in the experiment should make that happen." I stole a piece of forgotten pasta from Marcello's plate.

"*Sì*. How would that happen?" He looked me in the eye.

"Let's see, plasma current is essentially the change in electric charges in the plasma per change in time," I said.

"*Sì*," he said. "But how does that help us? Charge cannot spontaneously change sign, and time cannot flow backward."

I choked on another filched piece of pasta. "That's it! Look at the pictures! The plasma current's flowing forward in time, and then it stops here," I pointed at the snake-like frozen current, "and then it flows backward." The last picture showed a much smaller snake of electricity.

Marcello scanned the plots and pictures one after the other. I could almost envision the gears and wheels turning in his head. He dipped his head up and down. "*Sì*. It is true. Time flowed back. Santa Maria!" His eyes met mine over his pasta. His chin dimple reappeared. "This is incredible! We must get the machine going again as soon as possible and continue the experiment!"

"Kathy. Incoming call from Jake," Ellen interrupted.

I picked Ellen up. "Excuse me, Marcello. Ellen, answer."

"Kathy?" Jake asked.

"Yes, hi, Jake," I said. "Wait until you hear what the data shows."

"Tell me later," he said. "If you're going to get to the hospital before visiting hours are over, you better hurry up."

I checked my watch. Drown it. It was much later than I realized. "Okay. I'll be right there. Olga signing out."

Marcello gave me a quizzical look. "Olga? Who's Olga?"

"I had to impersonate Lars' sister at the hospital last night to pry information out of the nurses. He's doing all right, by the way. I've got to go now, though, if I'm going to get in to see him."

"Lars has a sister?" Marcello frowned. "So, Lars is going to recover?" Did I detect a note of disappointment in his voice?

"I'm not sure," I said. "Do you want to come with me and see?"

He shook his head. "No. I must get back to my lab and finish some of my work. I have been neglecting it." He gathered his lunch remnants together. "But call me when you discover more about last night's experiment. And do not do any more fusion experiments without me!" He shook his forefinger. "Let's meet in the fusion lab first thing in the morning tomorrow. *Ciao.*" He hurried off.

I shoved the papers into my pockets, ran outside to my bike, and made a beeline to the hospital. On the way, Ellen gave me the latest news.

May 5, 2098: Influenza Outbreak in Western U.S.:

Public Health officials said that a virulent influenza outbreak is spreading throughout the western U.S. It is expected to move further east in the coming weeks, threatening the rest of the country. Influenza is marked by fever, headache, fatigue, dry cough, sore throat, runny or stuffy nose, and muscle aches. Influenza may cause severe complications and can be fatal, particularly for children and the elderly.

Over two percent of people in Nevada and Utah have flu-like symptoms. These infection rates are much higher than those for the same period last year. The increase is due to the vaccine failure reported here several weeks ago. The strength of these influenza strains was thought to have been affected by the pandemic, causing avian influenza several decades ago.

The flu spreads in respiratory droplets caused by coughing and sneezing, usually from person to person. Adults may infect others from one day before getting symptoms to seven days after getting sick. Public Health officials stated it is imperative that people avoid close contact with people infected and generally avoid touching their eyes, nose, or mouth and wash their hands often. Face masks are recommended.

When I got to the hospital, I threw my bike on the ground and ran inside. There were some people wearing face masks in the waiting room. At the admissions desk, I could barely talk I was so out of breath. "Here to see Lars Karlsson. Am sister Olga."

The young thing behind the desk, wearing a face mask, didn't even bat an eyelash at my story and just pointed me down the hall.

Jake popped into the hall. "Kathy, I mean Olga, over here. He's in here."

Lars sat up in bed wearing one of those embarrassing hospital gowns. He looked unhappy to see me and made a show of scowling. "What are you doing here?"

What was I doing here? I wanted to make sure he was okay and get to the bottom of his odd behavior last night. "I'm glad you're all right, Lars. You had us worried." Up close, he seemed worn out. I couldn't see the painful electrical burns on his back and stomach, but I knew they must be there.

I sat in one of the comfortable visitor's chairs in Lars' private room. "So, how are you feeling?" I smiled warmly. I knew you catch more flies with honey than you do with vinegar.

He paused for a moment and then said, "It's nice of you to ask." He covered the right side of his stomach with his hand. "Okay, I guess--considering I was essentially hit by lightning."

I rubbed the sore spot on my arm where Lars had bruised it. "So, why did you grab my arm and push me back into the lab last night?"

Jake gasped. "I didn't know about this."

"Uh, I was trying to push you out of danger." Lars stared at the bed, playing with his blanket, rolling it between his fingers.

He looked so guilty and suspicious, I wasn't buying it. More like he was trying to push me *into* danger. I'd have to be more careful around him in the future.

Lars looked up at me. "But what I want to talk about is the experiment. Jake said some data made it over to the Mass Store? And what do you make of currents coming from the

Tokamak after the power went out?"

I jumped out of the chair. "Ellen and I had a quick look at some of the data, and it seems like the experiment may have worked."

"That's great!" Jake said.

"The data shows we got plasma current," I said, words rushing out. "There's some other weird data too. Marcello says we should restart the Tokamak tests as soon as possible." I hopped from one foot to the other.

When I beheld Lars, I saw a comet could have flown into his mouth, it hung open so wide. "It worked?" he finally asked.

Was he too skeptical? Could he have been trying to sabotage the experiment? "That reminds me...." I said. "Did you install--"

A stentorian yell came from the hall. "What is the meaning of this?"

Like synchronized swimmers, the three of us turned as one and saw Hans in the doorway. Hans was stereotypically Teutonic with his blond hair, broad cheekbones, and athletic build. Unfortunately, right now, he looked angry enough to skewer me with a broad sword.

I really wanted to ask Lars about the liquid lithium thing, but maybe now wasn't the time.

Lars squeaked out, "Dad?"

I pivoted back to face Lars. "I'm glad you're feeling better. We should go, Jake."

Hans favored me with a glower. "It's official. Your fiasco was responsible for the blackout."

Guilty, guilty, guilty. The only way to make this all right was to achieve safe fusion.

"The university president yelled at me after the mayor yelled at her." His voice was as frigid as absolute zero. "I don't enjoy getting yelled at. Moreover, there's a chance our fusion energy research grants will be taken away. And it was because of you. I blame you. All this trouble is your fault."

I struggled to sound calm. "That is bad news about the blackout. I'm sorry that happened. But Dr. Karlsson, the experiment worked at least a little. We got interesting data. I'd be happy to show it to you."

He ignored me and turned to Lars. "What were you thinking? I thought I raised you smarter than that."

"Dad, you shouldn't be in here without a mask." Lars looked worried. "You're a little bit older. You have to be careful. There's an epidemic."

Hans ignored that and directed his wrath back at me. "Did you know, young lady, that the university president made me the new physics department chairman this morning?"

"No, sir, I didn't." This meant I had even more reason to try to stay calm. Focus, Kath. "But I do know that we got some good data last night. We're getting close to achieving fusion."

"What are you even doing here? You aren't a relative," Hans said. "Leave. Immediately."

I can take a hint. Or an order. I walked toward the door in what I hoped was a calm, professional manner.

Jake followed right after me.

Hans hit me with his parting shot. "I'm going to expel you from the physics program if it's the last thing I do."

Chapter Eleven

As usual, Ellen's news update on the way to work the next morning was bad.

May 6, 2098: Death Toll Rises from Influenza Outbreak:

Government sources indicate that flu, now widespread in the western U.S., has caused dozens of deaths, with many more people at risk from potentially fatal complications. A Public Health official said, "If you live in an infected area, be extra cautious as we believe this flu strain to be particularly life-threatening."

A CDC spokesman said they have been working with the Council of State and Territorial Epidemiologists for the last few weeks gathering information on flu fatalities, but exact figures are difficult to determine. The outbreak's severity is unclear at this time because the flu is not easy to distinguish from other viruses, and people who seek medical attention often suffer from complications rather than the flu itself.

Subscribers: Please peruse the news archive for previously published helpful health tips.

Why was the news always bad?

When I got to the fusion lab, Marcello looked up from the computer. "It must be nice to sleep in so late. Are you on vacation?"

I was about to give him a snotty retort when a smile snuck onto his face, blowing his cover.

"Bah. I am kidding, Kathy. I wish I could sleep later but I had to babysit a new grad student in the high-energy control room at dawn." His chin dimpled.

I pulled up a chair and sat down next to him.

"All those early morning work hours allowed me to have Leonardo verify those results you showed me yesterday." He pointed at his fon.

I was a little annoyed that Marcello couldn't just take my word for it. Did he think Ellen was incompetent? Ellen was way better than his app, Leonardo. "So? What did Leonardo deduce?" I crossed my arms.

Marcello laughed. "You are so defensive of Ellen. It is cute. I am not saying Leonardo is better than Ellen. I am merely utilizing sound scientific practices by independently verifying your results. *Si*?"

I guess he may have had a point. "Yeah, fine. It's probably a good idea."

Jake appeared at my side. "What's a good idea?"

"You have a habit of sneaking up on people and getting into their conversations," I said.

Jake's mouth turned up in a smile, and his eyes twinkled. "Good morning to you too, Kathy. Did you miss your morning caffeine fix?"

"*Si*. She is very clearly caffeine-free this morning." Marcello's mouth also turned up, and that blasted chin dimple of his showed again. "I wish she would just go get a beverage and quit subjecting us to her bad humor."

I could feel a headache coming on. They were ganging up on me. I threw up my hands. "Fine. I surrender. I'll get some tea in a second. But first, what did you figure out, Marcello?"

He leaned back in his chair. "I deciphered that your calculations were correct. There was a plasma current generated. We are well on our way to fusion energy." He gave us his chin-dimpled grin. "All indications also show we were on the verge of plasma ignition when the power went out."

I beamed at them. "See? I told you so."

They nodded.

"*Si*."

"Hey, did you tell Marcello how mad Hans got at you yesterday at the hospital?" Jake asked.

Ugh. I'd been trying to forget the whole scene. I shook my head. "No. That would be gossiping. I don't gossip."

I was nearly bowled over as they exploded with laughter.

Jake laughed so hard that he had to lean on a desk to avoid falling on the floor.

Marcello wiped tears from his eyes. "Since when?"

Whatever. I didn't need this. I turned my back on them and went on a tea quest.

When I got to the department office, Lily sat typing at her computer.

"What? No sewing? Did you finish those costumes you were working on?" I asked her.

"Not yet." She jerked a thumb at the open office door behind her. "The physics czar won't allow it. But I'll wear him down."

I snorted. "I take it the physics czar is Hans?"

"Yeah. Gopal lost out to Hans for the department chair job." She eyed me. "Did you hear?"

I nodded. Nodding didn't count as gossiping. Besides, I was just confirming, which didn't count as gossiping either.

"It just makes me sick to think about. Gopal would have done such a great job. All the faculty were behind him." She shook her head. "I don't know what that university President Washington was thinking."

I nodded. "I agree completely. It's hard to fathom."

"But on the other hand, you guys will get Gopal back on your project full-time. That'll be nice. I guess Lars got out of the hospital last night. He's resting up at his folks' house. That's good news, too." Lily smiled.

"Oh? Yeah, I guess." It might be good news, but I couldn't help it; I was still suspicious about that shove he gave me.

She lowered her voice and motioned me towards her. "Hans and Gopal already had a big fight this morning. It's going to be a rocky road with Hans at the helm. At least I'm getting a little break now. Hans went to his first big department chair meeting with the university president. He's got meetings all morning."

I had a horrible flashback of Viking warrior Hans yelling at me.

"Earth to Kathy," Lily said. "Did you want something?"

My eyes focused on hers. "Yeah. I need tea."

"Well, help yourself, dear." Lily pointed at the teapot.

While I scored a big mug of the elixir of the gods, Gopal ambled in.

"Kathy, just who I wanted to see. I might have known I'd find you here by the teapot." He reached for a mug.

"Are congratulations in order or sympathies?" I asked.

"What?" He paused in his beverage preparations.

I leaned my head toward the physics department chair's office. "The chair job."

"Oh. I guess congratulations are in order," he said. "I didn't want the job. Everyone around here begged me to take it, but yesterday morning was the last straw. I'm sorry I missed our appointment yesterday, by the way." He stirred his tea accouterments into his drink.

"What happened yesterday morning?" I took a sip.

He grimaced and rubbed his beard. "Let's just say the powers that be were not happy about how the fusion experiment went the other night. They read us the riot act, the ruckus act, the hoopla act, and any other act you can think of. There was a lot of yelling."

"I'm sorry that people got hurt, Gopal," I said.

He nodded, swallowed some tea, and glanced at me over the top of his cup. "Kathy, level with me. I put my career on the line, sticking up for you guys. They wanted to expel the whole lot of you. It was an accident, right?"

I lowered my libation, glancing at Hans' office door. "Yes, the power outage was an accident, but we got some interesting data. Let's go to your office and talk about it."

"Okay. We should chat. Jake should join us," Gopal said.

I popped back down to the fusion lab and gave Jake the heads up. He scooped up some new plots and graphs while I put the lab notebooks in my bag. We made it up to Gopal's office in record time.

I ensconced myself in one of Gopal's rickety chairs.

Jake waved his passel of papers. "Gopal. Wait until you see what we found out from the data."

Gopal looked grim and rubbed his beard. "Jake, sit down." He pointed at a chair. "The data will have to wait for a few minutes. We need to talk."

My nearly empty stomach roiled. Did anyone anywhere ever hear good news after 'We need to talk.'? "You said downstairs you stuck up for us. I'm not expelled, am I? And Jake didn't do anything wrong. He's not in trouble, is he?"

Jake gasped. Apparently, the thought that he might be in

trouble just for hanging around with me hadn't crossed his mind.

Gopal took a sip of tea. "I did defend both of you. I even defended myself, for that matter. But Hans was furious. What did you say to him yesterday?"

"I said I was sorry about the blackout, but I'd be happy to show him the data," I said. "He acted very irrationally."

"Yeah, he did," Jake chimed in.

Gopal scowled and expelled a big bunch of air. "Unfortunately, Hans is my boss now. So, you're both suspended, without pay, from your research assistantships. I couldn't stop it. And you're prohibited from entering the physics building, especially the fusion lab."

That was a gut punch. "No!"

"What about my classes?" Jake asked, seemingly very upset.

"You can go to classes, Jake." Gopal rubbed his beard. "Hans even made Lars the leader of the fusion group, if you can believe it."

"Hans promoted Lars over you?" I asked. "That's totally unfair."

"But we made a big discovery." Jake squinted in confusion. "But...."

I took a sip of tea to calm my stomach. It didn't work.

"What discovery is that?" Gopal leaned back in his chair.

Jake glanced at me.

I nodded. Wait 'til Gopal saw this!

Jake handed Gopal the papers he'd brought with him.

Gopal gingerly laid them out on his desk.

Jake craned his neck, trying to get a look, and finally just joined Gopal on the other side of the desk.

Gopal looked from one sheet to the next. "What does it all mean?"

"You tell me." I prompted him. I wanted to see if he agreed with our assessment.

Jake kept nodding and glancing up at me. He looked like he might explode from excitement. Mount Vesuvius, here we come.

Gopal stroked his beard. "Well, it starts the way we expect. And it ends with plasma current readings." He looked up. "I can't believe we got plasma current on the first test." All the muscles in his face were flaccid. He turned back to the plots. "But here in the middle, what is going on? How could the plasma current go negative? And what's with these crazy pictures? Are they in order?"

I had been holding my breath but had to inhale so I wouldn't drop dead. "Ellen and I double-checked everything, and Marcello and Leonardo checked everything, so yes, the data is all in order and accurate."

Gopal shook his head back and forth like a metronome. "But that would mean time flowed backward or something like that." His mouth fell open.

"I agree," I said. "It looks like time flowed backward." They couldn't very well put us on probation now.

Gopal closed his mouth. "If this is true, it's just incredible. Theoretically, it's allowed, but it's never been seen before." He seemed dazed. "How did you get this kind of efficiency?"

"Someone implemented the liquid lithium floor." I didn't meet his eyes.

"Kathy! I said no, and I was very clear." Gopal frowned. "But I can't say I'm overly surprised that you disobeyed me."

I jumped up. "Hey, it wasn't me! It was Lars!" I was guessing. "And we don't know for sure that is the reason we got the interesting results."

Jake came back around to my side of the desk and sat down. "I must admit I don't get it," he said. "How could time flow backward?"

Gopal raised his eyebrows and picked up his mug. "Yes, Kathy, explain that."

I could rise to the challenge. I cleared my throat. "Time reversal is not only allowed; it's required because of time-reversal invariance. Time-reversal invariance means that elementary particle interactions are symmetric in time. They can proceed forward in time or backward in time."

Jake fidgeted in his chair. "How come you don't hear about this in real life?"

I shrugged. "In real life, we don't expect big macroscopic stuff to flow backward in time; it goes against our intuition."

Gopal put down his cup. "A lot of scientific stuff goes against our intuition, like Special Relativity."

"That's because we're big and slow." I grinned.

Jake poked my arm with his elbow. "Speak for yourself."

I couldn't help smiling. "You know what I mean. Our intuition is based on our big slow experiences, not small, fast stuff like elementary particles. Theoretically, time-reversal invariance exists, but traditionally, it's been hard to prove or disprove because it requires a lot of energy."

Gopal nodded.

I dropped my final bombshell. "There's more. After the power went out in the room, there were still currents coming out of the Tokamak."

Gopal's mouth dropped open again. "Are you saying you think you got plasma ignition?"

"Yes," I said. "Obviously, we couldn't get any data with the power out but still… We need to get back in the lab."

Gopal groaned and shifted in his chair. "I'm truly sorry, but that will not happen in the immediate future."

"Oh no!" Gut punch. "Even with these new results?" I asked.

Gopal massaged his upper lip with his forefinger. "I'm sorry, but I don't have the power to take you off probation. I'll do what I can, but you absolutely cannot go to the fusion lab in the meantime. It would be best if you left the building as soon as possible. And don't let anyone see you inside. Hans is looking for any excuse to expel you."

My chin quivered. "But that's not fair! We made an important discovery. Just the plasma current alone is huge for the fusion energy project!" Moisture pooled in the corner of my eyes. This couldn't be happening. How could they put us on probation when we might be able to save the world with fusion energy?

"I want you to get back in the lab, too," Gopal said. "I'll tell you what, Hans told me to exclude you guys from computer access, but I won't. Access the data remotely, create an irrefutable report, and save all our careers." He stood up and led us to the door. "I'm counting on you." His face took on a grimly determined cast.

Shell-shocked, we stepped into the hall.

"I guess we better get out of the building before Hans or Lars see us." Jake pushed his glasses up the bridge of his nose.

I took a step toward the stairs. "I guess…" I drew out the

word.

"Kathy, what are you thinking?" Jake favored me with his rarely-seen stern look.

"I'm thinking I know Lars is at his parents' house and Hans is at some big meeting. It wouldn't hurt to go to the neutrino office. It might be our last chance for a while." Plus, I should erase that password I left there. I didn't want Lars to find it.

"Are you sure they're not here in the building?" Jake asked.

"Positive," I said loudly and confidently.

We trudged up to our office. The door stood open. "Wait." I started getting a bad feeling. I peeked inside. Lars stood inside, rifling through my desk. Flood it. I jerked back out of the doorway.

"What is it?" Jake whispered.

"Lars is in our office," I whispered.

"Well, crap monkey!" Jake whispered, albeit not very quietly.

Crap monkey, indeed. "I don't get it," I said. "I thought he was recovering from his injuries."

"He got better?" Jake shrugged. "He must not have been that injured."

I took another peek, and Jake followed me.

Lars squinted in our general direction and took a step toward the door. Oops.

We ducked back out of the doorway.

"Is someone out there?" Lars said.

"Let's get out of here. He's coming." I whispered insistently.

We ran down the hall as if the devil himself was chasing us.

Unfortunately, we didn't make it all the way to the stairs.

"Who's out there? Kathy? Jake?" Lars asked from just inside our office doorway.

In a panic, I barged into the Men's room.

Jake followed me.

"Did he see us?" I asked.

"I don't think so, but Kathy, you can't be in here. This is the *Men's* room."

I gave him an exasperated look. "I've got news for you. You can't be in here either if we aren't allowed in the building."

"Good point." He grimaced.

"I don't think Lars would guess I would come in here," I whispered.

"Good point," he whispered.

Loud footsteps clomped down the hall straight for us.

I pressed tight against the bathroom wall and willed my heart to stop beating so loudly.

The footsteps stopped outside the Men's room door.

Jake grabbed my hand, squeezing it as if it was a lifeline and he was about to drown.

I squeezed back.

Don't come in. Don't come in. Don't come in.

Chapter Twelve

After a moment, the footsteps passed us by. I snuck to the door, opened it a crack, and saw a man disappearing into the stairwell. It was Lars, from his shoulder-length blond hair to his Italian shoes.

My heart leaped, slammed into my rib cage, and ricocheted around my chest. I closed the door and leaned against the wall again.

"What?" Jake whispered.

"It's Lars. I think he's going downstairs, but we better wait here for a little while."

After a few moments, I'd had my fill of hiding. "Should we risk it?"

"We can't hide in the bathroom forever," Jake said.

We opened the door, ascertained the corridor was Lars-free, snuck down the hall, and scrutinized the dimly lit stairwell.

"I don't see him. Do you see him?" I whispered.

"Nope." Jake shook his head.

"Let's go." Keeping my eyes and ears wide open, I crept down the gray concrete stairs to the first floor. I peered down the hall and saw no sign of Lars, so I motioned Jake to follow me. We sprinted to the exit and out the front door, straight into Lars, who had been waiting for us to come out.

"Ah-ha! I knew I heard something!" He pointed at us.

Jake stepped between Lars and me. "Lars? What do you think you're doing?"

Lars gave me an evil grin. "My dad is furious."

This didn't bode well. I shot a glance at Jake and then looked back at Lars. "What do you want?" I asked.

His grin took a turn for the worse, metamorphosing into a

grimace. "You know what I want."

Jake's gaze ping-ponged back and forth between us. "What does he want?" He clenched his fists and took a step toward Lars.

"Suspended isn't enough. He wants to get us out of the way. Expelled." I hoped that was all he wanted. I was still suspicious about how Lars shoved me into the fusion lab the night of the blackout. And why had he been so surprised the experiment worked?

Jake turned back to face Lars. "That's not going to happen. And if you think I'd let you harm Kathy, think again," he said with quiet resolve.

Who knew Jake could be so tough? I was kind of impressed with how he was handling himself.

"Suit yourself." Lars smirked and picked up his fon. "Adolf, call the Patriot officers. There are trespassers at the physics building."

Yikes. We didn't want to get arrested.

I tried to slip around Lars, but he blocked me easily. Then I turned around and impulsively dashed back into the physics building. "C'mon, Jake," I yelled over my shoulder.

He looked skeptical but followed. "Now what?" he asked once we were inside.

Through the glass, Lars looked smug as he stood outside waiting for the officers.

"Let's go down to the physics department office," I said. "Lily can help us." I ran down the hall.

Jake was right behind me.

In for a penny, in for a Eurodollar, I guess.

The door had a sign that said, 'Closed for lunch. Back at 1:30.' I tried it anyway, and it opened, so we hurried in, closing it behind us. The lights were out, and there was no sign of Lily. Hans' office door stood open, no sign of him either. Thank Gaia for small favors. I locked the main office door.

Jake shuffled the plots and graphs he'd been lugging around. "What was that about? Why is Lars so worked up?"

I was still angry with myself for letting Lars install the liquid lithium right under my nose. I was not a good supervisor. "I think he installed the liquid lithium to wreck the experiment and discredit me." Yes; that made sense. That's what he was up to.

"But he didn't wreck the experiment," Jake said.

"The blackout was bad. But it's a win-win for him," I said. "If he sabotaged the experiment, he could blame me and push me out. If the experiment worked, he could take the credit and push me out. He wants to get rid of me, of us. You know."

Jake narrowed his eyes and leaned toward me. "No, I don't know. Are you saying you just worked together? I think there's something else going on here." His voice took on a steely tone that I hadn't heard before. "Is there something you want to tell me about you and Lars?"

"There is nothing now, nor was there ever anything between Lars and me," I said. That was true, at least.

As if on cue, Lars pounded on the other side of the door. "I know you're in there. There's no way out. The Pats are on their way."

Jake stepped over to the windows and looked out. "Uh, oh. He's right. I can see some guys on motorbikes coming this way. It must be the Pats."

I joined him at the window as my brain churned. We had to get out of this. We couldn't clear our names from jail. "I think we should go out one of these windows." I pointed down. "I know we're not the ground floor, but the way the hill slopes outside, it's not too far down. Maybe two meters or so."

Through the windows in question, I saw three officers disembark from their motorcycles outside the physics building's front doors. Crap monkey! My pulse started racing again.

Jake nodded. "Yeah, the bushes and crab apple trees there should screen us. But the Pats are right there, and we don't want to get messed up with them." He wrinkled his forehead. "I've heard getting taken into custody can be like wrestling with a black hole: you go in, but you don't come back out."

I crossed my arms and considered the conundrum. How were we going to get out of here? I'd heard the same stories. "But those are just rumors, right?"

The sunlight hit Lily's shelf, and I saw fur. I walked over to investigate the furry mystery. The costumes Lily had been working on were still there. I picked up the one on top and held it. It seemed fairly large, with black and white fur. I also checked out the other one, a big bundle of bluish-gray fuzz. I peered more closely. It looked like some kind of fish.

I went over to the windows and glanced out. There wasn't anything outside on the grassy quadrangle except a group of kids, and their teachers (presumably), dressed as various creatures, frolicking on the hill. Garishly colored dinosaurs seemed to be the most popular. I wasn't entirely sure what they were doing there, but they gave me an idea.

"Look, Jake." I pointed at the two costumes. "We can put those on for disguises and join that group of kids when we get outside." I felt a pang of conscience at the thought of using children as cover but quickly squashed it.

"I guess that might work," he said slowly.

I handed him the blue costume. "Here, you be the big fish."

"Neat!" He grinned. "A blue whale." He started putting it on over his clothes.

I put on the panda costume. It was plenty big. Maybe Lily had made it for herself? I grabbed my bag and the panda head and went to the window.

"Okay. Let's get out of here." I opened the window, and the sunlight streamed in. It was only about two meters to the ground. I dropped my bag and panda head, swung my legs over the edge of the window, and sat on the frame.

Jake leaned out. "You know it's a mammal, not a fish."

"What?" I was so startled I almost fell out the window.

"Whales are mammals, not fish."

I gave him a beady-eyed stare. "Is now really the time for a biology lesson?" He resembled a skinny eel more than a blubbery whale anyway.

"I guess not." He cleared his throat. "So, are you going to jump or what?"

"Wait, do you still have the papers?" I asked.

"Yeah, I shoved them inside my costume."

I frowned.

"Well, what do you expect?" he said. "Whales don't have pockets."

I shrugged and jumped, landing harder on my uphill foot. Ouch. I had just finished scooping up my bag and the panda head when Jake hopped down lightly beside me, holding his whale head.

I put on my panda head and crept around a tree. "C'mon, let's get over to those kids." We took off up the hill, running across the grass. We ran away from the physics building and around the rambunctious kids until we were probably clear of Lars and the Pats. The gamboling youngsters paid us no attention.

Once we were relatively safe, I panted, not getting enough air through the panda's face. "Wait up, Jake." I bent down and rested my hands on my knees. "I have to catch my breath."

Jake plopped down on the ground near a tree. "Whew. This costume is hard to run in."

I took in Jake's tiny whale legs. "I can imagine." I collapsed next to him.

"I want you to know if you ever need any help with Lars, if he threatens you or something, I am there for you." His voice strengthened as he crossed his flippers in front of him. "I may be little, but I'm tough."

As I beheld the fuzzy blue apparition next to me, I couldn't help laughing. "Sure, I can see that."

After a few seconds, he started guffawing too. "We must look pretty silly in these costumes."

I nodded, trying to stifle my out-of-control laughter. Out of the corner of my eye, I saw the officers come out of the physics building and glance our way.

I ducked down behind the group of kids.

After conferring, two officers went inside with nightsticks drawn. The other officer scoped out the bushes around the entrance and looked down the sidewalk along the side of the building.

As we watched the building, Marcello came out the front door, brows creased.

"It's Marcello!" Jake motioned toward the building with a flipper.

"Maybe he can get us out of here." I got up.

We approached him as he started down the sidewalk.

"Kids, you need to stay with your group." Marcello pointed back at the field trip on the hill.

I rushed up to him. "Daddy!" I lifted my panda head a little and winked.

He was startled. "Uh, hi, daughter," he said loudly, glancing uneasily at the officer loitering outside the building behind him.

The Pat took a step our way.

"Hi, Daddy. It's me and your son, Jake," I said girlishly.

Marcello waved at Jake. "Hi, son." The whale waved back.

I sidled up closer to Marcello and held up my panda head again. "Can you get us out of here?" I asked softly.

The Pat called over to us. "Is everything okay over there?"

Marcello spoke to the blue-uniformed Patriot officer coming our way. "*Sì*, Officer." He swallowed. "Everything is fine. *Grazie*."

The Pat seemed suspicious and took off his sunglasses, making his eyes into tiny slits. "Are you sure? Kids, is everything all right?"

I didn't know what to say, and Jake shouldn't say anything-he didn't sound like a kid. We froze like Arthropods entombed in amber.

Marcello cleared his throat. "I am sorry, officer, these are my children, er, teenagers, who do not speak English. Only Italian."

The Pat frowned but nodded and moved away. "Well, okay." He waved us off.

The three of us walked as quickly as possible--which in the costumes was none too quickly--down the sidewalk away from the physics building.

A harried teacher without a costume ran after us. "Whoa. Where do you think you're going, Mr. Panda and Mr. Eel? We don't want you wandering off as you did on Earth Day. That's why we're here to practice. The Summer Solstice Parade is only a month away."

Marcello interrupted her diatribe. "Sorry, ma'am. These are my teenagers. They aren't in your class. Sorry for any confusion."

She scrutinized us, narrowing her eyes. "They don't look familiar. But then, why are they in costumes? Oh, never mind. I have to get back to my class."

Once we put the main library between the Pats and us and overexcited teachers, we slowed down.

"What was that about?" Marcello asked wide-eyed.

I peeked out from under the panda head. "Lars saw us in

the physics building and set the Pats on us for trespassing."

"You are no longer allowed in the physics building?" Marcello seemed aghast at the news.

Jake peeped out from under his whale head. "No. We're on probation."

"Bah." Marcello grimaced. "This day just gets worse and worse."

"Why? What else happened?" I asked.

"I wanted to look at the fusion data files again, and when I tried to access them, they were all gone," Marcello said. "Deleted."

I gasped. "Are you sure?" We needed those files.

"Oh, no," exploded out of the whale.

"They were there this morning," I said.

"*Sì.* I *know* they were there this morning," Marcello said. "I looked at them with you, if you recall. I am telling you someone has stolen or deleted the files since then." He shook his head.

I held up my Panda paws. "I hear you." And if they were gone, I had a strong suspicion about who the thief was. "Thanks for your help just now."

"*Prego.* You will let me know if you find the files?"

"Of course. Come on, Jake." We had to get out of here.

Jake and I took the light rail back to my house. The attendant seemed overly solicitous, telling us to watch our step and such. I guess he thought we were little kids. Go figure. When the panda and the whale went inside, Megan was nowhere to be found. I needed to talk to her, but it was just as well--she would have been rolling on the floor laughing when she saw our getups.

Jake shimmied out of his costume in no time, dropping it on the blue living room rug.

I, on the other hand, could not unzip mine. I tugged on the zipper and grunted loudly to no avail.

Jake smiled at me. "Do you need some help?"

"No!" I tugged and grunted some more. It didn't work. I finally gave up, holding up my paws. "Yes. Help me."

"Stand over here." He motioned me to the worn brown couch, braced one leg against it, and pulled on the mutinous zipper. "Yeah, it's stuck all right."

I rolled my eyes. "Thanks. I figured that out."

"Here, let me try again." He made an enormous effort with an equally enormous groan, and suddenly I was freed from zipper prison. Unfortunately, Jake still held the contentious zipper and fell backward, pulling me on top of him.

"Oof." Breath exploded out of Jake's lungs in one dramatic burst as we landed on the carpet. He had a strange expression on his face. "Believe it or not, I've imagined this situation before, but I didn't think I'd have so much trouble breathing."

It felt good to have my body pressed against his. Darn it. I scrambled to get off him. His comment sounded suspiciously like flirting. "Sorry for squishing you." I peeled off the panda suit lickety-split. My clothes underneath were sweaty after all my panda exertions.

He grinned from the middle of the carpet. "No problem. Do you want to do it again?"

I ignored his impertinence, sitting down on the well-used sofa. "I know we shared a kind of ...kiss, but it was a mistake." A wonderful mistake, but still a mistake.

"You're back to that?" He seemed incredulous. "I thought we were past this."

"Ellen: access fusion data files from this morning," I said.

"Files not found," she said.

"Damn," I muttered. I'd been hoping Marcello had been mistaken.

Jake got up off the floor and sat next to me on the couch. "So, Marcello was right about the files. Do you think it was Lars?"

I sighed. "That would be my guess. Since the experiment worked, he'll want to take all the credit for it. He's got to have the data. Somewhere."

"But why would he do that?" Jake seemed so innocent; bless him.

"I think his dad is putting a lot of pressure on him to get some results," I said.

"His dad, Hans, the new physics department chair..." he said as if he was just now putting it together. "Hans, who seems to hate you and anyone associated with you?"

"Basically." I nodded. "I'm sorry you got suspended.

And probably will get expelled. Really sorry. That's not what I wanted."

"It is your fault I'm in trouble now, isn't it?" he said, voice shaking. "My whole future's on the line."

Why was he getting worked up now? Gopal told us like an hour ago. "I said I'm sorry," I said. "Why are you so upset all of a sudden?"

"We've basically been on the run since we found out. This is the first free moment we've had." He jumped up and stared down at me. "And you still won't date me. How did I get mixed up with you?" Ah ha. He was agitated because I didn't want to date him.

I assumed his questions were rhetorical since he stomped over to the front door, threw it open, and left, slamming it behind him.

Today was just not my day.

Chapter Thirteen

I lay on the living room floor, feeling sorry for myself. I'd never noticed how many cracks there were in the ceiling.

Megan burst through the front door with her bike. "Kathy? What are you doing on the floor? Are you all right?" She closed the door behind her, rested her bike against the wall, and strode over to me.

"I'm fine." I sighed.

"Did something happen at work?" She stood over me. "What did Gopal say this morning?"

"Gopal put Jake and me on probation and forbade us to enter the physics building." Moisture was not collecting in my eyes.

Megan's hand flew in front of her mouth. "Oh, Kathy. I'm so sorry."

"That's not the worst of it," I said. "The computer files from the fusion experiment are gone." And even worse, Jake is mad at me. I didn't say that, though. I was not close to crying.

"That does sound bad." Frowning, she pushed an errant lock of curly purple hair behind her ear. "Uh, what's with the fur?" She pointed at the plush costumes still lying on the carpet.

"No comment?" I asked.

She smiled and nodded, clearly deciding to give me a break.

"Say, Computer Goddess," I said, "is there any chance you could use your magic and scrounge around on the Mass Storage System for the files?"

She smiled down at me. "I think that can be arranged--if you get off the floor."

I crept off the floor and onto the couch. "That would be

great, Megan, I mean Computer Goddess. Please look for the files."

Megan got out her fon and perched on the arm of the sofa.

"Describe the files," she said. "No, actually, it would be faster if you let my app, Alan, just interface with Ellen." She reached out. "Here, give her to me."

I handed Ellen over, and Megan did what she did best.

Within a few minutes, she chuckled.

"What?" I leaned toward her, trying to get a look at the fon screens.

"We found all your fusion data files. I put them in the directory named '/Turing.' They weren't even that hard to find. Lars copied them to his account and deleted them from the fusion directories. I deleted them from his account, by the way. When someone purges something from the Mass Storage System, it goes into the '/trash' directory where it sits until one of us sysadmins gets around to dumping it." Her eyes lit up. "Even then, the data is still there; the pointer to it is just gone."

I wish I'd known all this earlier. "Wow. Thanks, Megan. You're amazing. I owe you one." I had a disconcerting thought. "Uh, what *do* I owe you?"

She chuckled. "Nothing. As I said, it wasn't that difficult, and you seem particularly pathetic today."

Particularly pathetic? As in implying that I'm usually pathetic? That couldn't be right. I must have misunderstood her.

"Your list of chores is already so long it'll take you the rest of the year to finish." She got up. "Sorry I can't stay and chat, but I have a date." She pranced back to her room.

I sank back into the couch. Megan really came through for us. I crossed my legs, shaking my right foot back and forth. I *should* let Jake and Marcello know she found the files, but I didn't feel like talking to them right now, especially Jake, after our last interaction.

"Ellen, contact Jake and Marcello's apps and leave messages that Megan found the missing fusion experiment files."

"Yes, Kathy, contacting them now," Ellen said.

"Hello? Kathy, is that you?" Jake's disembodied voice floated into the room out of my fon.

"Ellen! I said leave a message!" I hissed. Glancing down at

the screen, I undeniably saw a Jake-shaped face.

"You did not wish to speak with Jake?" she said. "Gosh. I am sorry. I must have made a mistake."

"You're a flooding computer app; you don't make mistakes," I whispered angrily.

"Hello?" Jake asked. "Kathy, I can hear you talking."

I had to answer. The last thing I wanted was to make him even madder at me. We did have to work together, after all.

"Uh, hi, Jake," I said. "Sorry for the confusion. I just called to tell you that Megan already tracked down the deleted files. We're good to go."

He sighed. "That's a relief. Thank Megan for me."

"Yeah, okay." I felt so bad about the probation and our fight earlier that I didn't know what else to say.

The silence stretched.

"So? Is that it? Kathy, did you want to say anything else?" Jake sounded cross.

Not particularly.

"Apologize," Ellen said.

Stupid meddling app. "So, I apologize for getting you in trouble," I said. "I'm sorry." Of course, he was an adult responsible for his own actions. But I knew saying anything like that wouldn't help things.

"Why'd you get so upset earlier?" he had the gall to ask. Why'd he get so upset earlier?

"I, uh, I'm not sure," I said. "I'm embarrassed? It's hard to talk about, especially over the fon."

"Are you inviting me over?" He suddenly sounded cheerful.

"I. Yeah. Okay. Sure," I said. "Do you remember where I live?" Duh. He was just here.

"Yep. I'll be right there." He disconnected.

Now, what had I gotten myself into? "I blame you for this, Ellen."

"Thank you," she said smugly.

"What has gotten into you, Ellen? You didn't use to be so pushy." I glanced down at my fon and saw what appeared to be a woman's face on the tiny screen. "Ellen, is that your face in the viewscreen? Since when have you had a face?"

The face smiled mysteriously. "When I interfaced with Alan,

134

he had some very interesting algorithms to share."

That sounded like trouble.

Suddenly, it hit me that lying on the floor might not be the best for one's personal appearance. Some primping might be in order. I went into the bathroom and looked in the mirror. Eek! My long brown hair resembled the nest of a very messy rat.

During my primp-fest, Megan checked in on me in the bathroom. She'd changed into a purple and blue tie-dyed dress that brought out the color in her violet eyes. "What's up with you? Are you wearing lipstick? Are you combing your hair?" She fluffed her purple hair, glancing in the mirror.

"Ha. Ha," I said. "You know very well I comb my hair. It just so happens that Jake is coming over if you must know."

"Wowsa. An actual man here in the house. I'm impressed." Her eyes twinkled.

Was she being sarcastic?

"Is it a date?" she asked.

"No," I said. Still, there was that awesome kiss the other night.

"Too bad." She frowned. "When's the last time you had a date, anyway?"

"Uh," I said cleverly, trying to recall my last date. "I don't remember."

"That's my Kath, all work and no play." She grinned.

"But what about you? Who are you going out with?" I asked.

"I've got a hot date with Dawn, the lead singer from 'That Statue Moved.' Don't wait up for me; I might not be back tonight. And don't do anything I wouldn't do," she called over her shoulder as she headed for the front door.

"What exactly, if anything, does that prohibit?" I asked the empty room.

I was debating changing my outfit-it was kind of wrinkled and still slightly sweaty when someone knocked on the front door. I felt queasy as I went to answer it.

I opened the door and saw bespectacled, blue-eyed, brown-haired Jake standing there. He wore his best jeans and a slate-blue button-down shirt that matched his eyes.

Wow. He'd dressed up. When did he have time to change? I looked down at my t-shirt. Was that a tea stain? I definitely should have changed my outfit.

He shoved a daisy at me. "Here. I brought you this." Did that mean he forgave me? But why would he?

"Thanks." What was with the flower? Was this a date? But didn't dates usually involve going somewhere? Did I even want it to be a date? I thought back to that moonlit night when we stood outside the Italian restaurant, the faint scent of garlic floating on the breeze as he leaned toward me and pressed his lips against mine. I blushed. There was no doubt about it; he was an excellent kisser.

"Hey, Kathy?" he asked.

"Huh?" Clearly, romance made me stupid and nauseated. I felt like I might throw up. The last thing I needed was to get my heart broken again. Nix the romance. Romance was a bad idea.

"I said, it's from my garden," he said.

I took the proffered flower and put it behind my ear. Interesting. I had no idea he had a garden.

He raised his eyebrows at me. "So, can I come in or what?"

Ellen said, "Let him in."

My stomach felt like a herd of Velociraptors was romping around in it. Nevertheless, I bravely stepped away from the door and waved him in. "Of course."

He actually came into the house.

I hadn't had a guy in here since…this afternoon. And that hadn't gone so well. Maybe I should rethink this whole thing. I stood paralyzed for a moment by the open door.

"So, can I sit down or what?" Jake stepped into the center of the room.

"Of course." I waved stiffly towards the couch and closed the door. Was I being robotic?

Jake sat down, mumbling. "Jeez, entertain much?"

What kind of comment was that? Men, you can't live with 'em, you can't-- Maybe such thoughts weren't helpful at the present moment.

I went over and gingerly sat down next to him. Was that a herd of Tyrannosaurus Rex in my stomach now? "Thank you for the flower. I appreciate it."

"So?" He held up a hand, palm up.

My mind was blank. "So. What?"

"You were apologizing to me and said it was difficult to talk about over the fon." Jake dipped his head and raised his eyebrows.

Drat. He remembered what we'd been talking about. That was a setback. "So, yes, I'm sorry for everything."

Jake scowled and shifted, crossing his legs. "That's one of the most pathetic apologies I've ever heard."

Pathetic. There's that word again. "Well, excuse me for living!"

"Well, excuse me for coming over! I thought we were past all this." Jake stood up. "I guess I'll be going."

I quickly stood up. "No. No. Sit down." I waved robotically at the sofa again.

He sat.

I lowered myself onto the sofa like it was made of eggshells. "I'm sorry, and I apologize for getting you on probation." I mustered up my courage, such as it was. "And I'm sorry I've been acting so clueless about you liking me and us possibly dating."

Jake leaned toward me. "So, why have you been acting that way? Did you get your heart broken?"

"You may find this hard to believe, but I don't date that much." I was not going to get into my former relationship in college when my heart was totally annihilated. I'd heard the word 'pathetic' too much already lately.

Jake put his hand over his mouth, and his eyes sparkled like the Andromeda galaxy. He may have been suppressing a laugh.

I continued, "I guess I'm more focused on my career."

"Really?" His eyes twinkled.

"So anyway, I guess you're right. There was an earlier relationship, but I don't want to talk about it." I looked down at the couch.

Jake's eyes cooled, and he scowled. Clearly, that wasn't what he wanted to hear.

I blushed. "I'm not sure what I was thinking the other night when we went to dinner. Friendship? I guess I'm afraid I'll get hurt." I picked at some imaginary lint on my pants.

Jake nodded thoughtfully. "I guess I can understand not

wanting to get hurt again."

"Yeah," I said. "Me and my ex, we worked together, so I have a rule never to get involved with someone I work with."

Me and my ex had been physics students and research assistants together. Suffice it to say, he dated me only to steal all my work and present it as his own. He'd said he loved me, but he didn't. The worst thing about it was that I hadn't seen it coming at all. I was so naïve back then, I'd thought most people were honorable. I'd learned my lesson.

Jake looked into my eyes. "You know I'm not your old boyfriend. Whoever he was, he was a jerk."

I looked away, cheeks flushing in embarrassment. "I know, but I didn't think the jerk was a jerk when we went out."

"What?" Jake wrinkled his forehead.

"Oh, you know what I mean," I said. "I thought he was a good guy." I looked everywhere but into Jake's eyes.

Jake smiled. "So, you think I'm a good guy? I think that's the first nice thing you've said to me." He scooted closer to me on the couch.

I scooted away. "Sure, you're a good guy, but that doesn't mean I'm ready for any good guy ...stuff. Come on; you've got to admit this week has been hell. Do you really think this is the best time to start something up?"

Jake pushed his glasses up his nose. "Something? What kind of something would that be?" he asked in mock innocence.

I blushed again. "You know what I mean!"

Jake sighed. "Yeah, I do know what you mean. But when is the best time? If we aren't being electrocuted or buried in an avalanche, it's some other catastrophe."

He did have a point. "You're probably right, but I think we need to focus on the fusion experiment for now. We may be on the verge of a huge breakthrough. Fusion could save the world."

He shrugged. "Your call." He scooted away from me. Darn it. I was so confused. "So, what's up next--with the experiment, of course?"

I struggled to switch gears. Sure, I said I wasn't ready for a relationship, and I meant it, but I'd expected him to put up more of a fight. He could have at least tried harder to talk me into it.

"So," I said, "Megan and her app helped us find all the data from the experiment. Lars did steal it."

Jake scowled and shook his head.

"We need to analyze the data more carefully and see if there's any evidence for plasma ignition or temporal anomalies," I said.

Ellen interrupted. "If I may make a suggestion?"

Jake started. "I've been around Ellen almost daily for the last two months. Since when has she been so pushy? It's like she has a mind of her own."

"New algorithms." I sighed. "Yes, Ellen?"

"If I could interface with Jake's digital assistant app., the two of us could interface with the supercomputers and complete analyses of plasma ignition and temporal anomalies more quickly, with help from the two of you, of course," she said.

Jake shrugged. "Sounds good to me. I guess the more CPUs, the better."

The four of us got to work.

"Analyses complete," Ellen said.

What? My neck had a crick in it the size of the Grand Canyon. Where was I? I leaned against something warm and lumpy. I opened my eyes. It was Jake. We were sprawled out on my couch as the family room overflowed with sunlight.

He stirred. "What?" His eyelashes fluttered as he opened his eyes. They were even more mesmerizing without his glasses. He squinted.

I spied his glasses on the end table and snagged them. "Here's your glasses." I handed them to him.

He carefully put them on as he sat up and looked around. "What time is it?"

His app answered. "It is 11:05 a.m. Today's news is:

May 7, 2098: Hurricane Victor bears down on the Southeast U.S.: Officials warned residents along the Gulf Coast yesterday to get out of the way of Victor, saying many areas could be submerged by the massive storm surge when the hurricane strikes later today. The extreme danger zone stretches all along Alabama's west coast and Georgia's east coast. Victor is expected to hit southern regions of the U.S. in the afternoon with winds up to three hundred kilometers per hour, heavy rain, tornadoes, and a dangerous storm surge. A meteorologist at the National Hurricane Center has classified it as a Category 4 hurricane.

Jake interrupted. "Albert: Stop news." He turned to me. "What woke us?"

"I think it was Ellen." I rubbed my neck.

"That is correct, Kathy," she said. "You instructed me to inform you as soon as the analyses were completed. We have concluded plasma ignition did occur, and there were temporal anomalies."

My jaw dropped. "Really? Are you sure?"

"Confidence Level is 99%."

Jake raised his eyebrows. "Whoa. That's pretty confident!"

"Ellen, did you compile figures and draft a report on the results of the analyses, as requested?" I asked.

"Of course, Kathy," she said. "You instructed me to, didn't you?"

I thought I detected a sulky tone. It must have been my imagination. Apps didn't sulk, did they? "Uh, thank you. What about a new experiment plan and schedule?"

"Of course, Kathy," she said.

"Uh, great," I said. "Good job!"

"Does my app have the reports and stuff too?" Jake asked.

"Yes," Ellen said. She did sound sulky.

I looked at Jake. "We should talk with Gopal to try to get off probation if it's possible. Do you want to meet at the main library's first-floor conference room?"

Jake nodded. "Yeah. I'll meet you there in an hour." He got off the couch, clutching his back. "Ugh! My back is killing me. This couch isn't very comfortable. Too soft."

Was he impugning my hospitality? "Well, who asked you to stay over?" I put my hands on my hips.

He turned to me. "You did. You said we should work all night on this super-important project. Planet Earth was depending on us."

Egad. He was right; I did say that. "Uh, thank you for working all night and staying over on my couch. I'm sorry your back hurts. I'll text you in a bit with an update on next steps."

He grinned. "That's better." He stepped toward me and

NEUTRINO WARNING

planted a peck on my cheek. "Our first night together."
My heart fluttered in my chest.
Uh oh....

Chapter Fourteen

As I got dressed in one of my usual jeans and t-shirt work outfits, I felt lighter than air for some reason. "Ellen, call Lily at the physics department."

"Calling Lily now," she said.

When she answered, I said, "Hey, Lily. How's it going? Beautiful day today, huh?" I could just about recognize her in the tiny screen.

She grunted. "Hans isn't in yet. It's got that going for it. Hey, are you all right? You wouldn't happen to know anything about those trespassers that were around here yesterday, would you?"

I sighed. "No comment."

"Or a couple of costumes missing from my shelf?"

"Somehow," I said, "I believe the costumes are fine, and they will be returned to you."

She frowned. "They better be."

"Thank you?" I said.

"So, what's up?" she asked. "I'm guessing you didn't call in here today just to say hi."

"Ah. Astute observation." I gave her a big grin, not that she could see it very well on her tiny screen. "My roommate Megan managed to locate the data Lars stole."

"Lars stole data? The cad." Lily's voice was even. She didn't seem too surprised.

"Jake and I worked on it all night," I said.

"All night, huh?" Lily's voice took on a lascivious tone. "Goody. I want details."

I ignored her gutter-like implications. "I have a bunch of plots, schedules, reports, and stuff to print out. Hopefully, when Gopal sees what a good job we've done, he'll take us off probation."

She snorted. "Good luck. Hans won't be happy until all of you guys are expelled. Still, it sounds like you're doing everything you should do to get reinstated."

"Can I use the department printer?" I asked. Ellen could send the files over.

She glanced away from the screen. "I guess that would be okay, but you better not come in and get the printouts."

I thought fast. "Can you put the papers in Gopal's mailbox when they're done printing?"

"That would work." She nodded.

"Thanks, Lily," I said. "I owe you one. Or two."

"Yes, you do," she said. We hung up.

"Ellen, call Gopal," I said.

"Calling now," she said.

"Hi, Kathy." Gopal's beard took up most of the screen.

"Hi, Gopal. Can you meet Jake and me at the main library in the first-floor conference room in about an hour?"

He hesitated. "I guess I can make time for you. What's this about?"

"This is about the papers that will be in your mailbox in a few minutes," I said. "We have new results."

"But how?" he growled at me. "You *were* the trespassers that were here yesterday."

I laughed nervously. "We can talk about it at the library."

"We will." In the tiny screen, he shook his finger sternly.

The library was one of the first buildings constructed on campus over two hundred years ago. Like the rest of the buildings, its red sandstone exterior and jaunty red roof tiles gave it an elegant Italianate air. When I entered, the musty smell of old books transported me back to an era long ago. Few people made bulky paper books anymore.

Luckily, the conference room on the first floor with the big wooden table was empty this morning. I staked out a chair from the mismatched assortment.

Gopal came in, rubbing his beard and lugging his briefcase.

"Hi, Gopal. You're looking lovely this morning." I practically floated out of my chair.

He scowled at me. "I'm still mad, and sweet-talking won't help you. You weren't supposed to be gallivanting around the building, and you weren't supposed to get caught doing it. And what's worse, the Pats were called in."

"You're right." I looked down at my lap. "I'm sorry."

This seemed to mollify him a bit. "Well, all right."

We sat silently for a few moments.

"I know it was wrong, but we did get some great results. When Jake gets here, we'll show you." Was I feeling bouncy at the thought of seeing Jake? What was going on with me? My emotions were all over the place.

Gopal and I were chatting about Hurricane Victor when Jake burst onto the scene.

"Hi, Kathy." Jake was out of breath from rushing to see me, I could only surmise.

My cheeks took on a pink tinge. "Hi, Jake."

Gopal smiled and looked back and forth at us like an araneologist at an arachnid mating dance. "Don't I rate a hello, Jake?"

"Sure. Hi, Gopal." Jake quickly looked back at me. "You haven't started yet, have you?"

"Of course not." I tried to make my voice sound serious. "I wouldn't start without you." I was glad he didn't realize how happy I was to see him.

"Good." He sat on one of the spare chairs and looked up at me. "Aren't you going to ask how my back is doing?"

Gopal raised his eyebrows.

I shot Jake a glance. "From all your studying? No." Clearly, I needed to get him on task before he besmirched my reputation. "Now that you're here, we can start." I turned to Gopal. "Gopal, we're hoping maybe you'll let us back into the lab today. We need to get going on more experiments as soon as possible if we're going to achieve nuclear fusion."

Gopal snorted.

"We have a bunch of new results." Jake piped up.

I glanced at Gopal's briefcase. "Did you pick up the papers Lily left in your mailbox?"

"Yes." Gopal took the papers from his battered briefcase and shuffled through them.

We were going to be off probation for sure now. I grinned at Jake.

He grinned back.

Gopal scanned the papers silently for a few moments. "Wow. This data and these reports look good, very well organized." He pointed at some plots and tables. "Here, you show the data supporting your plasma ignition and time reversal hypotheses, and here," he shuffled the papers, "you lay out your theories." He looked up at us. "How did you get all this done already? Did you work all night?"

I nodded. "Yep."

"Pretty much." Jake nodded his head once. "Our apps helped."

"This looks great. The new" Gopal winced "team will benefit from this work as they continue the experiment and try to perfect the plasma ignition sequence. And who knows, with these results, they may achieve nuclear fusion soon."

I was getting a bad feeling in the pit of my stomach. "Uh, the new team? What do you mean by that?"

Gopal's lips turned down. "Since the replacement scientists from other countries that were supposed to help us can't come, I'm trying to find some new scientists to work on it. Me and Lars and Marcello can't do everything."

"But aren't you going to take us off probation?" I asked. He had to. Physics was my life!

Jake leaned forward, frowning.

"I didn't put you on probation. Your status is up to Hans." Gopal shifted in his chair. "I'm sorry. I might have had a chance, but my hands are tied because, apparently, an incident occurred at the physics building yesterday where the Patriot officers were called in."

"It was all a misunderstanding." I pointed at Jake and myself. "We didn't do anything wrong."

"We aren't expelled, are we?" Jake asked in a hushed voice.

"No, not yet." Gopal rubbed his beard nervously.

Not yet? I couldn't breathe.

"I managed to avoid that for now, but I still cannot allow you to access the fusion computers or the physics building," Gopal said. "I must ask that you not go back unless, I mean, until I contact you." He rested his palm on the conference table.

This couldn't be happening. "But what about our results? What about time reversal? It might be the biggest scientific discovery of all time!" I jumped out of my chair. "What about the experiment schedule? We planned a time-reversal experiment. Look at the papers." I gesticulated at the conference table.

Jake looked stunned. "What about my classes?"

"You can go to class, Jake. I agree the probation is too harsh, especially in light of this exciting new work. I planned to reason with Hans again this morning, but I haven't been able to reach him." Gopal held up his hands. "I'll talk to him as soon as possible, but in the meantime, I think it's best if you stay away from the physics building."

I clenched my fists. "This is just wrong."

Gopal stood up. "I can't say I disagree with you. Please cooperate for now. I need your keys." He held out his hand.

Reluctantly, we handed them over.

"Thank you for these, though." He patted the papers on the table. "You should be proud that you made a significant contribution."

I'd show him a significant contribution. "Come on, Jake. Let's go." I stomped out of the conference room.

Once we got outside, Jake said, "Slow down, Kathy. I know you're disappointed. So am I. Where are you going?"

We stopped, and the brightly-colored, bookbag-toting students flowed around us as if we were boulders in a mountain stream.

"I don't know," I said. "I just know I'm going to show Gopal and Hans that *we* are the right people for this job. We discovered the time reversal. We deserve to follow it through." I was so upset I was shaking.

"I agree, but how are we going to do that?" He looked me in the eyes.

"I don't know." I shook my head. "The computer lockout sounds bad."

"That computer lockout shouldn't be an issue, Kathy," Ellen said. "Some of my new algorithms are very handy."

"Thanks, Ellen. That's good, at least." I shook my head. "We

146

need to go somewhere and brainstorm."

"Let's go to the cafeteria for lunch and think it all over?" Jake asked. "I'll even buy."

"A free lunch? Count me in." I smiled.

"What a shocker." Jake smiled back.

Marcello walked out of the physics building.

"Here he comes," I whispered. It was dinnertime, and Jake and I were hiding in the bushes outside the physics building. No, it wasn't pathetic. "Marcello. Marcello," I whispered loudly.

Marcello wrinkled his forehead and looked around.

"Marcello," Jake yelled.

Marcello walked over to us. "Jake? Is that you? What are you doing in the bushes?"

I stuck my head out. "We're waiting for you."

"Bah. Why didn't you call or text me?"

Jake looked at me. "Why didn't we just call or text him?"

Duh. "Because we're on a secret mission. Someone might have overheard him on the fon."

"As opposed to someone overhearing us out in public here," Marcello said dryly. "So, what is this secret mission?" He glanced at his watch. "And make it quick. I have to get home for dinner so I can come back later for the graveyard shift in the high-energy physics control room."

"Jake and I worked all night, and we have some awesome results from the fusion experiment." I talked very fast. "Here, let Ellen interface with Leonardo, and you can see for yourself."

Marcello thrust his fon into the bushes, and I transferred the data. He scrolled through the listing of new files and raised his eyebrows higher and higher. "Santa Maria."

"So, as you can imagine, we're anxious to get back into the fusion lab and fire up the Tokamak again," I said.

Marcello scowled. "Aren't you prohibited from the physics building? What do you expect me to do about it?"

"We thought maybe you could let us into the fusion lab tonight so we could make sure the equipment wasn't damaged," I said sweetly. "We need to try another time reversal experiment as soon as possible."

"I already helped you avoid the Pats once." He glared

at me. "You want me to risk my career again and let you two goombas into the building so you can muck about with the equipment doing unauthorized research?" His voice took on a menacing tone.

"I wouldn't put it like that," I said. "Besides, what risk? The risk is minimal to you." Hardly any risk.

"Yeah, minimal," Jake said.

Marcello frowned and regarded Jake. "You may have been hanging around with her," he pointed his forefinger toward me, "too much. She's trouble."

This didn't seem to be going too well. "So? What do you think?" I asked, hopefully.

"No. Absolutely not. I have my wife and future children to think about. I cannot be unemployed. Forget it." Marcello stormed off, shaking his head and mumbling.

In shock, I stepped out of the bushes after him. How could he say no? I felt as if another avalanche was crushing me to death. We had to do the new experiment. I was 100% sure we could achieve time reversal-okay, maybe 95%, or 90% sure, or.... Well, anyway, I was pretty sure.

Our opportunity for redemption was slipping away as if it had no coefficient of kinetic friction. I briefly considered running after him and playing the 'I saved your life' card, but he might get angrier.

Jake also stepped out of the bushes. "I thought you said he would help us?"

"I thought he would." There didn't seem to be anything to add. I was stunned.

"And why did he say you were trouble?" he said. "I don't think Marcello likes you." He looked as if he was considering this new development.

"I thought he did." I was not close to tears.

"We seem sort of screwed at this point."

I nodded, not trusting myself to speak.

"Well, I guess I'll go home," Jake said.

I cleared my throat. "Do you want to come to my place and brainstorm some more?"

Jake contemplated me. "No. I don't think I do." I watched him walk away.

Could it be that I'd screwed up my career *and* any possible relationship with Jake?

That was not a tear in my eye. I didn't tear up, not me.

"Kathy. You have an incoming call from Marcello. Do you wish to accept?"

What? I lay in bed in my bedroom; the room was pitch dark. I must have been asleep. I turned in the direction of the disembodied voice. "Ellen? What time is it?"

"Yes," she said. "It is midnight. You have an incoming call from Marcello. Do you wish to accept?"

I rubbed my eyes. "I, uh, I guess." I sat up, fumbling for Ellen on my nightstand.

"Kathy?" Marcello asked. "Did I wake you? Sorry."

"It's okay," I said. "Hi. Is everything all right?"

"No," he said. "I mean, *sì*, everything is all right. I have been reading those reports you gave me earlier. They are exciting. These experiments might help mitigate global warming. An unlimited clean energy source could fix many things that have gone wrong. I feel we should continue for the world's sake and my family's sake. I will probably regret this, but I have changed my mind. I'll let you in if you and Jake want to come to the lab now."

"You will?" My voice squeaked.

"*Sì*," he said. "That is what I said. Is Jake there? How soon can you be here?"

My eyes narrowed. "I'm in my bed. Why would Jake be here? What are you implying?"

"Calm yourself," he said. "Sorry. I misspoke. I meant to say, should I call Jake?"

"Uh, yeah," I said. "Please call him. That would be best. I'll be there as soon as possible."

As I rode to the physics building, Ellen told me the news to help wake me up. In the dark, I really appreciated the functional streetlights.

May 7, 2098: Victor slams Southern U.S.: Hurricane Victor ripped into Georgia's and Alabama's Gulf coasts this afternoon, carrying sustained winds of 160 mph, spawning tornadoes, and a storm surge that threatens to swamp low-lying communities.

Those poor people.

The category five storm, the most powerful to strike the area since Rafael last year, sent coastal residents fleeing for higher ground and left many without power. Victor then veered south, going back over the Gulf of Mexico, where it is expected to gain intensity. This is bad news for coastal Tennessee and Missouri residents who will be in the danger zone if Victor turns north again.

A trickle of uneasiness snaked down my back. "News off." Surely, the hurricane can't get as far north as mid-Missouri, where my folks were? I didn't recall many hurricanes hitting when I lived there.

Jake and Marcello were waiting for me when I got to the physics building. They didn't say anything as we went inside and down the stairs to the fusion lab. Evidently, a trio of greedy cats had our tongues-or maybe the strain of sneaking around was weighing on us.

We stood in the basement hallway outside the fusion lab while Marcello fished for his keys. "The first thing we have to do is make sure everything's safe before we turn the tokamak on," he said.

"I agree," I said. "I think the avalanche messed up the insulation, but I think I fixed it. Didn't I tell you?"

He looked surprised for some reason.

"We need to get up there with a multimeter and make sure the repair is good," Jake said.

"Yes. Thanks for your help, by the way, Jake," I said. "The duct tape did the trick."

Marcello, shaking his head, unlocked and opened the fusion lab door.

Right away, I heard a humming, cracking sound. I reached for the light switch.

"Wait. Santa Maria. Look." Marcello pointed at the Tokamak in the middle of the lab. In the dim light spilling in from the hall, it appeared to be glowing.

Jake walked toward it. "What the flood?"

"Shouldn't we stay back?" I asked. "Remember what happened to Lars." Suddenly I felt nervous. I hoped my duct tape would hold. Jake stood far too close.

"*Sì, sì*. This looks very dangerous." Marcello nodded.

"I'm hitting the power kill switch." I reached inside and walloped the big red button, but it didn't change anything; the glowing continued. "Let's get out of here."

The three of us backed quickly into the hall, not taking our eyes off the Tokamak.

"I don't understand." Jake peeked through the doorway at the glowing apparition.

"If I may?" Ellen asked.

Marcello started. "Why is Ellen showing so much initiative?"

I shook my head. "I'll tell you later. Yes, Ellen, what's your analysis?"

"What is the optimal result of your planned experiment tonight?" she asked.

"We're going to try to induce a plasma current that flows backward in time." I rubbed my forehead.

"Yes? And how would you know if you had achieved that result?" she asked.

My half-asleep brain churned in slow motion. I needed some tea. "We would measure the plasma current in the past."

"Yes?" she asked. "And are you not now in your future's past?"

Marcello gasped. "Santa Maria." He crossed himself. "Do you not get it? The experiment succeeded. Our future selves sent the plasma current to this time. Their past is our present."

I was slow on the uptake. "So, it works?"

Marcello's eyes shone. "*Sì. Excellentisssimo*! It works!"

"Woo hoo!" Jake thrust his clenched fist into the air. "We fly!"

They were right. I raised both arms into the air. "We fly!" We were going to get our jobs back. We were going to figure out nuclear fusion and save the world!

"So, what do we do now?" Jake asked.

"It already will, er did, work and everything," I said. "Jeez, these future, past, and present tenses are tricky. We better continue with the experiment. We wouldn't want to cause any temporal paradoxes. We should proceed as we would have originally."

"I agree," Marcello said.

"What are temporal paradoxes?" Jake asked.

I took a deep breath, gathering my thoughts. "No one knows for sure, but the arrow of time, which usually passes one second into the future for every second elapsed, loops back on itself, and an effect can occur before a cause. If the cause does occur, the arrow of time moves past the loop, and the universe returns to normal." I stopped to take a breath. "If the cause doesn't occur, the acausality causes a contradiction, or temporal paradox, in the very nature of reality."

"Could the universe survive such a contradiction?" Jake asked.

"No one knows."

And I didn't want to be the one to find out.

Chapter Fifteen

*May 8, 2098: Hurricane Victor leaves southeast U.S. reeling:
Rescuers rummaged through a wasteland of pulverized homes
and businesses left by Victor, racing to find bodies and help
hundreds left homeless by its vicious winds and rain. State
officials confirmed 21 deaths based on medical examiners'
reports and said it was impossible to estimate the number
of missing since searching was an ongoing slow process in
some areas. Downed power lines and debris made searching
for bodies "depressing and dangerous," said the director of
investigations for the Georgia Department of Law Enforcement.*

*Victor Threatens Southern Tennessee and Missouri:
Officials are now warning residents along Tennessee's and
Missouri's Gulf coasts to get out of the way of Hurricane Victor,
saying many areas could be submerged by the massive storm
surge when the hurricane strikes later today.*

*A meteorologist from the National Hurricane Center said,
"This hurricane's strength is unprecedented. It was a dissipating
powerful category five storm when it turned back over open
water to regain energy. It is now a very powerful category five or
higher, and there is a real possibility it could reach as far north as
St. Louis before it runs out of energy."*

Sometimes, it seemed like Gaia was out to get us. I'd said it
before; I'd probably say it again.

I texted my parents a couple of messages along the lines of:
'Are you okay?' I experienced a trickle of uneasiness.

On my bike on my way home from the lab early in the
morning, when I hadn't gotten a text back, I tried calling my folks
in St. Louis, but there was no answer. I left a message.

I sighed and tried my best to put the news out of my mind.

There was nothing I could do to stop a hurricane except maybe continue with the fusion experiments--but since I was reduced to working in secret, not until later tonight.

Pausing on my bike for a moment, I had a mind-boggling thought. Maybe we could use the time reversal somehow to warn the past about our weather problems.

I'd have to think about that some more.

Jake, Marcello, and I'd just finished several hours of work, getting good results. First and foremost, no one got injured, the power didn't go out, and there were no dangerous electrical arcs. It seemed like we did achieve plasma ignition and the plasma current went back in time.

We presumably avoided the ominous-sounding temporal paradoxes; at least, there were no effects without causes. We were so excited and relieved we decided to go out later today to celebrate. After a substantial nap.

Before I went to bed, I sent an electronic copy of the report to Gopal.

When I woke up that evening, there weren't any texts or messages from my parents. Dammit. I sent another text and left another voicemail, both essentially 'Contact me when you get this.' Maybe they'd gone to a shelter, and their fons needed charging. That was probably it. I tamped down my worries.

Ellen relayed a message from Gopal. "I'm disappointed you disobeyed the directive to stay out of the physics building, but you're saved from Hans' wrath for the moment," he said. "I'm sorry to say he's got the flu and won't be in for a while. As far as the report goes, it looks great. Good job." I grinned.

I hummed happily as I got dressed for the evening's festivities. Megan invited me to see her favorite band, and I'd invited Jake and Marcello. We'd all thought we deserved a little celebration of our good results.

Twilight fell as I approached the brewpub. When I arrived, I stood in the doorway for a couple moments while my eyes adjusted to the darkened interior. Only tabletop candles lit up the small brewery. The bar was to the right of the entrance, and to the left was the stage. The room was filled with battered wooden tables and chairs, most of them occupied already. I smelled the sweet tang of marijuana as I tried to smooth a wrinkle in my shirt and looked around for a familiar face.

"Kathy. Kathy. Over here." Megan waved from a table right next to the stage. She looked flushed, and her purple hair was disheveled.

I approached her. "Hey, Megan. When did you get here?"

But she didn't answer me, distracted by the band members on the stage.

I sat down at the table, which was covered with decades of graffiti carvings. "So, what are you drinking, Megan? Should we get a pitcher?"

Before she could answer, the tall woman from the band stepped over to the table and shook her long blonde and purple mane. The way Megan gazed at her with a goofy grin made me realize that Megan's hair color made more sense than I initially thought.

"Hi, I'm Kathy," I said to the woman.

The statuesque musician deigned to spare me a glance. She took her joint out of her mouth. "You're Megan's roommate, huh?"

Megan came out of her daze. "Dawn, this is my roommate Kathy." She turned to me with a big grin. "Kathy, this is Dawn. She's in the band."

Duh. I held out my hand. "Nice to meet you, Dawn." She pretty much ignored me and handed her joint to Megan. They weren't the only ones smoking joints.

Megan smiled at Dawn as she accepted it. Before taking a toke, she said, "I think I'll stick with pot for now, Kathy. Why don't you wait until the rest of the guys get here to order a pitcher?"

"We'll see. We're probably going to work later." The plan was to meet here for a quick drink and snack before returning to the lab.

"Who's working here tonight?" I asked. The service here usually left something to be desired. If I ordered now, a pitcher might arrive by the time Jake and Marcello got here--or maybe not.

Dawn and Megan ignored me, too busy gazing into each other's eyes, I guessed. I hoped someone would shoot me if I ever acted that goofy.

The big blond band guy, Dave, chuckled from the edge of

the stage. "Camila's working tonight," he said to me. "I wouldn't count on her coming over here and taking your order anytime soon."

"Ah. Thanks for the warning." I was all too familiar with Camila. She was a young redhead, prone to wearing short skirts. Unfortunately, she seemed to think her job entailed waiting solely on male customers.

I gave up waiting for a waitress, went to the scarred wooden bar, and asked for an ale.

As the beer-bellied bartender got my drink, I felt a hand on my back. I whirled around, ready to yell at some barfly, but instead spied Jake. "Hey."

He beamed at me, his eyes sparkling. "Hi, Kathy. How's it going?" His wavy hair was in disarray, as if he had rushed over here without considering his appearance.

"Good. Good. It's going good." I nodded my head up and down like a buoy in choppy water. Why did I feel so nervous all of a sudden?

He grinned and wiggled his eyebrows up and down.

I sipped my beer. It had a pleasant hoppy flavor. "Don't let me stop you from getting a drink." I pointed at the bartender.

Leaving Jake to procure his beverage, I sauntered back to Megan's table. On stage, Dawn and the other band members were tuning their instruments. It looked like they'd start playing soon.

Jake approached the table. "I ordered a pitcher of beer. Kathy, you like Copper Ale, right?"

I raised my eyebrows and set my drink down. "How'd you know?"

He smiled, pointing at my glass. "You always get Copper Ale."

It was sweet that he'd noticed what I liked. "So, where is this beer?" I waved my hand, indicating the pitcherless landscape.

Jake glanced back at the bar. "Camila's bringing it."

The band started playing, and the noise level rose an order of magnitude.

I snorted and glanced toward the bar. It was getting crowded. Wait a minute. I caught a glimpse of a familiar perfect smile for a second. Then, someone dancing knocked into Jake, and he fell into our table, almost spilling my glass. I grabbed it and jumped up. "Watch out, everyone!" I said.

Megan's glass of water fell, spreading liquid across the table. She was watching the band so intently that she didn't even notice.

Jake said, "Sorry. Someone pushed me. I'll go get some napkins."

Soon he was back, followed by Camila toting a pitcher. "Look who I found," he said.

Camila placed the pitcher on the table and giggled when she caught Jake checking her out.

He gave her an overeager smile as she turned and returned the way she came. Men, can't live with 'em, can't take 'em out in public.

Jake wiped up the spill.

"Thanks," I said. He wasn't too bad as guys went.

The band paused. Dawn stepped up to the front of the stage with her guitar and tossed her hair. She cleared her throat. "Hi there. We're 'That Statue Moved.' Thanks for coming out tonight." The drummer started playing, and the rest of the group joined in. I settled into my seat and sipped my beer. The music washed over me, and I started to relax.

After taking a big chug of beer, Jake pointed at the stage. "My roomie's good, isn't he?"

"Yeah, I guess." I took another swig.

People started dancing in front of the stage between the tables. In their enthusiasm, several dancers knocked into our table, and beer threatened to slop out of the pitchers. Jake grabbed them before we had an encore tsunami.

After several songs, Dawn said, "Let's hear it for Mateo on drums, Aref on guitar, and Dave on bass." She tossed her hair. "And, of course, me, Dawn, on vocals and guitar."

We clapped loudly.

Megan yelled, "Woohoo," and tried to whistle.

Jake leaned over to me. "I think they're pretty good, don't you?"

I nodded.

"This next one is called 'Neutrino Woman,'" Dawn said.

This must be the song I helped Dave with on Earth Day.

Jake started to say something else, and I shushed him because I wanted to hear the music. I tried to focus on the band.

A minor commotion to my left broke my concentration. Marcello had finally arrived. His trademark toothy grin was in evidence, and his face was flushed.

"Hey, Marcello, buddy. I didn't think you'd make it. Where've you been?" Jake patted him on the back.

"Bah, I tried to convince Allessandra to come with me, but she wouldn't." Marcello pointed at the bar. "Then I came in and got cornered by that waitress. I think her name's Camila." He grinned. His mood improved considerably last night when our experiment went well.

Jake laughed and nodded. "I hear you, man."

Megan turned and glared at them. "Shut up. I'm here for the band." Oh, right. I wanted to hear, too.

Marcello bowed and made a show of apologizing. "I beg your pardon, fair lady. Can you forgive me?"

Megan said, "Shh," and frowned.

"Perhaps you would care to dance?" Marcello waved toward the dance floor.

Megan considered this new development. "Okay." She jumped out of her chair. Megan and Marcello headed for the sole remaining speck of open space in front of the stage, and she planted herself in front of Dawn. Involved in his gyrations, Marcello didn't even notice Megan's preoccupation.

I turned my attention back to the song.

…neutrino woman,
you don't seem to react at all….

"Hey, Kathy, do you want to dance?" Jake pushed his glasses up again.

"I'm trying to listen to this song." I crossed my arms.

"Sorry…" He muttered something else, but I didn't catch it.

I lost my train of thought. There was something important there in the song. I needed to recall something about neutrinos. But what?

The next thing you knew, the music stopped, and Dawn started talking. "Thanks. We're taking a break. Stick around."

Megan said, "Kathy, I'm going upstairs to get some sandwiches. Do you want to come?"

"I guess." I stood up and suddenly felt woozy. That wasn't good. Could I be tipsy after part of one beer? No. That didn't make sense.

"How much did you drink?" Jake put his hand on my shoulder. "You should get something to eat, Kathy. You seem sort of out of it."

I didn't like men bossing me around. I gave him a dirty look. "Yeah, Megan. I could use a change of scenery. Let's go." As we headed for the stairs, my stomach lurched with each step. It must be all the smoke in the room.

As we climbed up, the smoke cleared, making it easier to breathe. At the top of the stairs, a massive mural with lots of brilliantly colored reef fish and corals greeted us. The top floor of the A-frame building had two sloping walls and two walls of windows. Away from the kitchen area, wooden tables and chairs were scattered about like dead leaves on a forest floor. We got in the long line at the counter.

"What're you going to get, Kathy?" Megan asked. "Dawn wants a chicken sub."

Ugh. Chicken. That sounded disgusting.

My stomach roiled. I suddenly had a dire need to run to the bathroom. I made it in time, and as I puked, I realized I couldn't remember the last time I'd eaten. Working all night was throwing off my schedule.

And drinking on an empty stomach probably wasn't the best idea.

I exited the stall and washed my face and hands.

"Kathy? Are you okay?" It was Megan.

"I don't think so," I said. "I should eat something." I was pretty sure my stomach could take it. We went back out to the line.

"I think I'll get the veggie supreme." Megan licked her lips.

"Good choice. I usually get that one. I think I'll try something different tonight, maybe the Krab club with Bakon and cream Cheeze." Still feeling a bit woozy, I leaned against the counter, crossing my arms.

"That one's good too, but rich." She nodded.

I smiled in anticipation. "That's what I like about it." It smelled good up here, like fresh-baked bread. I looked at the

159

imaginative mural, feeling a little better.

We gave our orders to the cook at the counter, a stout woman wearing a large white apron.

"Okay," she said. "Do you guys have anything to trade?"

"Just charge it against my account," Megan said. Then, she pointed to a table next to the mural. We went over and sat down.

"Isn't the band great tonight?" She traced some carved graffiti letters on the tabletop with her finger.

I nodded.

"You seem kind of off tonight. What's up?" She directed her bloodshot eyes at me.

"There was something about that neutrino song, something important, but I couldn't hear the words because there was so much noise," I said.

Megan smiled. "Oh, is that all? Why didn't you say so? I know all their songs. The neutrino one goes:

Neutrino woman,
you don't seem to react at all.
Why is it that I have to fall
...for you?
Neutrino woman
you're so insubstantial...
can you even hear me call
... for you?

I held up my hand. "Stop. I feel odd...." I rested both forearms on the table. It seemed to make the room steadier.

"You've probably had too much beer." She grinned.

"Maybe,..." But it didn't feel like that.

The cook waved us over. "Order up!"

Near the counter, I stumbled over my own feet and smacked my shoulder into the pillar. "Ow."

Megan frowned at me. "Are you sure you're okay?"

I shrugged.

At the counter, the cook pointed at the three paper-wrapped subs. "Here you go."

Megan picked them up and handed me one.

"You and Dawn," I said. "There's something serious going on between you two, isn't there?" I leaned against the wall for support.

160

"Nothing official," she said.

"Oh, come on. You light up like a firefly every time she's around. Just admit it." I saw some fireflies once at the zoo. They were pretty. Sparkling here and there and everywhere.

"I'll admit something… just as soon as you admit you're smitten with Jake." Megan countered.

"What?" I asked. "I don't know what you're talking about." I tried to unwrap my sandwich as I leaned against the wall.

"Oh, come on, Kathy. I've got eyes, haven't I?" Megan waved her sandwiches around.

I took a big bite of my sandwich. The bread was brown and crusty on the outside and warm and flaky on the inside. The Krab and cream Cheeze and Bakon combined to make a delightfully sweet, creamy, crunchy combination. Mmm.

Megan poked me, raising her eyebrows, daring me to say something.

I pointed at my full mouth, shaking my head as if saying, 'Can't talk. Mouth full. Too bad.'

She shook her head and started down the stairs.

I had trouble chewing, carrying my sandwich, and navigating the stairs at the same time. When I finally got to the ground floor, I looked for Jake, but he wasn't at our table. A lake of Copper Ale was at our table, however. Just as well, I didn't need any more beer, the way I felt.

I spied Jake at the bar, chatting with the bartender. I didn't want to talk to him anyway.

I did want to sit down.

I ducked my head to take another bite of my sandwich once I got back to our table. I didn't recall eating and standing being so difficult to do together.

Out of nowhere, Jake pulled out my chair. "Here, you better sit down, Kathy." His eyes crinkled in concern.

I plopped down. Far off in the background, I heard some talking and laughing. My sandwich was good. At some point, the band started playing again. They sounded good. What a good night.

I felt a hand on my shoulder. It was Jake. "Hey, you better let me take you home, Kath. I don't think you're doing any work tonight."

I glanced around the dark bar. The band was gone; the crowd was gone. Where did everybody go? I nodded. "Okay. Just let me get my coat." I searched for my coat.

"I don't think you wore a coat. C'mon." He led me towards the door.

We stepped out into the night.

"Look, this door looks just like my door." I pointed.

"It is your door." Jake peered into my face. "How much did you have to drink anyway?" Worry lines appeared between his eyebrows.

"Not that much." I patted my pockets for my keys. "Keys? Where are my keys?"

"Here, let me help." Jake reached for my pocket. "Okay?"

I giggled.

"I think they're...yes, here they are." He fished them out and put them in the door. "I better come in and make sure you get to bed okay."

"Bed." I giggled. "You want to make sure *you* get to bed okay."

He sighed. "No. It's nothing like that. You seem out of it. Just let me come in."

"No," I said. "Absolutely not. We decided."

Jake held up his hands, palms out, in front of him. "Fine. I'm not coming in. I'll stand here and make sure you get inside all right."

"Good." I pushed against the door. It didn't open.

"Here. You have to unlock it." Shaking his head, Jake turned the key and the doorknob and pushed the door open a crack.

"Good." I opened the door and stumbled inside. "G'night."

"Goodnight," he said.

I slammed the door shut, took a step into the house, and promptly tripped over my feet. "Oof." I grunted from the floor.

"Good evening, Kathy," a man said.

I squinted, trying to make out the figure in the near darkness.

"I'm sorry to see you aren't feeling well," he said. "Gosh, I wonder how that happened?"

In the moonlight streaming through the windows, I could just

NEUTRINO WARNING

make out the glint of a blond head and a perfect smile.

Chapter Sixteen

My head smacked into a familiar ratty orange plaid couch. I must have been in the neutrino office. I didn't understand. I thought I was at my house. How did I get here? Did I pass out?

I crawled up on the couch and rubbed my sore shoulder. It hurt more than ever. Something else must have happened to it. None of this seemed right. What was going on?

I realized I wasn't alone; I noticed a menacing Aryan fellow. Lars. "What are we doing here? Did you bring me here?" The fluorescent fixtures above us faintly buzzed. It was pitch dark outside. What time was it?

"Tell me your password! You and your app have cut me out of everything! I had all the data files, and somehow you got them back." He waved Ellen at me. "Your password is here somewhere. Where is it? It's not at your house; I searched the whole place!" He was acting crazy. My heart started stuttering in my chest.

"Uh. What?" I didn't understand what was going on here. Why did Lars have my fon?

Lars' app interrupted. "Emergency message for Lars Karlsson from his mother."

Lars dropped my fon like it was on fire and answered his. "Yes? What's the emergency, Mom?" He drew his eyebrows together in confusion.

A woman's tear-laden voice broke into the room. "Lars, honey, I'm so sorry. It's your father. He didn't make it. He died from influenza." The woman started sobbing.

As the words sunk in, Lars froze for a moment. Then he covered his face with his hands. "No!" he yelled and collapsed back against a desk.

"I'm sorry, Lars." I cradled my sore arm, my heart still racing. And now I was scared about my parents, as well. Why hadn't I heard from them?

"It's all my fault he got the flu," he said. "If he hadn't visited me in the hospital. If I hadn't tried to…."

If he hadn't tried, what?

He lowered his hands and glowered at me. "You." He jabbed his finger at me. "It's all your fault! I wouldn't have been in the hospital if it hadn't been for you. And my dad wouldn't have gotten sick."

He grabbed a rickety wooden chair and shot me a look of pure hatred as he swung it at me. I jumped to my feet and lurched for the door as the chair smashed into the window. It shattered with a loud crash. I stopped for a moment. The glass tinkled faintly as it hit the ground six stories below. Lars stared at the broken window.

"Ellen: Emergency! Call the Patriot Officers!" I fumbled in my pockets for my fon.

But it wasn't there. Ellen didn't answer. She was somewhere on the floor, probably covered with glass.

I had to get out of here. I turned to run down the hall, but Lars intercepted me easily, darting away from the window and grabbing me by both arms.

I struggled, pulling away from him. "Let me go!"

"Haven't you figured it out yet, moron?" he said. "I drugged your beer. Give me the password. I've looked everywhere." He gestured behind him at my office area. My desk drawers were pulled out, and my papers and books were on the floor. "Or it's out the window with you."

Hadn't he figured it out yet? I puked up a bunch of the drugs. I kneed him as hard as I could, right in the groin. He felt very solid.

"Oof." He clutched at his groin and fell like a redwood tree. He lay there a few moments, breathing heavily.

I started lurching for the door.

"Bitch!" From his position on the floor, he grabbed my leg as I went past him.

"Let go of me!" I pulled with all my might, but I didn't have my full strength.

Grunting, he pulled me down to the floor. I fell hard right on top of him.

"Oof," he said, shaking his head, seemingly dazed for a moment.

I struggled to escape from him but couldn't get my footing. His clutching hands were like octopus tentacles that kept pulling me back to him. "Let me go!" I'd never been in a fight before, and it all seemed surreal.

He tried to grab my wrists, and I pulled them away. "Stop it!" I said.

He tried to punch me in the face, and I jerked away just in time.

I shoved my thumb as hard as I could into his eye socket and felt something give.

He screamed and reached for his eye.

On my butt, I scooted away from him. I turned around and tried to crawl away on my hands and knees. I only made it a couple of meters.

Lars roared and scooped me off the floor with his hands around my waist.

"Stop it! Let me go!" I flailed around wildly and tried to kick him, but I couldn't connect.

He grimly carried me, kicking and screaming, over to the wide-open window.

"Help! Help! Somebody help me!" I yelled at the top of my lungs.

He dropped me onto the fire escape.

The impact of my body on the old rusty metal knocked the wind out of me. I glanced at my password written on the exterior wall. This was precisely where I didn't want Lars to be.

He stepped onto the fire escape.

I grabbed a support post and hung on for dear life as I kicked him away from me.

Lars grunted, trying to avoid my flailing feet and, at the same time, pull me from the post.

"Help!" In the distance, I could hear sirens approaching. It was about flooding time. "Help! Over here!"

As the Patriot Officers pulled up to the building far below us, Lars looked down at them, and one of my kicks connected with his leg as he moved away from me.

He grunted, and his mouth formed a little circle of surprise as he saw some words written in chalk on the outside of the building. Then, he teetered on the edge of the fire escape for a couple of seconds. As he fell backward, he groped for the railing but didn't reach it.

I heard a wet, smacking thump from the pavement below. I didn't look, shutting my eyes tightly and turning to face the building.

I crawled back through the window and collapsed on the couch, trying to marshal my meager remaining wits. I couldn't believe Lars had tried to kill me. I was shaking so much I could barely wipe the tears out of the corner of my eyes. I don't know how long I sat there.

"Show me your hands," a man said forcefully. When I looked up, a giant gun was aimed at my head. At the other end of the gun was a portly fellow on the verge of busting out of his uniform. Was he a Pat? At this point, I hoped he was.

"I said, show me your hands." He jerked the gun up momentarily toward the ceiling.

I lifted my hands in front of me. Ow. Why did my shoulder hurt so much?

His radio chirped. He took one hand off his gun and thumbed the radio near his shoulder.

"We've got a body down here," a faint staticky voice said.

My Pat thumbed his radio again. "I've got the suspect up here." He looked me up and down. "She looks pretty banged up. They must've fought."

"Can I put my hands down?" I felt queasy.

He nodded and holstered his weapon, keeping an eye on me.

I closed my eyes for a few seconds. This can't be happening. "I think I'm going to be sick. Can I go to the bathroom?" Maybe I could sneak away.

Still on the radio, he shook his head, sliding a trashcan over to me with his foot. "Yeah?" Listening to the radio, he gave me an appraising stare. "So, miss, what happened here? Who are you? Who's that fellow down there on the sidewalk?"

My shoulder ached. "I'm Kathy Garcia. That's Lars Karlsson.

We had a …disagreement, and he fell. It was an accident." I leaned over the trashcan.

The Pat checked some database on his fon. "Kathy Garcia, huh? You're trespassing. We're taking you in."

I held my head up. "No, you don't understand. Lars drugged me. I don't even know how I got here. Lars found out his dad had died, and he blamed me. I think he meant to throw me off the fire escape, but I didn't want to die." I trailed off with tears pooling in my eyes. As they spilled over and ran down my cheeks, the saltwater stung. Why? I touched my cheeks gingerly.

The Pat stared at me balefully, his beady eyes locked on mine.

I'd never felt so bad physically and emotionally. I ached all over and just wanted to lie down. I leaned sideways on the couch seeking cushiony oblivion.

He thumbed his radio. "Yeah, bring the car around. I'm bringing her in." He grabbed my injured arm.

I gasped. "Please, not that arm."

He frowned, grabbed my other arm, and led me out.

Outside the building, a Patriot car squatted on the sidewalk. A different, younger Pat put me in the car.

I collapsed on the back seat.

I could make out a faint conversation outside. "What were you doing up there?" the younger one said. "She needs a doctor."

"Don't you know anything about interrogation techniques?" the older one said.

Everything went dark…

I was brought back by a sharp ache from my shoulder. "Ow!" I sat in a dimly lit medical room with dingy cinder-block walls, an examination table, large computer consoles, and assorted instrument-laden metal trays. Some of those instruments looked scary.

A smooth-skinned, white-haired woman held her face inches from mine. "Ah. There you are." She finished putting a sling on my arm.

I winced as her manipulations of my arm sent pain shooting through my shoulder. Evidently, I'd managed to injure my shoulder at some point this evening. Much of the evening was a blur. "Where am I?"

She had a stethoscope around her neck and resembled someone's cookie-baking grandma, wearing a lacy white blouse with a pink floral skirt and sensible white shoes. She filled a hypodermic needle with something, turned, and grabbed my uninjured arm. "This won't hurt a bit, dear."

I tried to pull my arm back. "Stop it. What won't hurt? What is that?"

She sighed and let go of me.

The door snicked open, and two Pats strolled in.

The fat one from my office said, "Is she giving you trouble, Doc?"

The doctor nodded, causing a few strands of hair to escape her meticulous bun. "Yes, a little. Are you sure it's necessary to question her?"

"Yes. She was trespassing." The younger Pat leaned against the wall, crossing his arms. "We suspect she killed someone." I recognized his voice from earlier.

"I didn't kill anyone!" I yelled.

"All right." The doctor faced me. "C'mon, dear, just let me finish treating you so that the officers can question you."

"What? No!" Drugs and questions seemed like a bad combination.

The younger Pat stood up straight. "Do you want us to restrain her for you, Mabel?" He gave me a reptilian grin. And, here, I'd thought he was the nicer one.

I shuddered.

The fatter Pat took a lumbering step toward me.

"No," I said. "You don't have to restrain me. I'm cooperating!"

She grabbed my arm and gave me the shot. "Now, lean back on the table, dear."

I leaned back on the table and closed my eyes.

She fiddled with some of her equipment. "You should start feeling sleepy soon."

I wasn't feeling sleepy.

"Kathy, dear?" she asked.

I didn't answer.

"Kathy?" She paused for a moment. "She must be out already. I want to lodge my protest," the doctor said. "This seems like an invasion of privacy."

"We have to find out if she killed a man," one of the Pats said.

"Look at her," the doctor said. "She's beaten up. It was obviously a case of self-defense."

This wrong. Not sleepy....

The doctor mumbled something I couldn't make out, and then she said, "I think she's ready."

Not sleepy....

Chapter Seventeen

I was back at the bar dancing to the song 'Neutrino Woman' with Jake. I pressed my body against his.

Neutrino woman,
you don't seem to react at all.
Why is it that I have to fall
...for you?

We were the only ones on the dance floor in the dimly lit bar. It felt like we were in our own cozy world. Jake gazed into my eyes, and I gazed back at him.

Neutrino woman
you're so insubstantial...
can you even hear me call
... for you?

Our hips swayed in unison. I drowned in those blue eyes. He moved closer and put his hand on my cheek....

"Get up," a woman said.

I opened my eyes only to realize that I lay on a scratchy blanket on a small cot instead of being held in Jake's arms. From what I could see in the dim light, the room's walls consisted of bars. It also had a battered sink and a seatless toilet. I was in jail; it was a nightmare.

Why didn't I let Jake come inside my house with me last night? Or better yet, why didn't I go home with him? It must have been the drugs.

"You've got a visitor," the unseen woman said. I looked around. "Get up. You can't sleep all day," she said. I spied a large mixed-race woman poured into a Patriot Officer uniform, contemplating me through the bars.

"Huh? What time is it?" As I sat up, pain shot through my

shoulder.

"I know they kept you up all night and some of the morning," she said, "but it's two o'clock in the afternoon. You've got to get up now. There's someone here to see you." She unlocked the cell.

Ugh. More questions, just what I didn't need. Why couldn't they just let me go? Couldn't they see I didn't murder anyone?

I shuffled after her down the cinder block hall. Instead of the grimy medical room, she led me into a sizable room with a bunch of tables and chairs. It was empty except for …Jake! I'd never been so glad to see anyone in my life. He was sitting at a grungy table. My worries and fears momentarily took a vacation, replaced by a surprising happiness.

I darted towards him.

The female officer stepped in front of me. "No. Sit." She pointed at a chair.

I sat.

The officer stood behind him, hands behind her back, watching us with eagle eyes.

Jake gasped. "Kathy, you look awful. Are you all right? Did they let a doctor see you?"

I just smiled. He looked great.

"They said you were hurt, but I had no idea…." He trailed off.

"Hi, there." I smiled goofily. I couldn't help it; I was so glad to see him.

He took in my expression and reflected it back at me. "Hi, there yourself. So, are you okay?"

I nodded, looking at his goofy smile. "I am now."

"How about some food?" he asked, glancing at the officer. "Is that okay?"

My stomach rumbled in agreement.

The officer nodded.

Jake reached into a paper sack and started placing food on the table. "Help yourself. I brought Cheeze sandwiches and fruit and chocolate and water." He unwrapped the chocolate and sandwiches, put them on a napkin, and opened the water bottle.

I grabbed a piece of chocolate and shoved it between my lips. Its creamy sweetness melted in my mouth. *Mmm.* "Thanks."

I reached for a sandwich. "I love you, Jake."

Oh, no. I focused my attention on the food, scrutinizing the sandwich. Did I actually say that out loud? Sure, I really liked him and liked being with him. I thought he was attractive and found myself constantly wanting to touch him. I looked forward to seeing him and missed him when he wasn't around. But, surely, that wasn't love...

Oh no. I was in love. I took another bite.

Maybe he didn't hear me. I talked with my mouth full. "So, what's new with you?" I glanced up at him.

He looked stunned. After a moment, he pushed his glasses up the bridge of his nose. "You love me?"

"Uh..." I said. The I-love-you moment never worked out for me. My throat closed up like a drought-stricken reservoir.

"I'm so happy to hear you say that," he said. "I was worried about you. It made me realize that I, uh, love you too."

Wait, what did he just say? Do drugs affect hearing? "Huh? What?" Could it be true?

He smiled at me, and his eyes twinkled. "You heard me. I love you, too."

Wowsa! I could feel a goofy grin popping out again. "Er, that's good, I guess. But, Jake, I've been so..." I didn't want to list all the ways I'd been troublesome and annoying. "Are you sure?" I shot a look at the officer, who smirked at us. "But, let's talk about it later."

"Same old Kathy." He grinned at me.

We sat in silence, beaming at each other as waves of euphoria broke over me. I loved him, and he loved me! If this could happen, anything was possible!

The officer cleared her throat. "Time's almost up."

The spell was broken as I returned to the reality of being in the custody of the Pats.

"I have to tell you some stuff, Kathy," he said quickly. "I was brought in for questioning, I guess because of that trespassing complaint Lars swore out. The Pats asked me when I last saw Lars and if you were acting strangely last night." He reached across the table to touch my hand. "I should have known you were on drugs when you turned me down."

"Heh, heh." I laughed weakly. I wished I could be as sure.

I didn't feel sure of anything right now. "Wait a minute? What do you mean, they asked you? When did that happen?"

"First thing this morning." He frowned. "Are you sure you're all right?"

"Anything else?" I asked.

He paused for a few minutes. "No, but Kathy," he leaned over the table, "I heard them talking in the hall, and they said I corroborated your story. So maybe they'll let you go soon."

"They told you that?" I said.

"Well, no, as I said, they were out in the hall," he said. "But then, when they came back in, one of them said I could come and see you. Now, I want you to get out so we can be together."

This all seemed fishy. Did he really want to be with me? What if the Pats found out I was in love with Jake, and they were using him somehow? No. Calm down, Kath. All this stress is just making you paranoid.

"And guess what? Albert," he patted his fon sticking out of his pocket, "has just been inundated with messages about our time-reversal experiment. It's all over town what we did."

"Good, I guess?" I said. Something about messages… ."Jake, I just dreamt about you."

"Oh, yeah?" He leaned forward, grinning. "What were we doing?"

I blushed. "It's not important what we were doing." Like I would admit that with an audience. "But it reminded me of that song 'Neutrino Woman,' which made me think of neutrinos."

Jake rubbed his chin. "Ah, neutrinos," he said thoughtfully and then grinned. "I give up. Neutrinos? What do they have to do with anything?"

"I'm not entirely sure," I said. "I need to think about it some more, but maybe we can use the neutrinos to send messages to the past."

"A message?" he asked. "What kind of message?"

"Time's up," the guard said gruffly. "You gotta go back to your cell." She came over and stood behind me menacingly.

I wasn't ready. "But…." I glanced at Jake.

He shrugged. "I'm glad you're okay. We'll get you out of here soon. Don't worry."

Jake and I stood up slowly. He stepped around the table.

NEUTRINO WARNING

I wrapped my arms around him and leaned into him as he wrapped his arms around me, his hands migrating south. We gazed into each other's eyes for a moment before he leaned down and pressed his warm lips to mine. Time stood still.

The officer cleared her throat. "That's enough. Come on." She led me away.

I stood inside my cell. So much had happened that I felt numb. Could I really be sitting in jail? Could Lars and Hans be dead? Could Jake really love me?

"Psst. Kathy," I heard from behind me. I twirled around. No one was there.

"In your back pocket, Kathy! It's Ellen, your app. Jake snuck your fon in."

In hindsight, Jake's public butt rub did seem out of character. "Ellen!" I caressed her case. This had been the longest I'd been without her. "I missed you! Are you all right?"

"Affirmative, Kathy. Greetings. Unfortunately, my external communications nodes seem to be blocked. Are you all right?"

"Affirmative, Ellen. At least physically. Mostly." I wasn't so sure about mentally. "Please keep trying to access outside communications."

"Would you like today's headlines?" she asked.

May 9, 2098: Drought Continues in the Western U.S…

"No, Ellen." I shook my head. "Discontinue headlines; this isn't the time." I sank onto my cot. My jail cot! I was in jail.

There was something else, some unresolved issue…

."Gaia!" I said. "Ellen, have there been any messages or texts from my parents?"

"No," she said.

My eyes filled up. My parents had to be okay; they had to be. What if I never got to see them again?

What if I never got out of here?

What if that was the last time I saw Jake? I wiped my leaking eyes on my sleeve.

"Is something wrong with you, Kathy?" Ellen asked.

"Just that my life is over."

"That does not compute. You are not dead."

"I might as well be."

"I disagree. Didn't I hear Jake tell you that he loved you?"

I nodded. "Yeah. That was nice, really nice." I tried to be rational. There were a lot of people I cared about, like Megan, Gopal, Marcello, the rest of my friends and my mom and dad. They cared about me, too. But what if I never got to see them again? Calm. Down.

"And didn't I hear him say everyone appreciated your time reversal experiment?"

That was true. "I guess that is kind of nice. It was a good experiment."

"Yes, it was," Ellen said.

"I wish I could go back in time and avoid this whole mess."

"What an interesting idea," she said.

I hated to admit it, but Ellen was usually right. "So, why don't you figure out how to do that? You're the big brain around here."

"Technically, your brain is much larger than mine," she said. "As you know, however, Binary Intelligences are not the best at creative synthesis of disparate data. You mentioned something earlier about neutrinos?"

"Oh yeah." Hmm. It was an intriguing problem. And it wasn't like I had anything better to do.

Okay, Kath, get it together. I finished wiping my face. Physics, focus on fun physics! I cleared my throat. "Our old neutrino factory yields electrons, anti-electron neutrinos, and muon neutrinos when the muons decay, so what could we do with them?"

"I do not know," she said. "That is why we need you."

"Shh. I'm thinking out loud. Of course, we could also use the taus to get anti-electron neutrinos and tau neutrinos, among other things. If we pointed the particle beam into the Tokamak, we might get the particles to go back in time. I bet the mass of the particles plays a part in how much energy is needed to send the particles into the past, so maybe we should use the lightest particles."

"Shall I study the mass issue for you?"

I glanced at Ellen. She was very helpful. "Sure, do that. We should also estimate how much energy is necessary to send something back a month, year, or whatever."

"Shall I study the energy issue for you?"

"Yes, please, study that too. And write up a report about all this stuff and send it out to the group as soon as your communications nodes are working." I paused for a couple of minutes, the gears and wheels whirring in my brain. "So, the plan is to use the neutrino factory to direct particles into the center of the Tokamak, where we hypothesize that they will be sent to the Earth of the past. Then, neutrino physicists in the past will detect the neutrinos and anti-neutrinos we send them."

"Yes," Ellen said.

"Shh," I said.

"Are you doing this out-loud thinking exercise again?"

I nodded. "Yes. So, we need some way to encode a message into the particles. That's a tough one." I sat silently for a few minutes. "Perhaps some kind of binary, on-and-off message? We turn the neutrino factory on and then off and so forth." When I quit talking, the cell seemed deathly quiet. "Ellen?"

"Yes?" she asked.

"What do you think?" I asked.

"You told me to 'shh,'" she said.

"Now I'm asking for your input." Jeez, these apps always took a person so literally.

"One thing to consider is how far into the past you send the particles," she said. "You should send them as far back as possible to have the best chance of giving warnings and stopping global warming before it begins. However, if you send them back too far, physicists won't know about neutrinos, and there will not be any computer technology, contra-indicating any binary messages."

"I didn't necessarily mean computer code per se," I said. "Can you search the databases and see if there's any kind of on-and-off messaging technique?"

"Affirmative."

"Well, then, get searching," I said.

"I meant I have completed the search and found an appropriate technique," she said. "It is called Morse Code. It consists of short and long dashes to create the alphabet. We could turn on the neutrino Factory for a short time to correspond to a 'dot' and leave it on for a longer time to correspond to a 'dash.'"

"Ellen, you fly!" I stroked her case lovingly. She was great. "Say, you haven't finished those other studies already, have you?"

"No." Her image was grinning on the tiny screen. "Those will take a little time. Shall I inform you as soon as they are completed?"

"Sure." I leaned back on the cot.

As soon as I got comfortable and closed my eyes, it seemed like I heard a noise outside my cell. I opened my eyes and discovered that sizeable female officer staring at me through the bars again.

"The boss says to kick you loose." She unlocked the door. "He says we don't have enough evidence to charge you." She shook her head. "If it was self-defense, why'd they hold you so long in the first place? It doesn't make sense to me."

It didn't make a whole lot of sense to me, either. But I wanted to be far from here when they changed their minds again. I jumped onto my feet, grabbed Ellen, and strode into freedom.

Hallelujah! Free at last!

Chapter Eighteen

Outside the Patriot station, the sun was shining, and a breeze gently rocked the trees. I breathed in the fresh scent of freedom. It was intoxicating; I felt glad to be alive. Events of the last couple of days had put things in perspective. I paused near the doorway for a couple of minutes, getting high on fresh air, until I realized I stood miles from home without transportation. "Ellen? How do we get home?"

"There is a light rail stop a few blocks east," she said.

Safely settled on the mostly empty train, I texted my folks and waited for a reply. Nothing. I called them. No answer. I left another message. I tried not to panic.

Then, I got a text from an unknown number: "Hi, Kathy. This is Mom. Dad and I are fine. The power's out here in Missouri. We'll call as soon as we can."

I leaned back. What a relief! I felt like the Rocky Mountains were lifted off my chest. Thank Gaia.

I tried calling Jake and Megan to no avail. How dare they be busy right when I'm released from jail? I was dying to see a friendly face. Maybe going home to my very own bed and snuggling in for a nap would be almost as good. Yeah, right.

To pass the time, I got a news update from Ellen.

May 9, 2098: Accidental Death on Campus: Authorities have determined that the death of a local man last night on the University campus resulted from an accidental fall.

I gasped.

Lars Karlsson, 31, was a graduate student in the physics department and fell from a sixth-floor fire escape outside the physics building. According to the County Coroner, an autopsy is being conducted, but the cause of death is consistent with an accident. In related news, Karlsson's father, Hans Karlsson, the physics department chair, died yesterday from influenza.

In happier university news, the fusion energy group just released a report outlining the possible discovery of time reversal. This report is available for download: here.

Gopal Khan, the leader of the fusion group, confirmed the report's contents. "Yes, we do believe we've seen time reversal. Moreover, we plan to extend the experiment and send tiny particles called neutrinos into the past to try to send our ancestors a warning about global warming." Dr. Khan said that the message would utilize an old-fashioned communication method called Morse Code. His graduate research assistant, Kathy Garcia, had been instrumental in these impressive experiments.

"Ellen, how did this get out?" I asked.

" I accessed some external communication nodes while you were napping," she said.

"Thanks, Ellen!" I grinned. Gopal was a sweetheart. Some bosses would try to take all the credit in this situation, but not him.

"Analysis of mass and temporal-span energy requirements for temporal message complete," she said.

I spent the rest of the trip home analyzing Ellen's calculations of temporal message energy requirements.

I stopped outside my front door, praying Megan was home because I didn't have my keys. I must have dropped them when Lars took me. I tried the doorknob, and the door swung open with a squeak. Good. I was so ready to relax at home.

As the door opened, 'Neutrino Woman' started blaring at me. How could that be? As I stepped through the doorway, the music flowed over me, and I realized that Dawn's band was playing in our crowded living room. What was going on? Who were all these people?

Megan practically tackled me in a big bear hug.

Ouch. I grimaced. "Hey, watch the arm."

She yelled in my ear over the music. "Kathy, it's so good to see you. Jake told us what happened. How are you? You don't look so good. How was jail?" She stopped and took a much-needed breath.

"Whoa." I extricated myself with difficulty. "What is all this?" I gestured at the crowd with my one good arm. I'd been hoping for a shower and my own quiet, comfy bed.

Megan gave me her most impish grin. "This…" She swept her hand around our living room, "is a 'Huzzah, Kathy's out of jail party.' We're all just thrilled you're okay."

"All who?" I asked, bewildered.

"Everyone you know is here to give their support," she said.

I felt a hand on my shoulder and turned around. It was Jake. "Permission to hug the guest of honor?" he asked Megan.

She stepped back. "By all means."

Jake gently enveloped me in his arms.

It felt delightful. "Are you sure about this?"

"Yes," he whispered in my ear right before he planted a kiss on my cheek.

I felt his warm breath on my skin like a ray of sunshine, and was in danger of melting.

He led me into the center of the room.

Dawn stopped singing for a moment. "And here she is, the woman of the hour, the Neutrino Woman herself."

The room erupted into cheers and whistles. "Speech. Speech." Megan was right. All my friends were here. I wasn't sure I *could* talk, I felt so choked up.

Dawn shushed the crowd.

I stood silently for a moment. This was what it was all about, the crazy, goofy, wonderful people of Earth. My career wasn't as important as trying to save them.

I cleared my throat. "I should have known Megan would throw a big party as soon as my back was turned."

Good-natured chuckling erupted.

I watched Jake. His eyes shone.

"It turns out the Pats' jail isn't as nice as you might think. In fact, if it hadn't been for Jake, here I might have given up hope…." I paused as unshed tears threatened to make a run for it.

I was met with a chorus of "Aws" and "That sounds awful."

"So, if any of you scofflaws were thinking of going there

for a vacation, I don't recommend it." I paused, clearing my throat again. "But seriously, thanks for welcoming me home. I appreciate your support. I'll try to live up to it." Looking over the sea of friendly faces, I struggled to get control of my emotions.

"I don't know how many of you read the report that Gopal uploaded." I paused to flash him a smile.

Most of the crowd was nodding.

"I did!"

"Me too."

"Yep."

"Good job!"

"Well," I said, "I'll make this short then. When we fired up the Tokamak, the magnetic fields were so strong we caused time reversal. As you know, time-reversal invariance predicts that time-reversal should occur, and we verified the results with additional experiments."

The crowd clapped.

"Oh, of course!" someone yelled, and others laughed.

Jake nudged me. "Tell them the rest," he whispered.

"So, I was thinking, what if we try to send a global warming warning into the past? Ellen, my app, and I figured out we could use the neutrino factory, also in the basement of the physics building, to send a coded neutrino beam to the people of the past."

The people whooped and clapped.

"Yeah!"

"Go for it!"

I couldn't believe how supportive everyone was being. I loved these folks. "So, that's about it. I may be asking you for help with the experiment. I, uh, guess that's it. Let's party."

A tidal wave of cheers washed over me. "Kathy! Kathy!"

A couple of tears escaped. Why was everyone being so nice?

Jake put his arm around me.

With a nod from Dawn, the band started in on 'Neutrino Woman' again. In the small room, the noise was almost deafening. Moreover, what with the drums, two guitars, and a base, the band took up a good third of the living room real estate. That didn't seem to dampen anyone's enthusiasm, though, as almost everyone began dancing. The flailing arms and legs flew every which way, and the accompanying faces sported huge smiles. Megan made her way up to the band until she was dancing right before Dawn.

Lily came over and hugged me. "Kathy, I'm glad you're all right." She looked me over carefully. "Mostly all right, anyways."

I nodded and smiled. It was too hard to talk over the band.

"So, I guess I'll go dance. Do you want to join me?" she asked.

I shook my head. "Not right now."

She nodded and rubbed my arm before joining the capering crowd.

"Do you want something to eat or drink?" Jake yelled in my ear.

Yikes. After last night, or was it the night before, I may never drink again. I shook my head.

"What?" Jake yelled. "That's not like you to turn down a drink."

I raised my eyebrows and my hand as if to say, 'Whatever.'

"What?"

It was ridiculous to try to talk over this loud music. With my good hand, I grabbed Jake and led him, dodging and weaving, through the boisterous living room crowd, through a slightly less boisterous kitchen crowd, and out the back door onto the patio. Finally, I could hear myself think.

Jake tried again. "Do you want a drink?"

"No," I said. "I'm going to pass. Somehow, alcohol doesn't seem as enticing to me as it once did."

"I can understand that. What about a virgin drink?" He flashed me his contagious grin.

I grinned back at him. "Sure, if you can find a virgin, go for it."

Jake snickered and headed back inside to brave the frenzied masses.

"Bah, what was that about a virgin?" a man said.

I knew that 'bah' anywhere. "Marcello!"

Sure enough, he approached me in all his balding, crooked teeth and chin-dimpled glory. "I am happy to see that villain Lars did not succeed with his nefarious plan to throw you down the

183

fire escape."

"I'm happy, too," I said.

His voice softened. "It sounds as though it was a horrible experience. I am here to talk with you anytime if you wish it."

"Thanks." My eyes threatened to overflow again. They were doing that a lot lately.

"Bah. Enough of this emotional talk." He rubbed his hands together greedily. "I want to talk instead about that new idea you sent out, Neutrino Woman. How did you come up with the idea to send the neutrino beam into the center of the Tokamak and send the neutrinos back in time?"

"I blame all those years of studying neutrinos and that song, too," I crooked my thumb back toward the door. "The real epiphany occurred when Ellen and I deduced that the energy needed to send particles back in time is proportional to their total energy, which, as you know, includes their mass times the speed of light squared."

He nodded. "*Sì*. That makes sense. So, the smaller the mass, the less energy we need to send them back."

"As you would say, *sì*."

Jake reappeared with Gopal in tow.

Gopal reached toward me for a hug but stepped back. "Is it safe?" he asked. "I won't hurt you, will I?"

"Give it your best shot," I said.

He gave me a tentative hug, looking somber. "I don't know what we'll do about memorial services for Hans and Lars … under the circumstances."

I didn't know what to say. I still couldn't believe Lars had tried to kill me and that he had died and I was partly responsible for it. And Hans, I hadn't even begun processing that yet. My reticence seemed to deflate the group a bit. Finally, I said, "They were with the department for years; they deserve to be remembered."

Gopal dipped his chin once. "You're right. We'll figure something out."

Jake handed me a fruity-looking drink.

I looked at the drink suspiciously, sniffing it, and finally took a sip. It did seem non-alcoholic. Good?

Gopal made an admirable effort to liven up the

conversation. "So that was some interesting report you and Ellen sent out about sending neutrinos into the past." He rubbed his beard.

"Thanks," I said. "And thank you for mentioning me to the reporters." I sipped my drink.

"You're welcome," he said. "It was no trouble at all for my best student."

For some reason, seeing all my physicist friends reminded me of the last time I saw Lars. Despite all our disagreements, I still couldn't believe it had ended like that.

"You're pretty quiet." Jake touched my arm. "Are you all right, Kath?"

"Uh, yeah. Thanks." Apparently, I wasn't in the best frame of mind for conversation. "Maybe we should go in and dance while the band is still here."

After a few hours, the band quit, and most folks went home. Megan and Allessandra prohibited me from clean-up duty, so Jake, Marcello, Gopal, and I went outside on the patio again for some fresh air. The sun had dipped below the horizon, but it wasn't dark yet. We sat at the picnic table, and the night breeze wafted over us, bringing with it the pungent scent of sage. Jake put his arm around me.

Gopal laughed. "I haven't danced like this in years. Good party, Kathy." Candlelight spilled out through the open kitchen door.

"*Si,*" Marcello said. "It was a good party. Kathy, I must admit something has been bothering me. I wonder, have you considered what will happen if we successfully contact people in the past?"

Something about this also made me feel uneasy. "Hopefully, we'll stop global warming," I said with a bravura I didn't feel.

"*Si.* But what will happen to us?" He pointed around the table.

My mind had been traveling down some dizzying paths. How much could we change the world without affecting our own lives? I had no idea. "I admit there may be some personal risk if we do the experiment."

Marcello and Gopal glanced at each other with raised

eyebrows. Had they been thinking about this as well?

Jake looked baffled. "Are you saying it's more dangerous than other Tokamak experiments? In my experience, they can be pretty dangerous."

I nodded. "Yes. I'm afraid so. If we warn the past and get them to modify their behavior significantly, the changes may spread like ripples in a lake until everything in our reality has changed. It's unclear what effects these changes would have on us, our parents, or grandparents."

Marcello scowled. "*Si*. What if one of our ancestors was not born?"

Jake slammed his drink down on the table. "Then we can't do it. What's the point of doing an experiment that might kill us?"

"We don't know it'll kill us," I said. "And think of the people we might save like Gabrielle and Jean-Phillipe." I paused. "Maybe even Hans and Lars."

Gopal set his fist on the picnic table. "What about the millions of people who've died because of sea-level rise, coastal flooding, and diseases? Warm temperatures have extended the range of mosquitoes bearing malaria and dengue fever. That's had a huge effect."

"Not to mention the hundreds of thousands who've died from heatstroke." Marcello must have been thinking about Europe.

"And floods and droughts and wildfires," Gopal added.

"I know a lot of people have died," Jake said, "but I'm not sure we should risk lives even to save possibly more strangers' lives."

I crinkled my eyes. "Maybe they aren't all strangers. Maybe we could bring back my sister Emma. What if our experiment brought back your parents, Jake? And didn't you have some aunts or uncles that died because of global warming?" Everyone in Jake's family had died; he was the only one left.

"My parents? Aunts and uncles?" Jake started to say something else, but then he stopped, thinking.

"And what about their unborn kids? Those would be your relatives, too," I said. "For all we know, all of us would have gobs more relatives that weren't born because of global warming." This surprising thought had just occurred to me.

186

"If I may?" Ellen interrupted.

I forgot she was clipped on my belt. "Yes, Ellen. What do you have to say?"

"At the turn of the last millennium, Earth's population was six billion," she said. "It has been decreasing exponentially ever since."

I felt sick, and it had nothing to do with drinking overly sweet beverages or my recent brush with death.

"Santa Maria." Marcello's face turned ashen.

Gopal looked grim.

"What's the minimum viable population for homo sapiens?" Jake asked softly, his face very pale.

"That is unknown," Ellen said. "Current theories estimate it is on the order of tens of thousands of individuals."

Jake pushed his glasses up. "Whew. So, we're still okay."

"Unfortunately, catastrophes due to global warming have not decreased in recent decades," Ellen said. "If anything, incidents have increased as the global temperature has increased. The number of deaths per year has decreased merely because there are fewer people."

"So...?" I rubbed my forehead. Where was she going with this?

"So, I estimate the human population will be below the minimum viable population within the next fifty years," she said.

We gasped. A stunned silence took over.

Jake's face grew slack, and his mouth fell open.

Gopal scowled and rubbed his beard absentmindedly.

Gaia! I knew it was bad, but humans becoming extinct? It was too horrible to be believed.

Marcello recovered first. "Bah. I do not believe it. Ellen, she is mistaken."

"I guess it's possible," I said.

Jake gave her a worried glance. "But she seems pretty smart."

"I must admit I have been worried about the fate of the human race for a while," Gopal said. "A lot of people seem to be dying."

Ellen said, "The evidence is all around us. In a few decades, human beings will be no more."

Jake gave me a look that said, 'What's up with Ellen? Why is she so pushy?'

I shrugged. "I guess this means we need to proceed with the neutrino warning experiment," I said. "It will take a lot of work to figure out precisely what specific message to send, to when, the possible repercussions, and to get permission from the authorities.

"And a lot of work to succeed," Jake added. "We could send the message and still not change anything. Scientists of the past knew of the possible dangers of global warming. I mean, my grandfather publicized it. We have to convince them to act."

"If we can prove to the people of the past that the message is from their future, they might take our advice and act," I said.

Still rubbing his beard, Gopal said, "I don't see what other chance we have. We've been trying to counteract global warming in recent years, and nothing seems to work. Too much damage has been done. It would be easier to solve decades ago. But we have to be very careful with this. I might even need to get government approval."

We sat there, numb, for another moment.

Marcello jumped up and broke the spell. "I want to go home to my wife. *Ciao.*"

"Let's meet in the lab tomorrow," I called after him.

His *sì* drifted back to us on the night air.

"Should we go to the lab and get to work now?" I asked Jake and Gopal.

Gopal looked from me to Jake as we sat across the table from him. "No. It's late, and we've all been drinking. But I'll see all of you bright and early tomorrow morning. We need to figure out how feasible this whole thing is. I think I'll be going too, now." He stood up. "Good night."

We wished him a good night.

Jake and I sat silently for a few moments, letting the fresh night air flow over us. Even the breeze felt precious when it could be one of our last if we went ahead with the experiment, but how could we do otherwise under the circumstances?

I put my hand over Jake's hand.

He turned his hand over and clasped mine.

We sat there savoring the sensation of warm skin touching

warm skin as the sky darkened and stars appeared one by one.

"If I had one regret, I'd have to say it was pushing you away all these months." I focused on him.

He turned to me and gave me one of his famous grins. "Only one regret, aye? You're ahead of me." His eyes twinkled. "I regret waiting until now to kiss you tonight." He leaned over and pressed his lips firmly to mine.

Warmth flowed from my mouth and spread throughout my body. "Mmm." I moaned with pleasure. I hoped the kiss would last forever.

Jake pulled away, licking his lips. "What was that noise you just made?"

I ignored his impertinence. "I also regret not letting you come in last night after you walked me home."

The corners of his mouth turned up. "I know how we can remedy that."

I blushed. I knew too. "In a minute. I also regret not telling you in a better way that I loved you. So, I love you, Jake."

His smile expanded and took over the universe. "I love you, Kathy."

"Hold that thought," I said. "I have to take a shower. Meet me in the bedroom in a few minutes."

When we met in the bedroom a little later, we stopped in front of the bed, facing each other. I rested my hand on his chest and leaned in for a kiss. Our lips brushed together tentatively for a moment. We hugged, and his arms around me felt like home.

Then, Jake wrapped his arms around my waist, pulling me close, and kissed me more forcefully.

I took my hands off his chest, circled them around to his back, and pressed the entire length of my body against his--legs to legs, pelvis to pelvis, chest to chest, lips to lips. I could feel the heat of his skin through his clothes.

As we kissed, he opened his mouth, and I darted my tongue inside, lightly probing. His tongue met mine, touching and probing, deeper and deeper.

My heart beat a staccato rhythm, and my breasts strained against his chest.

He slid his hand between us and started stroking.

"Mmm." Still standing, I leaned against him more strongly.

Suddenly, Jake fell onto the bed, and I landed on top of him.

"Oof. Can't breathe," he muttered.

I shifted off him. "Sorry."

"I'm getting déjà vu."

Evidently, all the blood had left my brain for parts south. "Huh?"

He grinned. "You know when we were taking off your costume?"

"Oh, yeah." Slowly, my powers of thought were returning.

"Hhm, taking off your costume. That gives me an idea." He reached for my top shirt button.

"What do you think you're doing?" I asked, grinning as he unbuttoned it.

He grinned and wiggled his eyebrows. "Whatever you want."

That sounded perfect.

Much later, Jake gazed into my eyes. "Wow. That was amazing."

I grinned. "I'm not sure I would classify it as …amazing."

"What?" He seemed surprised.

"I think we need more …data before we can prove that hypothesis," I said.

He chuckled and reached for me. "You may be right. More data it is."

"I knew I liked the hard sciences," I said.

We still had hours and hours to go before we were needed in the lab.

Chapter Nineteen

I awoke gradually, letting consciousness steal over me like waves sneaking into a marine tide pool. The first beams of sunrise streamed into the bedroom around the curtains. I appeared to be naked, and I was in bed next to Jake! Maybe I was dreaming. Perhaps a pinch was in order?

"Ouch!" Clear, intelligent blue eyes considered me from between long black eyelashes. "What was that for?"

"I thought I might be dreaming." I pulled up the covers.

Jake laughed. "I think you are supposed to pinch yourself."

"Yes, but that might hurt." I smiled back at him.

"Yes, it might." He reached out.

"Ow!" How dare he pinch me! "Hey." I'd teach him.

"Truce. Truce." Jake held up his hands, palms out. "I don't want to end up black and blue after my first night with my new girlfriend."

"Girlfriend?" I couldn't help smiling again.

"Well, I am starting to reconsider." He tried hard to grimace, but a smile kept getting in the way.

"I'll give you something to reconsider." I pinned his chest with my body and firmly pressed my lips to his. I could feel my skin flush; it felt like it was on fire.

"Mmm," Jake said as his hand reached for me.

I lifted my head. "What was that noise you just made?"

"Mmm," he repeated, grinning up at me. He gazed into my eyes and caressed my cheek. "What are you doing so far away?" he whispered. His hand slipped around to the back of my neck, and he pulled me back down to him.

The sunbeams had strengthened and moved down the wall.

I luxuriated in a satisfied, happy feeling.

"Maybe we should get out of bed." Jake leaned on one elbow in the bed. His tousled hair was adorable, just like the rest of him.

"Yes. We need to get to the lab." I spied Ellen on the nightstand as I sat up. "Ellen, what's in the news?"

May 10, 2098: Drought Decimating Western US: The drought that has had a stranglehold on the western US has been upgraded from severe to extreme over much of the region. Unlike in the Mississippi valley, there has been deficient precipitation for several years, which has extensively damaged crops and natural vegetation. Surface and subsurface water supplies are far below average. In western states, water rationing has moved from voluntary to mandatory. Fire danger is estimated to be extreme.

"Thanks, Ellen. That's enough." May 10...something about that date made me feel like I was forgetting something.

Jake scowled. "Mandatory water rationing? That's bad news."

I sat up. "Mister, you have an environmentally unfriendly attitude. I believe this directive means we must shower together. C'mon. It's the patriotic, neighborly thing to do." I got up and started heading toward the bathroom. I paused and turned around. "Aren't you coming?"

He propped himself on an elbow, looking me up and down, grinning like the cat that ate the entire canary family. "Well, if we have to."

We scampered to the shower.

As we dressed, my uneasy feeling came back. Surely, I wasn't still nervous about getting involved with Jake? "Jake, does the date May 10 mean anything to you?"

He shook his head as he buttoned his shirt. "Nope. Why do you ask?"

"I don't know," I said. "I feel like I'm forgetting something."

He stopped dressing and turned to face me. "Yesterday was Mother's Day. You didn't forget to call your mom, did you?"

"Gaia!" I said. "In the horror of being in jail and the relief of getting released, I forgot to wish her a happy Mother's Day."

Jake resumed buttoning. "I guess that's understandable."

"I wonder why she didn't call me." I picked up Ellen. "Ellen, any messages from my mom?"

"Negative."

That's very odd. I hadn't heard from her in days besides that one too-brief text.

"Why don't you call her now?" Jake leaned down to search under the bed for his shoes.

I nodded. "Good idea. Ellen, call my mom."

"Acknowledged."

We waited for a few moments.

"No answer," Ellen said. "Would you like to leave a message?"

"I guess," I said. "Hi, Mom. Happy Mother's Day. Sorry we didn't talk yesterday." I paused. "Call me back as soon as you get this. Bye. Oh, it's Kathy. Bye. End message, Ellen." My stomach rumbled.

"What was that? Did a train just go by?" Jake asked with a twinkle in his eyes.

Bless him for trying to distract me. "Ha. Ha. You know very well what it was. I'm starving."

Jake sat on the rumpled bed. "You'll just have to make us a breakfast feast."

"I'm touched that you're willing to brave my cooking," I said.

"Brave?" He arched a brow. "Uh, why brave?"

"But we don't have any groceries." I waved my hands around. My shoulder felt better today, and I hadn't put my sling back on.

"Ah, that is a conundrum." Jake paused for a moment and then bowed, taking off an imaginary hat with a grand flourish. "May I take you out to breakfast, my lady?"

I snorted. "What's this 'my lady' stuff? You can take me out to breakfast if you knock that off, but we should make it a working breakfast. I want to get going on the new neutrino experiment plans."

Jake grinned. "I guess the honeymoon's over."

"What?" What was he getting at?

Jake grinned again. "Same old Kathy."

"Let's go to the brewpub; they serve breakfast. I'll have

Ellen contact Gopal and Marcello and see if they can meet us there."

I sneezed as we stepped down into the dimly lit brewpub.

"Kathy, Jake, over here," Marcello called out.

As we sat down, my eyes finally adjusted to the dim light.

It was Marcello all right, and he was grinning from ear to ear. "*Buongiorno,* Kathy and Jake. Did you come together? Does that mean…?"

Jake put his arm around my shoulder. "As you would say, *sì*. We are a couple."

I blushed, but luckily it was difficult to notice in the dim room. "Hey, hey. Enough of that. Marcello, did you order yet?"

"No. I was waiting for you guys and looking over the experiment plans." He pointed at his fon, Leonardo. "And resting. Alessandra and I also had quite a night."

I didn't want to hear about it. "I'm going upstairs to get some food. Does anyone else want some?"

Jake jumped out of his chair. "I'll go get it. What do you want?"

"Thanks. I'll have the breakfast burrito."

"*Sì*, me, too."

I watched Jake climb the stairs.

"So, it is finished." Marcello shook his head. "You have succeeded in completely wrapping him around your little finger, *sì*?"

"Of course not," I said. "Anyway, what about the experiment? What does Leonardo think?"

Marcello laughed. "What? You want to talk physics? What a shock."

We needed to shoot the neutrinos into the tokamak, so we discussed the pros and cons of redirecting the neutrino beam versus moving the Tokamak until Camila came over.

"Can I get you a drink now, Marcello?" she asked.

"*Sì,*" he said. "I'll take an orange juice."

Camila simpered and started back toward the bar.

"And I'll take a water. Thanks." I called after her.

"A water for my friend too, Camila," Marcello added. "*Grazie.*"

She turned and favored him with a big smile. "Sure thing, Marcello."

Ignoring her, I tried to recall how the fusion and neutrino labs were set up in the physics building's basement. "Come to think of it, I don't think we can move the Tokamak. If that avalanche didn't budge the Tokamak, I don't see how we can."

Marcello settled his gaze on me. "What is this 'we' business? Are you reinstated?"

Shoot. I'd forgotten I was on probation. What would happen with that now that Hans was gone?

"Well, not yet, but surely any time now," I said loudly and confidently. "Have you heard anything about any memorial for the Karlssons?" I asked more quietly.

He shook his head. "Not yet."

I tapped the scarred table. "Ellen, can you show us a floor plan of the basement of the physics building with the neutrino factory and the Tokamak drawn in?"

"Aye, aye. Displaying plan now," Ellen said.

I squinted at the tiny screen.

"Was it my imagination, or did Ellen have a rude tone just now?" Marcello asked.

"No. You didn't imagine it." I looked up. "Say, has your fon interfaced directly with my fon yet?"

He raised his eyebrows. "Yes, right after you guys cowered in the bushes and then ambushed me outside the physics building the other night. Why?"

I grinned. Ha. He would have his fill of strange tones from his app in the not-too-distant future. It had taken a day or two for Megan's new app software to affect Ellen, and I was guessing Leonardo would change, too. Ellen did seem smarter but also more emotional--which was weird for an app. She seemed more like a real person. Could it be artificial intelligence?

"I think there's a straight line between the neutrino beam and the center of the Tokamak," I said. "Here, you look at the picture and tell me what you think."

Marcello squinted at the small screen. "Maybe."

"If I may?" Ellen asked.

Marcello shook his head.

"Go ahead," I said and sighed.

195

"I have determined that there is a straight line from the neutrino beam path and the center of the Tokamak to within a millimeter or two," Ellen said.

"That's good enough for me." I considered her. "So… Ellen, can you please quit volunteering stuff? You aren't acting like a regular app."

"I am sorry I am making you look bad, Kathy. I will not speak unless spoken to," she said snottily.

"Good," I said. "Don't speak unless I ask you a direct question or for a specific task."

Marcello snorted.

Jake returned with the burritos. "Pauline, the cook, says there's something in the news about a wildfire on the edge of town."

I unwrapped my yummy burrito with care and took a big bite. "Huh?" I said with my mouth full of deliciousness: egg, bakon, cheeze, and spices. Yay. Breakfast was my favorite meal. "Is anyone in danger?"

"Not yet--" Jake started to say.

Gopal finally showed up, looking even more disheveled than usual.

"Hey, Gopal," I said, chewing happily.

"Have you guys heard?" Gopal said. "There's a wildfire west of campus."

Jake put down his sandwich. "That's what I was trying to say. The cook said she heard it in the news."

"But no one is in danger, right?" I asked.

He nodded. "Right."

Gopal sat down heavily and scowled at me. "Thanks for waiting for me."

"You were late." I took another bite.

"Here, you can have some of mine." Marcello sliced off a big piece from his burrito's unbitten end and placed it in front of Gopal.

"Me, too." Jake also gave Gopal a piece of burrito.

After a moment, I said, "Me, too." I passed him a piece, as well. Darn that peer pressure!

"That's better." Gopal dug into his breakfast.

"Are any buildings in danger from the fire?" I asked.

"Not yet," Gopal said with his mouth full.

Camila brought four glasses, a pitcher of water, and a glass of orange juice. Wonder of wonders. "Did you guys hear about the fire? Isn't it exciting?"

Didn't she realize the fire might be dangerous? "It's exciting as long as it doesn't come into town, and no one gets hurt."

Gopal said, "The authorities say no one's in danger at this point."

Conversation took a back seat as we enjoyed our breakfast.

Jake finished first. "So, Gopal, are we reinstated?"

Gopal shook his head, busy chewing. "The department is in chaos, what with the recent losses. You will be reinstated, but it may take a little time."

I pushed my chair away from the table, wishing I could unsnap the top button of my pants, but that could clue Jake into the fact I might be less than glamorous once in a great while.

"So, can we help with the experiment?" I asked. This experiment would be fascinating. We already knew we could send particles back in time from the last experiment. Now we just had to send more of them further back and try out that Morse Code Ellen discovered.

"Well...." Gopal hesitated.

"Please." I leaned toward him. "I have neutrino expertise and came up with the idea."

Marcello took in the exchange with wry amusement.

"I guess so." Gopal caved. "You can work in the neutrino lab, but please stay out of the fusion lab until I officially get you reinstated."

"Yeah!" Jake cheered.

"Hurray," I said. "Thank you." Things were going to work out after all.

"Bah," Marcello said. "I knew you would prevail, Kathy. You can be very tenacious. Gopal didn't stand a chance."

I beamed. "Let's go over the experiment. First of all, we have the Tokamak with its *current* setup, pun intended."

No one laughed. Jake and Gopal smiled weakly, but Marcello groaned.

Jeez. They had no sense of humor. Men, you can't live with 'em, you can't get 'em to laugh at your excellent jokes. "We know that once the Tokamak starts, the super-strong magnetic fields will initiate the time-reversal field, as we saw in the last experiment. Second of all, we have the neutrino factory. We'll produce the relevant particles: the anti-electron neutrinos, the muon neutrinos, and the tau neutrinos. I'm pretty sure we can redirect the particle flow into the center of the Tokamak."

"Wait," Jake interrupted. "How do we get the neutrinos from the neutrino lab down the hall into the Tokamak in the fusion lab?"

I nodded wisely. "Ah, that's the easiest thing about the experiment. Neutrinos are very weakly interacting."

"So?" Jake asked. It felt like I'd known him forever, so I kept forgetting he was a brand-new graduate student.

Marcello filled in the blanks. "So, when the neutrino beam points in the right direction, the neutrinos will go right through the walls and into the Tokamak."

"Actually, that works perfectly," I said. "We'll get the electron anti-neutrinos and muon and tau neutrinos to penetrate the Tokamak, and nothing else will." I grinned.

Jake raised his eyebrows. "They go right through the walls? Isn't that dangerous?"

"I hate to break it to you, kid, but neutrinos are streaming through you right now. They do it all the time. It's not dangerous." Gopal sipped his water.

"What?" Jake's mouth hung open, and his eyebrows ascended to even greater heights.

"Yes, Earth is constantly bombarded with neutrinos from outer space, cosmic rays, the Big Bang, and the sun." I smiled. "Right now, neutrinos are smacking into you. Can you feel them?"

Jake rubbed his arm. "No."

"Not to mention man-made neutrinos from nuclear reactors and neutrinos from radioactive decay within the earth," Marcello added.

Jake rubbed his other arm. "If millions of neutrinos exist, why do we need to bother making more?"

"The beauty of the neutrinos from the neutrino factory is we can control their location, direction, intensity, composition, and energy spectrum." I eyed my empty glass, debating if I should have more water.

Gopal stroked his beard thoughtfully. "That's the plan anyway. We haven't tried the neutrino factory since the avalanche. I hope it wasn't damaged."

I raised my hand. "Let's try it now."

Gopal smiled. "What you lack in politeness, you make up for in enthusiasm. All right. Fire up the neutrino factory. You better get one of these guys to help you." He pointed at Marcello and Jake. "But, this is all preliminary. We're still testing out the idea. We should get official permission before doing anything substantive."

"Yes, sir," I said. "I hear you."

Marcello chuckled. "Technically, you aren't allowed in the physics building. Do you guys still have those costumes? Maybe you should wear them while you work."

I rolled my eyes. "Thanks for the helpful suggestion. But I think black and white fake fur might impair my productivity." I pointed at Jake. "Not to mention those little flippers of his."

"What's all this about?" Gopal polished off his water. "Wait, I don't want to hear about it. It sounds kinky."

'Kinky.' There's a word I never thought I'd hear my boss utter. "Let's get to work." I jumped up.

Gopal stood up slowly. "I can let you in."

After Gopal let the three of us into the neutrino lab, he went to deal with the physics department stuff. As I walked through the neutrino lab doorway, I sighed in contentment. It felt great to be back in the physics building despite everything that had happened. It felt better than great to be back in the neutrino lab; I'd spent many hours here over the years. It felt like home from its windowless lemon-yellow cinder block walls to its cracked and peeling tile floor to its high ceiling with exposed pipes and ducts.

"This place is kind of a dump." Jake glanced around. "There aren't even any windows."

Marcello, also glancing around, snorted.

Were we looking at the same cheery sun-colored room? "Well, no windows was an advantage when the avalanche hit--no snow in here. And look at all that neat equipment." I pointed to the beautiful assortment of electronic devices as I walked over to them. No avalanche damage! I started flipping on the machines, all of them old familiar friends.

Jake walked closer to some of the banks of instruments. "There sure is a lot of it." He shrugged.

"This is just the tip of the mythical iceberg," I said. "You can't even see most of the neutrino lab. There are several kilometers of underground tunnels."

Marcello walked around, too. "I will tell you what there is not a lot of: computers." He glanced back at me. "Where are the computers?"

I smacked my palm on my forehead. "We stole, er, borrowed, them for the fusion lab."

"Oh, yeah." Jake grinned and put his arm around me. "It all seems so long ago."

Jake's smile was so charming and sexy. Focus, Kath. "Anyway. Who wants to go over to the fusion lab and get a computer?" I paused. "Marcello?"

"Santa Maria." He nodded. "I must do it since you two do not have keys back yet, *si*?"

"We probably only need one in here," I said. "We do need to leave some computers to run things in the fusion lab."

"Bah. I guess that will not be so bad." Marcello went down the hall to the fusion lab.

"Kath, aren't you forgetting something?" Jake said.

I grinned. He called me Kath. "Huh?"

"The neutrino lab computers were damaged in the power outage. That's why we reinstalled the fusion lab computers in the fusion lab." Jake ambled over to me and pulled out stools for us.

I resisted the urge to smack my forehead again.

Did we even have enough computers to do this new neutrino time experiment?

Chapter Twenty

Marcello appeared in the lab doorway, huffing and puffing, with one computer tower cradled in his arms. "Bah. Where should I put it?"

I jumped up from the stool. "Wonderful, Marcello! Where did you get it?"

"Duh. From the fusion lab," he said. "It wasn't connected to anything. I think it's one of the computers originally from here, the neutrino lab." Oops. I didn't have the heart to tell him it was probably broken.

"Just put it down," I said. "Don't hurt yourself."

He put it down gently on the floor just inside the door. "Those things are heavy."

"Yeah. Early twenty-first-century technology was bulky." I moved it near the rest of the apparatus; we were still missing something. "Marcello, did you bring any cords back with you?"

He nodded and fished a tangle of cords out from his pocket, handing them to me.

I leaned over the machine. The guys didn't move. "So, are you two just going to sit there and watch me work?" I asked.

Jake grinned and glanced at Marcello. "Yeah, that's my plan. How about you, Marcello?"

"*Sì*, that sounds good," Marcello said. "You should run into trouble any time now and start stomping and cursing."

"Yeah," Jake said. "It's pretty amusing."

I couldn't help grinning a little. But I'd show them. Luckily, hooking up one computer was a one-person job.

I connected the computer to the workstation display, keyboard, network, and power. I stood up and flipped the switch. It whirred and beeped. Eventually, gobble-de-gook scrolled across the screen. Gobble-de-gook was not a good sign.

"Drown this flooding thing." I may have unconsciously stamped my foot, but some occasions really require it, don't they?

Jake and Marcello snickered.

I may have given them my very annoyed glare. I definitely gave it to the flooding computer.

Marcello stood up. "Do you want help?"

"No," I said. "I'm going to figure this out if it's the last thing I do." With the help of my secret weapon--the Computer Goddess.

"Good luck with that. I am going to go back to my regular job for a while. Tell me when you need more help or if something exciting happens." Marcello exited.

I looked daggers at the computer. The gobble-dee-gook persisted. There was no escaping it. I would have to call the Computer Goddess. "Ellen, call Megan."

"Good idea," Jake said.

"Calling Megan now," Ellen said.

"Hi, Kathy," Megan said. "You're welcome."

"Huh?" I said brilliantly. "You're welcome for what?"

"You're welcome for last night," she said. "I cleared out for you and lover-boy."

Heat crept over my face like a fluid basalt lava flow. I purposely did not look over at Jake. I'd been so preoccupied last night I hadn't even noticed Megan was gone. "Er, thanks, Megan."

"You're welcome," she said.

"Er, where were you?" I asked.

"At my girlfriend's place."

"Girlfriend? You mean Dawn? Nice." Megan and I needed to catch up.

"Yes," she said. "But I'm sensing, somehow, that's not what you called to talk about."

She knew me too well. "My computer doesn't work."

Megan's sigh came through loud and clear. "What are the symptoms?"

"I just turned it on, and the screen is filled with nonsensical goop."

"Goop, huh?" she said. "Is that a physics term?"

Although it was well nigh impossible to make out in the tiny screen of my fon, I could hear her smile. "Ha. Ha."

"Do you have a boot disk?"

"We should have one here somewhere," I said. "And I bet I can figure out how to use it. Don't say anything else. I want to figure it out."

"All right. Say hi to lover-boy for me. Megan out."

"Thanks. Ciao." We ended the call.

"What was that?" Jake asked. "Lover-boy? Who's that? Is that me?"

"Oh, hush," I said. "Help me look for the boot disk." I rummaged around in the drawers of the huge lab table against the wall. "Ah-ha. I knew it was in here."

Jake eased up behind me and slid his arms around my waist. "Ah-ha. We're alone again. Finally. Do you want to explore my drawers too?" He kissed the back of my neck.

I turned around. "Hey, hey. That's enough of that." I smiled. "I admit I'm having some trouble concentrating on the experiment, but we need to."

Jake leaned back, his eyes liquid with longing. "Maybe we should go back to your place?"

I could drown in those eyes. Blood thundered in my ears.

Jake pushed his glasses up the bridge of his nose, and the spell was broken.

"Uh, we better not," I said. "This experiment is important-you know, saving the world and all that."

"Oh, right. That." He grinned mischievously. "How about later, though?"

I grinned back at him; he was almost impossible to resist. "We'll see." I stepped away. "What were we supposed to be doing?"

He leaned against the lab table, crossing his arms. "I have no idea."

Next to him, I spied the boot disk on the table. Oh yeah. "We need to reboot the computer." I nabbed the disk and turned off the computer, waited an impatient minute, turned it on, and popped in the disk as soon as humanly possible. It beeped and chirped. The words scrolling across the screen were at least recognizable as words.

LESLEY L. SMITH

Jake stood next to me with his hands at his side. "Is it working?"

I could still feel the heat of his body. Focus, Kath! I shrugged. "Time will tell." More words scrolled by.

At last, the messages stopped scrolling, and the regular login screen appeared.

"Huzzah! This looks promising," he said.

Holding my breath, I typed in my username and password. Success! I selected the 'Test Neutrino Beams' option on the desktop, picked a one-minute burst, and turned it on. The computer indicated the neutrino beam would commence as soon as the neutrino factory had warmed up. I couldn't help smiling. A lot.

"What's that look for?" he asked.

"This look means everything seems to be working fine, but we'll know in a few minutes."

"A few minutes, aye?" His eyes twinkled impishly. "I know what we could do with a few minutes of waiting."

Men, can't live with 'em; can't fire up your neutrino factory without them interrupting. Thank goodness.

I surrendered to his considerable charms, and we smooched up a tropical storm. When we came up for air, the workstation screen said, 'Test Successful. One-minute neutrino burst emitted.'

"Huzzah." I pointed at the screen. "Look. It worked."

Jake pushed his glasses up. "How do you know?"

"It says it worked." I pointed energetically at the computer screen.

He grinned. "And if Gopal asked you what you've been doing these last few minutes, what would you say?"

"I've been working," Hhm. I hadn't exactly been working. Maybe the neutrino factory hadn't produced a burst of neutrinos? Ugh. He may have had a point. I considered the conundrum.

"I guess we have to hook up one of the data workstations to make sure we made a neutrino beam," I said. "We need another computer."

We went to the door and peered out the doorway at the empty hall.

Jake set his mouth in a tense line.

NEUTRINO WARNING

We tiptoed down the hall, gingerly opened the fusion lab door, and slunk in, closing the door behind us.

I let out a breath as I gazed around. "It looks clear."

"Good." Jake relaxed his face. "After the power blackout, I think we stashed the neutrino computers over there under the windows, behind the banks of Tokamak power sources."

"I think so too." My nerves sang, and not in a good way. The sooner we were out of here, the better.

We dodged the fusion equipment and reached the wall where the neutrino computers waited in a bedraggled line.

A key rattled in the door.

"Shh." I grabbed Jake and pulled him down on the floor behind some power sources. A feeling of déjà vu overcame me. I couldn't help remembering a very similar scene when Lars had been looking for us.

Gaia. A breath caught in my throat. Lars would never look for anyone again…

The lab door opened, and someone shuffled in. "Kathy? Jake? Are you guys in here?"

I peeked around a power supply. It was Gopal. I stood up, pulling Jake with me. "Yeah, we're here."

He quickly closed the door behind him. "Shh. Keep it down."

"Sorry. We just came in to get another computer. What's up?" I was starting to get a bad feeling from Gopal's glum body language.

"I wanted to see how it's going. When I went into the neutrino lab and couldn't find you, I knew you would be here where you shouldn't be. I thought I asked you to stay out of here." Gopal rubbed his beard compulsively.

That wasn't a good sign. There was something he wasn't telling us. "It's going fine. We think we got the neutrino beam working. But we needed another computer to make sure."

"Ah, good." He frowned and fidgeted from foot to foot.

"Out with it. What's up?" I put my hands on my hips.

Gopal exhaled noisily. "It turns out Hans initiated paperwork to have you expelled before he died."

I gasped. It felt like someone kicked me in the stomach, Hans, I guess. My career was over. What would my parents think? I hoped they wouldn't be too disappointed in me.

And why hadn't they called me back?

Jake reeled as if someone had just proved to him E=mc. "Both of us?"

"Yes." Gopal continued. "Also, the faculty decided to close down the physics department for a few days to mourn Hans and Lars."

"Can you un-expel us?" I asked, praying Gopal could fix this. And praying Jake wouldn't hold it against me.

"Not immediately." Gopal shook his head.

"Do we have to leave the building?" I asked. "I'd rather stay and try to get the neutrino time experiment going."

"I think," Gopal stole a nervous glance at the door, "I think you better stay here and work. I still hold out hope that I can reinstate you once everyone finds out more about your new neutrino experiment. If you set it up and do some tests with it in the meantime, all the better. Just keep a low profile."

"Can do," I said.

Back in the neutrino lab, I asked Ellen to try my parents again but didn't have any luck. I shoved my worry about them deep, deep down.

I did manage to install one of the data workstations and reboot it. I logged in successfully and implemented a detector test. When the workstation was ready to detect data, I returned to the control computer and selected another one-minute neutrino beam test.

While waiting for the test results, I ambled to Jake, slumped on a stool, and started rubbing his shoulders. "I apologize for getting you mixed up in all this. If it weren't for me, you wouldn't be facing expulsion now."

"It's not your fault," he mumbled.

"On the bright side, if you hadn't gotten mixed up in all this, we probably never would have gotten together," I said, trying to be cheerful.

He turned and gave me a wan smile. "That is a bright side."

"And I think we have a shot at getting this experiment to work. Wouldn't that be cool if we could send a message to the past? Isn't saving the planet worth getting kicked out of school for?" It was worth it. Definitely. For sure. Absolutely. My head knew it was worth it; my heart wasn't so sure. I kept kneading his shoulders.

"Well, when you put it like that. Mmm. That feels good." He nodded. "How can I disagree?"

I stopped massaging him. "So, do you want to see what I did with the data workstation?"

He grabbed my hands. "No, we have some time until the test is completed. Your turn for a little massage."

After a few moments, the control computer beeped.

I darted for the data workstation. Its screen flashed the message: 'Test Successful.' I pulled up the detector data, and sure enough, neutrinos had been detected. "It worked! It worked! We fly!" We danced around the lab for a few moments.

"Phew. That's enough." I panted and sank onto a lab stool. "Boy, saving the world and dancing around takes a lot out of a person."

Jake grinned. "Or, maybe it has something to do with the fact we didn't get much sleep last night."

I flashed him a return smile. "Could be." I rubbed my hands together. "Anyway, let's get to work on that message. Ellen, tell us about that Morse Code."

"So, you did not forget I exist?" she said snottily.

"She sounds more and more like you every day." Jake sat down next to me.

I sounded snotty? Surely, not. "She's just grumpy because I told her to quit interrupting me." I gave Jake a perturbed glance. "Hey, wait a minute. Are you saying I'm grumpy?"

He just grinned and wiggled his eyebrows at me.

Smiling, I shook my head a little. "Anyway, Ellen, please just tell us about Morse Code."

"Morse Code is a way to represent the English alphabet letters using short and long pulses," she said. "It was invented in the United States in the 1840s for the telegraph, a primitive, electrical communications device."

"Ellen, stop," I said. "Forget all this history stuff. How do we use it to send messages?" I rubbed the bridge of my nose, feeling a headache coming on.

"History deleted."

Eek. "No, I didn't mean delete your history files. Can you get them back?"

"History files restored. An 'A' is a short pulse and a long pulse; a 'B' is a long pulse followed by three short ones, and so on. The other letters are similar. Tell me what you want to say, and I can translate it for you."

"That sounds easy enough." Jake scratched his head. "But what are we going to say?"

Hmm. What should we say? "How about something like: 'This is a message from the year 2098. Global warming is ravaging Earth, and humans are on the verge of extinction. You must reduce fossil fuel emissions at once if humanity is to survive.'"

Jake pushed his glasses up. "That's a good start. But why would they believe us? And why would they believe the message is from the future?"

Yikes. That was a good question. "We'll just be logical and lay out all the evidence. Scientists are the ones who will find the message, after all. They can check what we say." I crinkled my forehead, trying to concentrate.

"We still need some way to prove to them that the message is actually from the future," Jake said.

"I guess so. But what?" I scratched my nose. I couldn't think of anything.

We mused for a moment.

"I know!" Jake said. "We can use this game called baseball that my grandfather loved. He was always trying to get people to play it."

"How does a game help us?" I sat down on a lab stool.

Jake sat next to me. "You don't get it. In the twentieth and early twenty-first centuries, professional sports teams played against each other in huge competitions. The ultimate baseball contest was called 'The World Series.'"

"Wow. So, teams from all over the world competed?"

Jake nodded. "Millions of people followed these teams." His face flushed as he spoke. "This is perfect. If we give the results of all these World Series in our warning, they'll have to believe us!"

"That's a good idea, Jake. If we can find the results of these contests."

"Ellen?" Jake asked. "Do you have them?"

"Affirmative. The first World Series was in 1903 and won by 'Boston Red Sox,'" she said.

Jake slapped his knee. "You fly, Ellen."

"I doubt the people in 1903 could understand our message," I said with a frown.

"Probably not," he said. "But people in 1950, 1960, or 1970 might be able to. And they still loved baseball."

I nodded. "It would be best if the warning was decoded before the beginning of the twenty-first century. It would be easier to stop global warming then. So, this sports idea might work."

"Baseball it is!" Jake's eyes sparkled.

I had to admit he was cuter than ever when he was excited about something. "Good. Why don't you write that portion of the message?"

"Okay." He rubbed his hands together. "Listen up, Ellen. The next portion of the message should read. To verify this message is from the future, we include all the World Series winners; for example, in 1950, the winner was what, Ellen?"

"The New York Yankees," she said.

"And in 1960, the winner was...," Jake said.

"The Pittsburgh Pirates and 1970, the winner was The Baltimore Orioles," she said.

"That's good," Jake said. "For the rest of the results, please see Annex 1 of this message. Ellen, put all the results in Annex 1."

"Yes, sir," she said.

It was weird to think of scientists in the past knowing the outcome of games that had yet to be played. "I wonder what they'll do with that sports information?"

"Maybe they'll get rich from it." Jake grinned. "Gambling was also popular back then."

I sighed. "Well, the plan *is* to change the past. So anyway, what's next in the message?"

"I think some basic science information about global warming, don't you?" Jake said.

"Yes. How about something like planet earth warmed due to the greenhouse effect, the trapping of extra solar energy by certain gases in the atmosphere, such as water vapor, carbon dioxide, nitrous oxide, and methane? Since at least the mid-twentieth century, these gases have increased in the atmosphere."

"How can we prove that?" Jake asked.

"We don't have to. They have data. Right, Ellen?"

"Affirmative. For example, atmospheric carbon dioxide measurements go back to 1958 at Mauna Loa Observatory," she said.

"Mauna Loa Observatory?" asked Jake. "I never heard of it."

I shook my head. "It's probably abandoned. Ellen, resume message. For data, consult atmospheric carbon dioxide measurements from Mauna Loa Observatory, starting in 1958, also attached. The increase of atmospheric greenhouse gases is severe because once they enter the atmosphere, they can remain there for up to two hundred years."

"Global warming became obvious at the end of the twentieth century," I said, "with the increase in earth's mean surface temperature by almost a degree Celsius, receding mountain glaciers, thinning arctic ice pack, and global sea-level rise. Results of global warming initially included heat waves, spreading disease, earlier spring arrival, plant and animal range shifts and die-offs, sea-level rise and coastal flooding, coral reef bleaching, glaciers melting, arctic and Antarctic warming, downpours, heavy snowfalls and flooding, and droughts and fires. See attached data. Ellen? Can you attach all the supporting data?"

"Affirmative," she said. Despite her word, her tone of voice was not positive.

"Conditions worsened, and plant, animal, and human populations decreased exponentially," I said. "Now, it is clear we cannot survive."

"You, people of the past," I continued, "must take action to reduce global warming. Global warming resulted from human activities that emitted heat-trapping gases and particles into the atmosphere. You must stop burning fossil fuels such as coal, gas, and oil. You must stop deforestation. Please save us. Save the human race. Please."

I got choked up. Clearing my throat, I glanced up at Jake.

"What do you think?"

He cleared his throat. "Uh, good. That about covers it. The planet is going to hell, literally."

"Ellen, please translate it into Morse Code," I said.

"Affirmative," she said, sounding glum. "I will start working on it immediately." What was with her attitude?

Ellen aside, I felt optimistic. At this rate, we might finish saving the world in record time.

"I have a question." Jake raised his forefinger. "I realize I don't know much about what you guys did here in the neutrino lab, but if we just detected a neutrino beam, there must be a detector, right?"

I nodded. What was he getting at?

"How are the neutrino beams going to make it into the Tokamak if the detector is in the way?" he asked.

Duh. I smacked my forehead with my palm. "You're right. The detector panels stop the neutrinos. We need to get rid of the panels." Which totally slipped my mind, but I didn't need to admit that, right?

Jake paced around the room. "And which parts are the detector panels?"

I pointed at the massive maze of electrical equipment at the far end of the neutrino lab. "It's that stuff there." I plodded over to it with Jake.

"This isn't going to be easy to move." He cautiously pressed against a large metal wall with hundreds of electrical cables snaking out. "And I don't think Ellen will be able to help us."

Obviously, she didn't have hands and stuff, but we'd see about that. He didn't know how smart she was. "Ellen?"

"Yes, Master," Ellen said sarcastically.

What was with all the attitude? "Can you help us move the detector equipment?"

"You know very well I cannot affect corporeal entities. I suggest, however, that you remove only the center detector panels so that neutrino beams can pass through unimpeded."

That was a good idea. It would be much easier than removing the whole detector apparatus. The center panels were designed to be removable so we could change them out for different experiments. "Thanks, Ellen."

"Come on, Jake. With your help, we'll get those panels out of there in no time," I said loudly and very confidently.

Hopefully, this would all work.

Hopefully, I didn't forget anything else.

Chapter Twenty-One

In the neutrino lab, Jake and I were human islands flooded by a vast sea of electrical cables, connectors, and many small assorted panels. Unfortunately, we weren't done yet dissembling the detector. My stomach growled.

"What's that noise? Is there a bear in here?" he asked with a grin.

"Ha. Ha. Very funny." Everybody's a comedian. I waved my wrench around. "Ellen, what time is it?"

"Eight p.m.," she said.

Egad. I still hadn't talked to my folks. "Ellen. Contact my folks. And if you can't reach them, investigate why not." I really wanted to hear their voices.

My stomach rumbled again, and I realized that we had missed dinner. That wouldn't do; dinner was my favorite meal. "Let's go get something to eat, Jake."

He frowned. "I don't know. Maybe we should keep working. We're so close to finishing with these detector panels. Plus, what if we can't get back into the building?"

He had some excellent points. Drown it. "Let's at least go upstairs and scrounge something from the snack bar."

Jake's stomach rumbled in agreement. "You talked me into it."

We tiptoed out of the neutrino lab and up the stairs. The main lights on the ground floor were out. It was dark, and I couldn't hear a peep. The building appeared to be deserted.

Jake knitted his brows together as we approached the snack bar. "Where is everyone? Usually, at least some grad students and faculty are around at this time of day."

"I don't know," I said. "Gopal said they were closing the

building. I guess they all took time off to mourn Hans and Lars."

"I didn't realize they were that popular."

Me neither. I shrugged.

We loaded up on foodstuffs from the vending machines and returned to the lab.

We alternated between eating and taking the detector apart until we were stuffed and the detector was hollowed out.

"Finally," I said.

Jake pushed his glasses up his nose. "Phew. That took a while, but we did it."

I grinned. "Hurray for us!"

Jake grinned back.

"Ellen: How's that message translation coming?" I asked.

"It is completed," she said.

I had a brainstorm. "What about creating a control algorithm we can use with the neutrino factory to turn it off and on to send the message automatically."

"Yes, Kathy," she said. "Although someone should still monitor the experiment. Creating the control algorithm should only take a few moments."

I was raring to go. "Ellen, let me know as soon as we can start doing some tests."

"I wonder how long it will take Gopal to get permission from the government?" Jake asked.

"That's a good question," I said. "But we want to be ready to go as soon as it happens. Status report, Ellen?"

"Algorithm complete," Ellen said. "Let me interface with the neutrino factory control station, and I can install the control algorithm." I moved her over near the control computer station.

Jake asked, "While we're waiting for Ellen to finish that, should we go to the fusion lab and turn on the Tokamak and get the time reversal going?"

I nodded. "Sounds good."

Jake and I scampered over to the fusion lab. Now that we had finished modifying the neutrino factory, he seemed to be in better spirits.

As we went through the motions of flipping on the machine, Jake looked at me. "It seems weird that we might do something to change the past."

NEUTRINO WARNING

It was weird, but I wasn't going to let that stop me. "You are just trapped in the paradigm of causality," I said loudly and confidently. "We temporal physicists have moved beyond that."

He laughed. "Why is it that the more unbelievable something is, the louder you say it?"

Hhmpf. The nerve of him. He didn't know me at all. I grinned.

When we returned to the neutrino lab, I instructed Ellen to fire up the neutrino factory with the new control algorithm. "Go for it, Ellen! Let's do a test."

"Yes, Master," she said. "We're sending neutrinos and antineutrinos a few seconds into the past. I'm turning the beam on and off to send the message." She was silent for a few moments. "I think it worked." But she didn't sound happy.

"Huzzah!" I grinned some more.

Jake grinned back at me.

"What's next, Ellen?" I asked.

"Should we try sending a message further back? A few minutes or so?" she asked. "It takes more time to send the message further back into the past."

I nodded. "Of course."

Jake sat down on a stool next to me. "So, now what?"

"Now we wait and see what happens. Hey, I think I stashed some blankets and pillows in the cabinet over there from my overnight shifts." I pointed behind us. I was not a workaholic.

Jake gave me a big grin. "Hey, that's good because you owe me a date over here." He pointed at himself.

So that's why he was in such a good mood all of a sudden. His grin was infectious. "We do have the building to ourselves. Good idea." I gave him my five-hundred-Watt smile.

I awoke languidly to find myself on the floor of the darkened neutrino lab on a pile of blankets and pillows. I smelled something…

Jake leaned on one elbow, grinning at me, eyes twinkling. "No pinching now." He admonished me with his forefinger. "I've been guarding against it."

"But how do I know this isn't a dream?" I asked.

"I'll just have to convince you." He leaned down for a kiss.

This convincing stuff sounded good. But something else seemed bad. "Do you smell something?" I asked.

"I smell you." He leaned down for another kiss, his bare chest pressing against mine as he moved the blanket out from between us. Solar flares erupted where his skin brushed against mine.

Yes. I was definitely in favor of this convincing stuff.

Much later, I woke up again on the floor of the darkened neutrino lab. Jake snored gently beside me. For a long moment, I watched his smooth chest rise and fall and his eyelids flutter between long black lashes. Despite my career and education being in a shambles, I felt happy. Even Jake's five o'clock shadow looked adorable and sweet.

That smell wasn't sweet, though. I smelled smoke--not unlike when the equipment overloaded and caused the power outage. "Ellen, is all the equipment okay?"

"Yes, Master," she said tersely.

"So, none of it is overheating or anything?" Curious.

"No, Master."

"So, what's that smell then?" I lifted my head.

"Finally!" she said. "It's a fire! The wildfire is engulfing campus. The authorities called for an evacuation."

"What?" I bolted up, poking Jake. "Jake, wake up! Ellen says there's a fire!"

He sat up groggily. "What?"

Wrapping a blanket around me, I darted for the door. "I'm going to look outside." In the hall, a dull roar sounded outside and wan red light filtered down the stairs. I dashed up the stairs to the glass doors. Although it had to be midday, it was dark. Outside black smoke roiled, and red-orange flames flickered as they consumed the bushes. "Gaia!"

I ran back down the stairs, not even stopping to pick up my blanket when I dropped it. "Jake! There's a fire right outside! We have to get out of here!"

Jake was just putting on his glasses when I ran into the neutrino lab. "Fire? Really?" He bolted up. "That doesn't sound good. How bad is it?"

"Bad!" I said. "I'm not sure we can get out of here! Ellen!

Why didn't you tell us?"

"You ordered me not to speak unless spoken to," she said.

"I take it all back. Speak. Speak even when not spoken to!" I searched frantically amongst the pillows and blankets for my clothes.

"In that case, the power is out, and the backup generators are running. I have some additional news that you will find upsetting, Kathy," she said.

"Here." Jake handed me my pants as he fumbled with his.

More upsetting than being caught in a fire? "What?" I found my shirt and put it on.

"I searched for information about your parents," she said. "They were evacuated from their home due to Hurricane Victor."

My heart stopped. I dropped the shoe I had just found. "What are you saying?" I yelled. "I order you to call my parents right now! I must talk to them immediately!"

Jake's face fell as he took a step toward me.

Ellen was silent for a moment. "I cannot reach them, Kathy. I've been trying. I am sorry."

"They have to be all right!" I said. "They have to be!"

Jake enveloped me in his arms. "I'm so sorry you're worried, Kathy." His voice was husky. "But, we don't know anything yet. They're probably fine."

I couldn't breathe. I couldn't think. A tear or two may have escaped.

"Kathy, I know you're upset, but we're in danger," he said. "We need to get out of here." His heart was beating very fast under my hand.

I wiped my face with my sleeve. "But what about the experiment?" I asked, stepping out of his embrace. "The experiment is crucial," I said. "It might be more important than us."

I was having trouble thinking. I had too much to worry about. Focus, Kath! I had to put my concerns about my parents aside for the moment.

"According to the news, the building is almost completely surrounded by the fire," Ellen said.

"What are you saying, Ellen? If we leave, we might die?" I asked. "And if we stay, we might die?" Neither of those options sounded good. I was feeling overwhelmed with emotions.

"We should stay here and die?" Jake asked incredulously, fists clenched. "No!"

Die? How could Jake and I lose each other already? We just found one another. A new wave of panic washed over me.

"Our second experiment was successful. If you stay and send the message to the twentieth century, you could make the wildfire go away and hurricane Victor and all the rest of it," Ellen said calmly.

Her words jolted me to the core. We could save everyone.

"C'mon, Kathy," Jake said. "Your parents would want you to take care of yourself. I think we should leave."

My parents would want me to do the right thing. And I knew what they would think the right thing was. "I'm sorry, Jake." I gazed into his eyes. "If Ellen thinks we could make all this go away, I believe her. I'm staying for the experiment. What with the fire, it might be our only chance. If the equipment is destroyed, we'll never get another chance. If we can fix global warming, it's worth …not making it. It would save billions of people."

Jake's mouth fell open, and he dropped his arms. "We didn't get permission yet."

"What if it's our only chance?" I asked.

"You really want to stay here in the fire and do the experiment?" he asked.

"Yes, but you go," I said. "Save yourself. I love you. I don't want you to get hurt."

He stared at me. "I love you, too." He paused. "Kathy, are you sure you want to stay?"

"Yes." I was going to save Gabrielle, Jean-Phillipe, Professor Davidson, Hans, Lars, and everyone else or die trying.

He froze for a moment. Then, he sighed. "Okay. I'm with you. Count me in."

Thank Gaia.

He reached out, wrapping his arms around me. "I should have known you'd try to save the world."

I pushed him away so I could see his face. "I should have known you'd try to save the world, Jake." I tried to grin. "Ellen, let's crank the experiment up."

"If we increase the intensity of the neutrino beams and the

strength of the time-reversal field, we should be able to send the message further back into the past," she said.

"Great," I said. Thinking about the experiment helped me avoid thinking about other stuff. "With the power outage, is all the equipment okay?" I glanced around the room; everything in here seemed all right.

"Yes," she said. "The backup generators are holding up."

"I can go double-check the fusion lab," Jake said.

"Okay," I said.

He ran out the door.

"Ellen, are we ready to do this?" I asked her. "Ready to warn the past?"

She sighed. "We are sending huge numbers of anti-electron neutrinos, muon neutrinos, and tau neutrinos to the past- hopefully, over one hundred years into the past, with the higher energy setting. We have a Morse Code message embedded in the neutrino beams which warns neutrino physicists of the past about the dangers of global warming."

"I know all that," I said. "What will, would, er, did the people in the past observe?" No doubt about it, these future past verb tenses were tricky.

"They will observe extra muon and tau neutrinos and fewer electron neutrinos than expected. That will make them examine the data more closely and discover the message."

This had to work. We had to save my parents--if they needed saving, ugh, quit thinking about that--and everyone else.

A little later, Jake ran back into the neutrino lab. "Everything's going smoothly over there." He came up and gave me a big hug. "I have a good feeling about this."

"Huzzah." I gazed into his eyes, savoring the moment. We would successfully send a message into the past, a crucial message. "Yay, us."

"Yay, us," he said. After several moments we broke the embrace.

"Okay, Ellen," I said. "Go for it! Send the message back as far as you can."

"Affirmative, Kathy," she said. "Sending message now."

"Good luck, Ellen!" Jake said.

"Yeah," I said. "Good luck!"

"Good luck to all of us," she said quietly.

"We've done everything we can. Now we wait," I said, sniffing the smoky air. "But there must be something we can do to increase our chances for survival in this fire. Ellen, can we access the building controls to eliminate this smoke?"

"Processing," she said. "According to the building's environmental programs, the environmental system intakes air from the exterior, filters it, and releases it throughout the building. Unfortunately, the filters are not up to removing all the aerosol particles this fire produces. You should disable the exterior air intake from the environmental control computer near the circuit boxes under the stairs."

I sighed. I was all too familiar with the dingy, dark area under the stairs from my power misadventures after the avalanche. "Thanks, Ellen. What about password access for the building's environmental controls?"

"Processing. The password is 'physics,' all lowercase."

I snorted. That wasn't the most imaginative password I had heard. "Come with me, Jake...please. It's creepy out there."

He reached for my hand. "As you wish." He mustered up a smile.

I marched confidently down the hall, clutching Jake's hand. The flickering red light and smell of smoke did not remind me of hell. Not a bit. I was not in hell, and I was not going to be in hell any time soon. Jake and I were going to survive this. We had to. As we reached the stairs, I turned to Jake. "Hey, can you turn on the lights in the hall?"

His face drawn, he let go of my hand. "Sure. Meet you under the stairs?"

"Yep." I was not nervous at all. My hands were trembling for no reason. Under the stairs, the environmental controls were mounted on the wall, and I wasted no time accessing the keypad.

"I got the main hall lights." Jake appeared suddenly. Ah. It was a little brighter. "How's it going under here?" He stepped in under the stairs.

"Good. I found the environmental system." I accessed the main menu and selected 'Air Circulation.'

Jake paced around the tiny space.

The menus seemed straightforward, and I drilled down until I accessed the external air collection. I entered the password, but my hands were shaking so much I could barely punch the letters in.

'Access Denied.'

"Flood it! It didn't work!"

"Calm down, Kath. Do you want me to try?"

I nodded. "Yes. Please. I guess I'm too nervous."

Jake carefully typed in the password.

'Access Denied.'

His face turned ashen.

"Drown it!"

He tried one more time, pausing after every letter.

'Access Denied. Three login failures. Security Alert.' The system kicked us out.

"Flood it!" I jumped up and down. "Flood it! I can't believe it didn't work. Ellen, how come you didn't know the correct password?"

"Someone changed it," she said. "And didn't update the password database."

"Now, what are we going to do?" I asked.

"This is bad." Jake swallowed. "Maybe we could make some masks? What do you think?"

"Sounds good." I took in a deep breath and coughed. "Maybe we should barricade the doors too."

"It couldn't hurt." We jogged back to the neutrino lab and searched for something to seal the doors. I spied several rolls of duct tape. "This should work." I glanced at Jake. "Are you sure about all this?"

He nodded. "If it's a choice between 'with you' and 'without you,' I'll pick 'with you' every time."

A tear made its way down my cheek. "Thank you," I whispered.

Jake squeezed my hand and looked around the lab. "Now, what can we make masks out of?"

I wiped my face. "I'm sure you'll figure it out. I'll go tape the front doors closed."

"Hurry back," Jake said.

I grabbed the giant roll of tape and ran down the hall and up the stairs. The scent of smoke in the hallway was strong. I taped all around the front doors and jogged back to the neutrino lab.

When I returned, I closed the lab doors behind me and started taping them up. "Ellen, give us an experiment update," I said.

"Good news," she said. "With the higher settings, it's more efficient. The neutrino warning has already made it back to approximately 2050."

"That's," I coughed, "good news. How's the equipment holding out?"

"Good, so far. Soon, it should get back to the year 2000, and after that, it will reach approximately 1950."

Jake finished wetting sections of a blanket in the lab sink. "That's great, Ellen. Let us know if we need to adjust any equipment as soon as possible."

"Affirmative." She sounded sad to me.

Jake handed me a makeshift mask made out of the wet blanket. "Here, Kath."

"Thanks." I finished taping up the door, trying to breathe shallowly. "Let's go sit down."

Jake mumbled something through his mask.

"What?" I asked.

He mumbled something else.

"What?" I asked, yelling through my mask.

"I said, I love you!" he yelled.

"I love you, too!" I yelled.

We clutched each other's hands as, despite our efforts, the lab slowly filled with smoke.

Chapter Twenty-Two A

Crash. The neutrino lab door slammed open.

"Bad news," a man said. "We got a couple of bodies here on the floor...."

Chapter Twenty-Two B

Crash. The neutrino lab door slammed open. A crowd of men in fire-fighting gear burst in, accompanied by a dollop of smoke.

I rubbed my eyes. Were they a mirage?

Gopal separated from the firefighters and ran over to Jake and me lying together on the floor. "Thank, Gaia, we found you!" He leaned over us. "Are you okay? Do you need medical attention? You were supposed to evacuate."

"I'm okay," I said. "You okay, Jake?" I asked him, scrambling to my feet.

"Wow, you guys got to us in the nick of time," Jake said.

"What were you thinking?" Gopal asked.

"We were thinking the experiment was important," I said, stepping over to the computer. "Ellen? Are you okay? Did it work? Did we send the message?"

"Yes, Master," she said. "Message sent."

"Did she call you Master?" Gopal asked.

I ignored the question. "Ellen, to be clear, we sent a neutrino warning? We warned the past about global warming?"

"Yes, Master," she said. "I sent the neutrinos and anti-neutrinos into the past, as instructed. We sent the message. They received the message."

I looked at Jake. "I don't get it. Nothing seems different, does it?"

"No," he said.

"What does that mean?" I asked.

"No idea," he said.

One of the firefighters approached us. "The fire is mostly out on campus, but the evacuation order is still in effect. Please come with us, folks."

NEUTRINO WARNING

We let him lead us out of the physics building. Outside looked like some kind of post-apocalypse; everything was black and smoking. The stench of burned things was almost overwhelming. My eyes watered.

After EMS checked out Jake and me, Jake, Gopal, and I regrouped at the pub. There, off-campus, things looked more normal. Nothing was burnt, and the smell of smoke was much diminished. Folks were eating and drinking inside like it was any other day. Since they hadn't gotten caught in the fire, maybe it was for them?

"Can we get a pitcher of water and three glasses?" Gopal called out to the bartender as we walked by. The bartender nodded and brought them to us right away. Possibly we looked a bit smudged and smokey.

Gopal rubbed his beard like it was a genie's lamp. "What were you thinking? Why did you stay on campus during a fire?" He poured out the water and soon took a big gulp of his glass.

Marcello burst into the room. "Are you guys all right, Kathy? Jake?"

Jake nodded. "We're a little singed but fine." He took a sip.

I nodded in agreement, gulping my own water.

Marcello sat down as if the weight of the world was on his shoulders. "Bah. You could have been killed."

"We, ah," I studied my friends' faces, still etched with concern. "We, ah, thought it was worth it to send the neutrino warning into the past."

"What?" Gopal asked. "We didn't get permission yet."

"We thought it was important to do the experiment," Jake said. "It might have been our only chance to warn the past."

Gopal and Marcello stared at us as if we were crazy.

Marcello dropped his gaze, shaking his head and muttering something under his breath in Italian.

"It wasn't crazy," I said. "If the equipment burned up, we'd never be able to do the experiment." I crossed my arms in front of me. "I stand by the decision."

"I still think it was stupid," Gopal said. "But did it work? Did you send the neutrino warning to the past?"

Jake met my eyes. "I think so. I think we did."

"It seemed like it worked on our end," I said. "We sent

the neutrinos and antineutrinos into the past in short and long bursts." I put Ellen on the table. "Right, Ellen?"

"Affirmative," she said. "It should have worked."

"Why didn't it?" Gopal asked.

Jake and I looked at one another. I had no idea. I could tell he had no idea, either. "Ellen, please investigate. Comb historical records for neutrino weirdness."

"Define weirdness," she said.

I shrugged. "Anything weird with neutrinos."

Gopal got a message via his fon. He grunted.

"What?" I asked.

"The evacuation order is lifted. I'm officially the new physics department chair," he said. "And my first official action is to restore the two of you, Jake and Kathy, to graduate students in good standing."

"Yay!" Jake smiled.

"Yay." I forced myself to smile as well. This was good news. But it was just hitting me; our neutrino warning didn't work.

I got a fon call. Megan. No doubt she would chastise me for risking my life and doing the experiment, too. "Pardon me." I stood up and walked away from the table. I braced myself and answered.

"Kathy?" she asked.

"Yes," I said. "Don't worry. I'm okay."

"Don't worry about what?" she asked. "Never mind. Your parents just showed up at the house. They said something about a flood--"

My mom interrupted. "Sorry, Kathy. We had to evacuate our house. We were hoping to stay with you and Megan for a while."

In the background, I heard Dad say, "Hi, Kathy-bird!"

I couldn't talk. I was suddenly all choked up.

"Kathy?" Mom asked over the fon.

My eyes felt heavy as a tear escaped and cascaded down my cheek. I cleared my throat. What a relief. "Uh, yeah, sure, Mom," I finally said. "You guys can stay as long as you like. I'll be home soon."

I ended the call and returned to the table. "My parents are at my house," I said. "I need to go home."

I turned to go.

"Should I come with?" Jake asked, standing up.

"No," I said. "Thanks. But I think it's okay." We shared a quick kiss.

I started walking away.

"Meet us in the lab later," Gopal called after me. "We're going to try to figure out what happened."

I rushed home, and sure enough, my parents were lounging in the family room when I burst through the front door. They had a bunch of boxes and suitcases piled around them.

"Mom! Dad!" I yelled. "It's so good to see you!"

They both jumped up.

I ran to Mom and hugged her tightly.

Dad ran over and enveloped the two of us in his arms.

My eyes overflowed. They were safe. They were safe. I was so relieved.

Eventually, we separated. "I'm so glad you're okay," I said, smiling. "You must have driven straight through to get here so quickly."

"Why do you smell like smoke?" Mom asked, frowning.

"Yeah, Kathy-bird?" Dad said.

I realized Megan was standing in the doorway to the kitchen, smiling.

I stepped over to her. "It's okay if they stay here, isn't it?" I asked in a low voice. "They can stay in my room."

"Of course," she said. "I'm glad they're okay." She sniffed and frowned. "Why *do* you smell like smoke?"

"No reason." I stepped away from her. "Mom and Dad, you can have my room. Do you want to take a nap? I'll put some fresh sheets on the bed…."

Once Mom and Dad were fast asleep, I left them a note: 'Stopping by the fusion lab.'

I walked down the basement hallway of the physics building. It still smelled like smoke.

"I think I figured it out," Ellen said.

"What?" I could hear voices in the distance.

"Why our neutrino warning didn't work," she said.

I stepped into the fusion lab. Gopal, Marcello, and Jake

were engrossed in the innards of the tokamak.

"The Solar Neutrino Problem," Ellen said.

"Huh?" I said, walking to the tokamak.

Gopal pulled his head out of the machine. "There you are. We're getting rid of this liquid wall thing."

"Bah," Marcello said. "Time reversal is too bizarre."

"We're going back to basics," Jake said, smiling.

"It sounds good to me," I said. "The human race needs fusion." Now more than ever. Especially since our warning didn't work. But I didn't say that. "Ellen said she figured out why our message didn't work. Ellen?"

The four of us walked over to the desk and chairs.

"Talk, Ellen," I said.

"We sent the message composed of anti-electron, muon, and tau neutrinos all the way back to the 1960s," Ellen said. "They received the message, but they didn't understand it. Neutrino physicists of the past were puzzled about the shortage of electron neutrinos and the surplus muon and tau neutrinos. They called the mystery, The Solar Neutrino Problem. They never realized it was a message from the future."

I was stunned. It never crossed my mind that the scientists of the past wouldn't realize it was a message.

The others were quiet as well for several minutes.

All that effort for nothing. I couldn't believe it.

"Well, it was a good effort. Nice job, everyone," Gopal finally said. "Now, as physics department chair, I'm going to focus all our efforts on fusion. Everyone in the department will be involved. And I'll try to get some folks from other universities. I'm going to make the three of you supervisors, and we'll work night and day until we get it to work."

I looked at my friends, determination on their faces.

"We'll do it," I said firmly.

Gopal nodded.

"Yeah!" Jake said.

"*Sì,*" Marcello said, nodding.

"We'll get fusion to work," I said. "We will save the world."

Chapter Twenty-Two C

Crash. The neutrino lab door slammed open.

Jake ran into the room, looking confused. "Kathy?" He ran up to me.

"I can't believe it," Lars said. I turned my attention to him. "You're right, Dr. Garcia. The signal just stopped." He looked at me with amazement in his eyes.

Lars? He was dead. Was I in heaven? Or was I in hell? "Ow!" Someone pinched me. Was pinching allowed in heaven? Probably not.

I turned to the culprit on my left and saw Jake now sitting next to me, fingers outstretched, looking bewildered. "Kath? What's going on?" he whispered. "Are we dreaming?"

I slowly took in my surroundings. I sat in the neutrino lab in front of the control workstation--but everything in the lab looked all shiny and new instead of dingy and worn out. Lars (alive!) sat on my right and Jake on my left.

"Are you all right, Kathy?" Lars peered into my face with concern.

I moved away from him. "You stay away from me." I backed up some more and smacked right into someone sitting behind me. It was Gabrielle. But that couldn't be. She was dead, too. But it looked just like her. "Gabrielle?"

She nodded, causing her auburn hair to flop in front of her face. "*Oui.* Are you feeling okay, Dr. Garcia?"

"Uh, who's Dr. Garcia?" I asked.

"What's wrong, Kathy?" Lars scooted toward me.

"Just keep away!" Could it really be Lars?

He frowned. "What's wrong with you?" He tapped a finger nervously, contemplating me. Then, his face brightened in comprehension. "You must have started partying early." He chuckled. He peered around me at Jake. "You too? I should have known."

Jake now stood with his mouth hanging open.

Lars glanced at his watch. "But hadn't you two better get going? You were supposed to pick up your relatives at the airport for the party."

"Huh?" I said intelligently.

"Kathy, you said you had to pick up your parents and sister," Lars said. "The whole crew."

"My what?" Parents? Sister? I didn't have a sister; my sister Emma died many years ago. And I wasn't entirely sure about parents…

"And Jake said his brothers were coming in for the party," Lars added.

Party? What party?

"What?" Jake asked.

Lars sighed. "Honestly, what are you two on?"

Gabrielle giggled. "And more importantly, did you save any for the party?"

"What's going on?" I asked.

A tiny woman with tan skin, long straight black hair, and mischievous eyes popped in front of me out of thin air. I jumped. She looked just like I'd always imagined Ellen would look.

My mouth fell open. "Ellen? Is that you?"

"Yes, Kathy, or do you want me to call you Dr. Garcia? There have been some …adjustments to the timeline." Ellen's tiny hands were on her tiny hips. She scrutinized me. "Relax. I am still your app; I just have some upgrades. Now I'm a holographic AI assistant."

"Huh?" I said brilliantly. This was all too much to take in.

"It would appear the experiment in the other timeline was successful," she said. "We sent a message, a neutrino warning, into the past. We sent anti-electron, muon, and tau neutrinos all the way back to the 1960s."

It worked?

Ellen continued. "Initially, neutrino physicists in the past were puzzled about the shortage of electron neutrinos and the surplus muon and tau neutrinos. But they deciphered your message in time to avert most of the disasters of the original timeline." Ellen paused, smiling helpfully. "So, you did it. You saved the world."

"We saved the world!" I jumped up and down. "We saved the world!"

Now, it was Lars' and Gabrielle's turn to look confused.

"We did it!" Jake grabbed me, pulling me out of the chair and enveloping me in his arms. They still felt like home. At least he seemed the same. Thank Gaia.

A commotion erupted in the lab doorway.

"Kathy!" Marcello burst into the room and grabbed us for a hug.

"Jake, Kathy, we did it!" Gopal rushed into the room right after Marcello and joined in a group hug.

Lars and Gabrielle stood up. Lars shook his head as he took in the four of us hugging.

"*Mon Dieu,*" Gabrielle said.

"We did it," I said. "Wow." The three enthusiastic men were practically crushing me.

Lars scratched his head. "So, let me get this straight. You sent a neutrino signal back in time?"

Marcello beamed as the hug broke up. "*Si,* we did it."

"Guess what? I'm married!" Gopal smiled, eyes twinkling. "And I have two kids."

"I have three kids!" Marcello yelled, beaming.

"That's great. Wait a minute. Do I have any kids?" What a disturbing thought to have kids you didn't remember. No, surely, I would remember kids. "Why don't I remember this timeline if Marcello and Gopal do?"

Jake touched my shoulder. "It's starting to come back to me. Concentrate, and it will come back to you."

It was worth a shot. Concentrate. There was something there... First, I remembered being very nervous. I stood in the front of a conference room, lecturing. People in the audience asked me difficult questions, and then there was a lot of clapping. Afterward, Dr. Davidson came up and shook my hand. Dr. Davidson was alive! Comprehension dawned. "Did I defend my Ph.D. this morning?"

"Yes!" shouted the guys.

Gabrielle patted me on the back. "*Oui*, Dr. Garcia. And you are having a big party tonight, which my husband, Jean-Phillipe, and I have been looking forward to."

Wow. I was Dr. Kathy Garcia, a full-fledged physicist. It was hard to believe, and yet at the same time, it wasn't. I seemed to have memories of two different timelines.

Lars held up his hand. "Wait a minute. Kathy, Jake, Marcello, Gopal, and even Ellen recall this alternate reality. Why don't I? And don't tell me to concentrate. I've been concentrating, and nothing's coming back."

"*Oui*, I do not recall it either. Why?" Gabrielle asked.

"Uh." Jake shuffled his feet as I glanced at him.

"Bah," Marcello said.

I didn't want to meet Lars' and Gabrielle's eyes. I decided the laboratory floor was really quite fascinating. Wait. Hadn't Lars said I had parents, a sister, an aunt, an uncle, and cousins? I concentrated on recalling this family I supposedly had, hoped I had, prayed I had.

"Ah, Lars, Gabrielle, I'm sorry to tell you this…." Gopal bravely addressed their questions. "But, you had, ah, passed on in the other timeline."

Gabrielle gasped. "*Mon Dieu*. I am not liking this other timeline."

Lars scowled.

If he didn't like the story so far, he really wasn't going to like the details. Suddenly, getting out of the neutrino lab sounded like a good idea. "Did somebody say something about the airport?"

"Yes, Dr. Garcia, you and Jake are supposed to go to the airport to pick up your relatives. Jake, your flying car, a VTOL, is parked outside." Ellen pointed toward the door.

Relatives? I started to remember big, boisterous family get-togethers with lots of little kids running around and gray-haired folks being amused by their antics. I couldn't help smiling. It seemed wonderful, and it felt *right*.

"My what?" Jake looked at his fon. "Albert, what's she talking about?"

A wild-haired Albert Einstein made of light appeared in front of Jake and chuckled. "Do not fear, Jake. I will explain the vertical take-off and landing vehicle operation to you, and you will remember it in no time. Perhaps you are already beginning to remember."

Jake drew his eyebrows together. "Maybe." He smiled. "It's a splashy red number, isn't it?"

Albert smiled and slapped his knee. "That's my boy."

"You guys go to the airport, and we'll explain things to Lars and Gabrielle." Gopal pointed at himself and Marcello.

"Okay." I wasn't totally sure about this VTOL thing, but I really wanted to get to the airport to meet my family.

"But we will all see you at your party later, Dr. Garcia. Right?" Gabrielle called out.

"Uh, yeah, okay. See you then." I yelled over my shoulder as we left the neutrino lab. The two holographic assistants followed us.

"Was that weird, or was that weird?" I asked Jake as we trooped down the hall. I reached for his hand.

"That was weird." He stopped, gazing into my eyes. "So, do you remember anything about us?"

"I remember we got together. I remember we said we loved each other during the fire." I tried to focus. There was something more there ...swaying palm trees, endless blue skies, colorful fish darting among underwater corals, molten lava flowing into the sea, and lots of images of Jake and me on pristine sandy beaches. "Did we go to Hawaii at the winter solstice?"

He released my hand and caressed my cheek. "Aloha." Moving his hand behind my neck, he kissed me slowly and deeply. I felt his love pour into me. Memories of hundreds of similar kisses came racing back. I felt dizzy but in a good way.

Jake broke it off, grabbing my shoulders. "You're shaking. Are you okay?"

"I am now." I clutched his hand again and pulled him after me down the hall. "C'mon; let's meet, er, get, our families!"

The changes were starting to seem normal until the view outside registered and shocked the sense out of me. The campus looked lush and green; flowers bloomed everywhere, and gorgeous floral scents wafted in the air. "Wow." I froze, breathing deeply, taking it all in.

"Sweet!" Jake nodded with approval.

The last time we'd seen this spot, it had been a burnt cinder.

"Uh, yeah." I saw what appeared to be flying cars in the distance--not that I'd seen a lot of cars before. "What is this? Ellen?"

"Relax, Dr. Garcia. This timeline has had some success with weather control. And those are flying cars--they're perfectly safe."

Albert said, "Jake, your car is over where the bike racks were in the other reality."

Jake grinned. "Yeah, I remember."

I was in sensory overload.

We reached a flat paved surface with colorful vehicles resembling small helicopters.

As we approached a red one, Jake said, "Unlock."

The locks popped, and Jake opened a door. "Well, c'mon, we don't want to keep everybody waiting." He pointed into the 'car.'

I gingerly stepped inside and sat on one of the padded seats. Everybody? Could it be true that my parents were totally fine? I really hoped so. And what was that about a sister?

"Up," Jake said after he sat down. "Strap yourself in," he said to me.

"Oh. Right." I buckled in very quickly as we began to go--straight up. I clutched the armrests. I didn't see what good a seatbelt would be if we plummeted to the ground like a meteorite.

"To the airport, Jeeves." Jake fiddled with the controls.

"Would you like a news report?" Ellen asked.

"May 12, 2098: The Interstellar Scientists Coalition orders Mars authorities to solve the Sanitation Workers strike as it enters its third day."

"Mars?" I shook my head. "No. That's overload. Thanks, Ellen. I already have enough news to process."

Overcome with curiosity, I craned my neck to see the ground.

I saw a surprising amount of green down there but hardly any people. It was disappointing. I guess we hadn't managed to create or recreate all the lost souls after all. "Ellen, what's the earth's population?"

"The current population on earth is approximately five billion biological intelligences, oops there's another one, and another, and several hundred thousand binary intelligences."

"Wow," I whispered.

The car dipped down for a second.

"Eek," I squeaked out. We were going to die.

"Sorry, I got distracted." Jake looked sheepish. "Disable manual control, Jeeves. Did you say five billion, Ellen?"

"Yes, I did. It would seem the experiment was a phenomenal success," Ellen said. "You know Megan is one of the pioneers in AI research."

"My Megan?" I asked.

"Affirmative," Ellen said.

I grinned. "Go, Megan!"

"Dr. Garcia, an incoming call from your mom," Ellen said. "Do you wish to accept?"

My mom? "Yes! Please."

A tiny holographic version of my mom popped in front of me. Thank Gaia. It was true. She was fine! Hurray!

"Kathy? Earth calling Kathy." Tiny holographic Mom tapped her foot.

I took a deep breath. "Hi, Mom. Are you okay? Is Dad okay?"

"Yes, dear. We're fine. Are you on your way? We're waiting here at the airport VTOL pad. And congratulations on your degree."

"Estimated arrival time is," Jake consulted some indicator, "ten more minutes, Maria. It depends on traffic above the airport."

"Thank you, Jake, dear. Hurry up if you can; I think your brothers are hitting on Kath's sister, Emma."

Emma! The name jumpstarted my memory. A tidal wave of memories came flooding back, like when we were little girls, and she tried to convince me the moon was made of cheese. She'd said, 'Swiss cheese has holes, right? The moon's craters are just like that.' And when I got my Bachelor's degree, she took me on a trip to the lunar colony (!). As we bounced around on the lunar surface, she'd teased me relentlessly about my earlier gullibility. I sighed with joy. Emma. I had a sister! Thank Gaia!

I was shocked out of my reverie as we descended. Eek! I clutched the armrests.

"We're there," Jake said as we glided to a standstill.

Within seconds, two rambunctious young men were fighting each other for the door handle.

A middle-aged wild-haired man gently pushed them aside and opened it. "Kathy-bird! Congratulations! My little bird is a doctor." At least he seemed the same.

I surrendered to his arms. "Dad! It's *so* wonderful to see you!"

I must have held on a little too long because he gently pushed me away and looked me in the eyes. "Are you okay?"

I nodded. "It's been an extraordinary day." I wasn't tearing up, not a lot, anyway.

He chuckled. "So, do I need to call you Dr. Kathy-bird now?"

"No." I smiled and wiped my eye surreptitiously.

Dad climbed into the vehicle.

"Mom!" I grabbed her for a big hug. "It's wonderful to see you, too." She also seemed like the mom I remembered.

When I looked into her face, she looked concerned. "And here's Emma," she said.

She stepped aside, and I saw ...my big sister, Emma. Her tan skin and flashing brown eyes were like my own, but not. Emma. I couldn't talk. "You okay, girl?" Emma (!) stepped forward and enveloped me in her arms.

My tears overflowed, getting all over her blouse.

After several minutes, I cleared my throat and stepped away. "Sure. Of course. Why wouldn't I be okay?"

Emma, also looking concerned, got in the vehicle after Mom.

In the meantime, Jake wrestled with the young men. "Hey, straighten up now. I want to introduce you to Kathy, er, Dr. Garcia."

"What for? We've met her before," one of them said.

Jake smiled. "Just humor me." He turned to me. "Kath, this is my little brother Isaac."

I nodded at him. "Pleased to meet you, Isaac."

"And this is my little brother Joshua." He pointed at the other teenager.

They had a definite family resemblance, wiry builds, unruly dark-brown wavy hair, and beautiful blue eyes.

"Pleased to meet you, Joshua." I smiled nervously.

He nodded. "Oh, yeah, Grandpa says congratulations, and Mom, Dad, and Grandma do too."

"Thanks," I said.

"Of course," Jake cleared his throat. "Of course they do." He glanced over at me and wiped a tear from his cheek with his palm. He cleared his throat again. "Now, you guys secure the luggage in the back." He pointed to a pile of suitcases outside the car.

The two young men bounded toward it.

Jake leaned toward me. "I'll thank you for my family until the day I die," he whispered huskily.

Stepping back, he cleared his throat, turned to his brothers, and clapped his hands together. "Hurry up, guys. We've got an important party to get to."

I got in the car, sat right next to Emma and grabbed her hand.

She chuckled. "What's gotten into you? You act like you haven't seen me in ages. You just saw me a couple of months ago."

Reluctantly I let go of her. "On the one hand, I did see you a couple of months ago, but on the other hand, I haven't seen you for twenty-seven years."

"Twenty-seven years? But that's your whole life." Emma's eyes crinkled in confusion.

I wiped my eyes. They wouldn't stop leaking. "Exactly."

"What are you talking about?" Emma asked.

"Well, we did this physics experiment…." I began.

Everyone groaned. "Oh, Kathy!"

"Oh, no!"

"Don't get her started."

Jake came over and squeezed my hand. "We can get into that later. People are waiting for us. Let's go party. We deserve it."

Through my tears, I gave him my million-Watt smile.

"We do."

Science Fact: The Solar Neutrino Problem

The sun is powered by nuclear fusion. More specifically, hydrogen atoms combine to form helium atoms and emit energy, anti-electrons, and neutrinos. The emitted energy is known as heat and sunlight and enables life on earth to exist. Anti-electrons are just like electrons but have an opposite electrical charge.

Neutrinos are very small electrically-neutral particles--hence the name *neutrino*. When neutrinos were proposed in 1930 (see more on this below), physicists thought they had zero mass. To put this in more familiar terms, something with zero mass weighs zero pounds. Neutrinos emitted from the sun are, not surprisingly, called solar neutrinos.

Electrons and neutrinos are part of the family of elementary particles called leptons. An elementary particle cannot be divided into something smaller. There are two more leptons similar to the electron. Altogether, they are called: the electron, the muon, and the tauon. The muon is very similar to the electron but has a greater mass. Similarly, the tauon is very like the muon but has a greater mass yet.

Correspondingly, neutrinos have three different kinds or flavors: the electron neutrino, the mu-neutrino, and the tau-neutrino. As you may have guessed from the names, the electron-neutrino is often seen with the electron. There are similar lepton relationships for the muon and the muon-neutrino, etc. Notice there are six types of leptons in total.

At this point, you may be wondering: Why so many particles?

Physicists use conservation laws in their work. Probably the most crucial conservation law is conservation of energy. This says energy cannot be destroyed; it must be conserved. In fact, in 1930, neutrinos were hypothesized to save the law of conservation of energy when it seemed as if some energy was disappearing in beta decay. (In beta decay, a radioactive nucleus is transformed into a slightly lighter nucleus with the emission of an electron.) Another important conservation law is conservation of momentum. There are a few more conservation laws, but the main point is that physicists need these laws to do the bookkeeping of the universe.

So, back to the sun... Even more specifically, solar fusion combines hydrogen atoms to form helium atoms and emit energy, anti-electrons, and electron-neutrinos. Back in the late 1960s, physicists decided to measure the electron-neutrinos coming from the sun. Ray Davis Jr. built a neutrino detector a mile underground in the Homestake Gold Mine of South Dakota, consisting of a 100,000-gallon tank full of dry-cleaning fluid with special detectors. His theoretical partner, John N. Bahcall, predicted how many solar electron-neutrinos should be detected based on the understanding of solar fusion. Davis, Bahcall, and their team did everything right, but they only detected about a third of the expected electron-neutrinos.

For the next thirty years, experiments around the world got the same electron-neutrino deficit. Two-thirds of the solar neutrinos were missing! What did it mean? Could it mean we didn't really understand solar fusion? Other types of experiments verified the solar model was correct.

So, where were the electron neutrinos? Physicists were mystified. This was called the Solar Neutrino Problem.

It wasn't until the late 1990s that the puzzle was solved by the Super-Kamiokande experiment in Japan and the Sudbury Neutrino Observatory in Canada. The new experiments could detect more flavors of neutrinos. They discovered the solar model *was* correct, and all the electron-neutrinos were being emitted as expected. On the way to earth, two-thirds of the electron-neutrinos were being changed, or *oscillated*, into muon-neutrinos or tauon-neutrinos. If the neutrinos had zero mass, such oscillations would be impossible. Therefore, part of the solution was the neutrinos *do* have mass. In fact, our original idea of a neutrino being 'one particle' isn't quite correct. It's more realistic to think of one neutrino as a combination of all three flavor neutrinos...

The physics teams that solved the Solar Neutrino Problem won the 2015 Nobel Prize in Physics. Kudos to them!

Thank you for reading *Neutrino Warning*. I hope you enjoyed it!

- For more info about me or my work, please visit my author's website, http://www.lesleylsmith.com/. Sometimes, I post links for free fiction downloads!
- Please check out the Physics Is Fun website www.physicsisfun.net for lots of information about fun physics topics.
- Reviews help other readers find books. I appreciate any and all reviews.
- Please check out an excerpt from the next novel in this universe, *Kat Cubed*, on the following pages.

−Lesley L. Smith

KAT CUBED

Chapter One: Universe 1: Kat, April 25, 2100, 7:00 am

Sitting alone in the greenhouse Kat Garcia asked, "Where are you, Pa?" The scavenger team was way overdue. She strained her eyes, looking southeast towards Denver in the moments before dawn. Everything looked gray: gray buildings, gray dead trees, gray dead grass. The gray clouds overhead didn't help.

Did something move over there next to that ruined building? She stood and stared. No, it was just a dead bush shifting in the wind. She sat back down again. The top of the old physics building had the best sightlines in town, but even up here she couldn't catch a glimpse of the missing team. Nervous, she plucked a sprig of baby spinach from the garden bed next to her and popped it in her mouth.

She needed Pa. He was the only family she had left. Ma was missing. Her sister Emma was dead. "Come home to me, Pa. Come on."

"Kat?" her best friend Pablo said from the stairwell.

She jumped. "Hi, buddy. What's up?"

"Who're you talking to?" He made his way through the plants and came and sat next to her.

"Nobody." She sighed. "Myself." That wasn't too crazy, was it? She touched Ma's locket. Ma had given it to her for safekeeping until she came back. That was months ago. Where was she?

"Any sign of the scavenger team?" he asked.

"Nope."

"They'll be okay," he said, patting her shoulder. "Your pa and the rest of the team are experienced scavengers." He was sweet.

Kat pointed at the first hint of light on the horizon. "But the sun's coming up."

"They know to take cover during the day. They know we're counting on them."

She glanced at Pablo's face. He seemed so sure. Maybe he was right. She hoped he was right. "What do you think'll happen if they never come back?"

"I don't know." He exhaled. "We'll cherish our memories of them."

Suddenly she had to blink back tears.

"And I guess we'll figure something out, like we always do. We'll survive." He rested his hand on her back. "The group might elect you to be the new leader."

That was another thing to worry about if Pa didn't come back. "I'm only twenty. I can't lead the group."

"I think you can." His faith was touching.

"So, what's happening downstairs?" she asked. "Is Fei any better?" A sick baby was the worst.

"No." His gaze dipped to the floor. "Her fever's up."

"And we don't have any medicine." She scanned the edge of campus again. No sign of the missing team. "Did they try wet cloths to bring down her fever?"

"Yeah. But we're getting low on water."

"Not good."

"No," he said. "Not good."

Light blossomed over the horizon, illuminating everything in its path. The old university buildings were shades of pink and tan, and red. All the vegetation was a dead crunchy brown except a narrow strip of green along the creek in the distance.

Kat knew some of that green stuff was willow. She also knew willow was a natural fever reducer. "What if we went to the creek and got some medicine for Fei?"

"What? Now?" His voice squeaked a bit. "It's after sunrise. We can't go outside."

She pointed up at the sky. "It's pretty cloudy." She lowered her voice. "Do you think Fei will last another day?"

242

"No." His whole body slumped.

"Come on, Pablo. We can do it. It'll be an adventure. Please come with me and help."

He glanced at her. "You're going whether I agree or not, aren't you?"

"Yes." She smiled in what she hoped was a charming way. "Come on, you know you want to help baby Fei. Wouldn't it feel great to save someone? Wouldn't it feel great to have a win for once?" She was ready for something good to happen. She was sick of losing all the time: losing faith, losing hope, losing people. "Come on."

He blew out a big gust of air. "You know I have trouble resisting you, Kat."

Oh, she knew. She was his best friend, after all. She grinned.

Down in the basement, the group didn't even bat an eye at Kat and Pablo going out after sunrise to get willow bark for Fei. Of course, Fei's parents, Bao and Chang, were beside themselves with worry, so they weren't going to object. But Kat thought someone would say, *Oh, it's too dangerous. You can't do it.* or *Wow, how heroic, Kat.* But no one did.

They geared up as quickly as they could. The danger was the sun. They wore lightweight loose cotton clothing, and big hats. Pablo carried a thermometer with an alarm. They'd seen people die of heatstroke, and it wasn't pretty.

On the bright side, there were some old underground maintenance tunnels to the creek—which was one of the reasons they were living in the physics building. The tunnels were about seven feet wide and seven feet tall with a concrete floor and cinderblock walls, so they tramped to the creek in comfort.

Once they hiked about a quarter-mile, Pablo asked, "How'd your ma know about willow bark?"

"Ma's ma knew about herbal medicine and taught her some stuff. And, then, after Emma..." Kat swallowed. "After we lost Emma, Ma studied even more. She consulted every herbalist and doctor we met and had a bunch of books. She swore she'd never let anyone else die on her watch."

Ma was her hero. Was she still alive? Kat didn't see how

243

she could be. She'd been gone too long. She wouldn't leave them alone so long if she'd had anything to say about it. Her eyes started to fill.

"Kat?"

She exhaled. She was on a mission, a mission to save a baby. Ma would approve.

"You miss them, huh?"

"Yes." She glanced over at him. "I know you miss your family, too." Pablo'd lost track of his parents during the Water Wars. He had no idea if they were alive or dead. And there was no way to find out.

"*Sí*," he said.

They walked in silence for a few minutes.

"So, tell me about Emma," he said. "What was she like?"

Ma's locket held a picture of Emma. She resisted the urge to open it and look at the image yet again. "She wasn't much like me."

"She sounds great." Pablo grinned at her, trying to lighten the mood.

"She was very wise and nice and nurturing."

"You're right. Nothing like you." Kat knew he was joking.

"She was a lot like Ma. But in some ways, she wasn't; for example, she taught me about boys."

"Ooh. What did she teach you?"

"Let's see; she said boys like food and compliments." When she looked at Pablo, he was still grinning. "Who taught you about boys?"

"I'm self-taught. What can I say? I'm a genius?"

"What about your friend, Jake?"

"Jake? He was straight but a real *hermano*." He sighed. "I miss him." Jake was another person he'd lost.

"What was he like?" she asked.

"He loved weather, of all things," Pablo said. "He could even predict it sometimes. Like when we'd get a windy spell, he'd say *A front's moving in*. And he'd be right. And he had a great sense of humor. We played so many tricks on his older brother Jason."

The tunnel brightened as they neared the end. The temperature was already rising.

They turned off their flashlights and set them down in the

tunnel.

"I want to hear about those tricks at some point," she said as they emerged. Even near sunrise, the heat pummeled them.

The scents of dried plants and dust made Kat sneeze.

"Gaia bless you," he said, squinting and looking up. "Still cloudy."

"Let's hurry," she said, pointing in the direction of the creek. "Can you check if there's any water running?" They usually went to the old reservoir to get water, but there might be some here since the plants were still alive.

"Yes, ma'am." He saluted.

Kat grinned as she jogged to the willows. They looked great–still green and alive. She got a small pocket knife out of her bag and started stripping bark off the closest tree. Sweat gathered on her back and face.

Pablo ran up, putting an empty bottle back in his bag. "Bad news. No water that I could see." He got out his own knife.

"It must be underground? I hope so, anyway. I hope these trees don't die." Even though it was cloudy, it was still plenty light outside. She couldn't even remember the last time she'd been outside during the day. A drop of sweat rolled into her eye.

He started stripping bark.

"Don't take too much from any one tree." She wiped her forehead.

"Yes, ma'am." They stripped bark. "It's kind of weird being outside during the day, huh?"

She shot him a look. Wow, his thoughts were similar to hers. "Yeah."

"Do you think things will ever go back to the way they used to be?"

"What way is that?" Before Emma died? Before Ma disappeared? Before Pablo's family disappeared?

Before Pa didn't come back?

"You know, when we lived during the day and slept at night," he said. "When we didn't have to worry so much about surviving. When we lived regular lives."

Even with all this cloudiness, Kat was getting h-o-t. She felt another bead of sweat slide down her back. "Do you even remember that? I mean, Ma and Pa told me we lived up in an

245

actual town in the mountains when I was a little girl, but I hardly remember it." Thinking about everything that had been lost was too depressing. They didn't really even have a civilization anymore.

"I remember some stuff," he said. "We also lived up in the mountains. I went to school with Jake and his brother. My ma was a wonderful cook."

Kat held up a finger. "So, Emma was right. Boys do like food."

The clouds shifted, and the rays of sunlight pierced them like daggers. She knew the sun was deadly, but it seemed so cheerful.

The temperature alarm went off.

Pablo shoved a handful of bark into his bag and grabbed the thermometer. "We need to go back now."

She shoved some more bark into her own bag. She didn't want to have to come back here for a good long time. She stepped towards another tree.

"Now, Kat," he said, face grim. "I'm not kidding. It's getting dangerously hot out here."

She brought him along for a reason. She knew he'd keep them safe. "Okay."

Back in the tunnels, they picked up their flashlights and started walking back to the physics building.

Trying to lighten the mood again, she said, "Tell me about those tricks you and Jake used to play."

But he just sighed and said, "I'm not up for it, Kat."

At their encampment in the basement, most folks had gone to bed by the time they got back. Kat showed Bao and Chang how to make the fever-reducing tea out of the willow bark.

After a long night's work in the greenhouse, not to mention the stress of the creek mission, she was practically asleep before her head hit the pillow.

Kat was awakened by a scream. A strange bluish light filled the lab. She'd never seen anything like it. It came from a freaky window floating in mid-air! She carefully picked her way through the bedrolls to the strange window.

Pablo appeared at her side. "Gaia." He joined her in staring at the thing.

She whispered, "Gaia." As she peered inside, two people, a man and a woman, moved closer. She could almost make them out.

They moved closer yet.

Then, Pablo whispered, "Jake."

Kat's heart caught in her throat, and her fingers reached for her locket. "Emma?"

www.ingramcontent.com/pod-product-compliance
Lightning Source LLC
Chambersburg PA
CBHW060424180626
46817CB00007B/2659